I1038854

# ALL THE
# RIGHT
# MISTAKES

SEP 2 0 2021

# ALL THE RIGHT MISTAKES

## A NOVEL

# LAURA JAMISON

SHE WRITES PRESS

Copyright © 2020, Laura Jamison

All rights reserved. No part of this publication may be reproduced, distributed, or transmitted in any form or by any means, including photocopying, recording, digital scanning, or other electronic or mechanical methods, without the prior written permission of the publisher, except in the case of brief quotations embodied in critical reviews and certain other noncommercial uses permitted by copyright law. For permission requests, please address She Writes Press.

Published 2020
Printed in the United States of America
ISBN: 978-1-63152-709-8
ISBN: 978-1-63152-710-4
Library of Congress Control Number: 2020900034

For information, address:
She Writes Press
1569 Solano Ave #546
Berkeley, CA 94707

She Writes Press is a division of SparkPoint Studio, LLC.

*Book design by Stacey Aaronson*

All company and/or product names may be trade names, logos, trademarks, and/or registered trademarks and are the property of their respective owners.

This is a work of fiction. Names, characters, places, and incidents either are the product of the author's imagination or are used fictitiously. Any resemblance to actual persons, living or dead, is entirely coincidental.

*For every mom who has ever felt*
*she is doing it the wrong way*

# PROLOGUE

12:15 PM, Sept. 1

**Elizabeth**: *DEFCON 5*

**Carmen**: Um, you know that DEFCON 5 is like the good one? Peace breaking out everywhere? Also, glad to see you figured out texting. Welcome to the 21st century.

**Elizabeth**: FINE, Carmen. DEFCON 1.

**Carmen**: OK, I'll bite. Did William finally go behind your back and repaint the living room the wrong gray?

**Elizabeth**: I'm just going to leave this here.

https://www.FLASHbooks.com/The-Four-BIG-Mistakes-of-Women-Who-Will-Never-Lead-or-Win/download

The Four BIG Mistakes of Women Who Will Never Lead or Win

Hardback/FLASHReader – September 1

by Heather Hall, COO, FLASH.com and CEO, The Hall Family

This sure-to-be runaway hit is a must-have for all women looking to get ahead in a man's world. FLASH executive Heather Hall has been there, done that—and so have her closest friends. Drawing on all their collective experience, she reveals a distinctive set of mistakes women make that ultimately sabotage their careers—and their lives.

Don't be another mistake—purchase Heather's book in a FLASH! This book can be purchased with the Official Book Circle Conversation Guide.

**Carmen**: I don't have time to read Heather's crap. I'm busy actually being a mom instead of writing about how fabulous I am in the workplace. I mean, whatever. Good for her.

**Sara**: Hey! Some of us have to work, Carmen. Be nice.

**Carmen**: OK, you know I don't mean you and Elizabeth. That's different. I'm sorry, but you can't be a superstar executive, wife, mom, and an author on top of it. I'm not buying it.

**Sara**: Carmen, I'm sure she has lots of help. We should try not to be so judgy. It's great that one of us is so successful.

**Carmen**: I don't accept your definition of success.

**Sara**: 🙄

**Martha**: While you guys were busy bickering, I clicked the link and started reading–not good.

**Elizabeth**: Right?! Sara, what's the emoji for "Holy shit, I can't believe I defended this bitch all these years?"

**Carmen**: Did Elizabeth Smith just say the "b" word? You have my full attention, and I'm finding the book right now.

2

# MARCH

# HEATHER

**From**: Heather Hall <heather.hall@flash.com>
**Sent**: Mon. 3/2 5:17 a.m.
**To**: Elizabeth Smith <esmith@gmail.com>
**Subject**: Girls' Weekend

So I got your message about doing our annual girls' weekend in June. I'd love to do it, but this year I have to pass. I can't tell you all the details, but I have a project in the works that may completely transform my career. I know that sounds melodramatic (even for me), but this project is really special. It should be ready in September if everything goes to plan.

I feel really bad that I can't get away this year. Would you let me treat you, Carmen, Martha, and Sara to a week at my Carmel cottage? You know what, I'm not letting you guys say no. The tickets are on their way.

Love and kisses,

Heather

P.S. Any news on the baby front? I have my fingers crossed for you. I know that this will be the year you get everything you want! No one deserves it more than you.

# ELIZABETH

Elizabeth's fingers hovered over her keyboard as she considered whether to reply to Heather's message. She was really disappointed that Heather was backing out of their girls' weekend. Heather was one of her oldest friends, and Elizabeth had spent the whole winter looking forward to their getaway with their other three college friends, Carmen, Martha, and Sara.

She would e-mail Heather later. She needed to get her head in the game today. The Old Man and Joe had invited her to lunch, and she suspected something was in the works. It felt like it was one of those days, a day when something happened that changed the arc of things. Elizabeth's world as a big firm attorney was characterized by long stretches of tedious, hard work punctuated by the rare day that brought a big win (or loss). A new client. A big deal. A breakup. A promotion.

Elizabeth had taken the time this morning to pick out her most flattering suit, straighten her fine, brown hair that she kept cut in a sharp bob, and apply a little more than her normal five-minute makeup. She hated that how she looked was an integral part of her success, but that's the ways things were, and she didn't see it changing anytime soon. She felt she was doing well enough in that department, though. The baby weight was nearly all off after months of coffee for breakfast, a salad for lunch, and the promise of a half bottle of wine on Friday if she kept it together during the week.

Elizabeth pushed back from her desk and headed for the elevator. Walking down the hall, she mentally prepared for the conversation that was to come. As she closed in on the elevator bank, Kenny strode out of his office and sidled up next to her.

"Hey, lucky," he said with a smile. "Nice break on the office. I thought they would give it to me, but I'm happy with my spot. And I'm sure it makes them look good to have a woman in the corner office. I don't mean that as an insult at all. You understand."

"No offense taken," Elizabeth replied, doing her best to mask her mild annoyance. She had developed an incredibly thick skin over the years, and it took way more than a comment like that to insult her. Getting the Old Man's corner office was no guarantee that she would be getting the Old Man's work or responsibility. It was just an office, after all.

Elizabeth added, "Sorry, I actually don't have time to chat. I'm late to lunch with the Old Man and Joe."

"Oh, didn't he tell you? I'm tagging along. I wonder if they've decided to pick a new cochair."

*Hmm*, thought Elizabeth. She had expected that the lunch would be an opportunity for the Old Man to dispense some of his famous "wisdom" on his way out, but it was equally plausible that with his departure they might decide to elevate someone to cochair the corporate transactions team with Joe. *But surely they would be speaking to us privately on something that important*, thought Elizabeth. If Kenny was coming along, it must be something else. And she doubted Kenny was in the running, a guy five years her junior, no matter how good everyone thought he was.

"I think it's just a friendly lunch, Kenny," replied Elizabeth calmly. "I wouldn't make too much of it." As they walked together toward the elevators, Elizabeth decided that she actually felt a little bad for Kenny. If they were really promoting someone, it was going to be her, and Kenny would be disappointed. Elizabeth supposed Kenny had a shot, but, in her heart, she felt certain she had the leg up, and not just because she had more experience. She was also confident that she was the better attorney. Kenny was good, too, but a lot of the big successes Kenny was known for were a result of Elizabeth's leading the team. He wasn't a particularly bad guy; in fact, he could be a lot of fun to work with, but he had a knack for hogging the credit. Elizabeth figured everyone knew who the real brains of the operation was, so she never drew any attention to it. Firm life was hard enough without making unnecessary enemies.

A few minutes later, they both pulled into the valet at Harbor House. The Old Man and Joe were waiting in the lobby.

The Old Man kind of still had it, Elizabeth had to admit. His six-foot-four frame was leaning over the hostess stand, and he was doing that thing where he made you feel like you were the only person in the room. That hostess was a goner. She was laughing at whatever he was whispering in her ear and tilting her head just so.

Poor Joe, on the other hand, would never get the time of day from that type of woman. A bull in a china shop, a good half foot shorter and half foot wider than the Old Man, and with less than half of what the Old Man had up top.

"Hey, it's my dream team!" the Old Man boomed as he shook Kenny's hand and turned to envelop Elizabeth in a hug. "I know you are going to miss me—don't try to hide it. Especially you, Elizabeth honey. My right-hand gal!"

Elizabeth wanted to be annoyed, but she felt a rush of pleasure at the compliment, hating herself a little bit for her response. *Give me a gold star and I'm all yours*, she thought.

The hostess led them to a round table right at the water's edge. A waitress scurried over, and the Old Man ordered a steak (rare, the only way it should be eaten, he said with authority). *Really, steak at a seafood restaurant?* thought Elizabeth, but she kept her mouth shut and nodded pleasantly as she ordered her usual salad.

"Your wife must be delighted to have more time with you at home these days," began Elizabeth politely.

"Are you kidding me?" The Old Man laughed. "A third wife doesn't want to spend time with you. She wants to spend time with your money."

Joe and Kenny laughed uproariously as if it was the funniest thing they had heard all month. Elizabeth managed an awkward smile at the old, tired line whose time had come and gone.

"In any case," the Old Man continued, "this lunch isn't about me. It's about the future of our group. Joe and I have some news we would like to share with you."

Elizabeth stiffened involuntarily. *Crap, maybe Kenny was right. Here it comes*, she thought.

"This is how we see it," Joe interjected, cutting off the Old Man. "You both are great. And you would both make a great cochair with me."

*Right*, Elizabeth thought. *But I am the clear choice.*

"Look," Joe continued, "we want a modern, fresh take on things, so we are looking hard at the both of you. You both would get it done."

*Well, I certainly would*, thought Elizabeth. *Kenny, not so much.*

"Here's what we are thinking," Joe went on. "Elizabeth, you are working on Project Greysteel for Grey Corp. There probably isn't a more important client for the firm."

"And they will need a new partner to take care of them," said the Old Man.

Elizabeth was surprised to hear this. Again, she knew the Old Man would be passing that relationship on to someone else. But she thought she had it in the bag. Since when was Kenny in the picture? Greysteel was her deal. Not her client yet, but definitely her deal.

Joe continued, "Elizabeth, I know you are running the merger, but we need Kenny to be brought in now too. I want you two to run it together. Share all key information with him, and run important strategic thinking by him. You guys have always been such a great team. We need to be sure we are covered, okay? Make sense? And we need to know how the client views you both before we make any big decisions."

She definitely got it. She would do all the hard work per

usual, and Kenny would get the credit. Kenny, the man who had signed her welcome back card after having George as follows: "Hope you had an awesome vacation!"

"Of course," replied Elizabeth tightly. "I don't think you gentlemen have anything to worry about in terms of coverage, but I agree we should always function as a team for our clients, and we will continue to do that."

"And I'm sure it will be helpful to have me around when you have that kid stuff, Elizabeth," interjected Kenny.

*Not cool, Kenny*, thought Elizabeth with a little flair of anger. *No, it's fine*, she told herself. *And it's not a secret that I'm a mom. Anyway, Joe and the Old Man are smarter than to fall for that shit.*

The food arrived, and Elizabeth was thankful for the interruption. Joe began complaining to the waitress because his tomato looked "just fucking unacceptable." The Old Man and Kenny started talking about a different deal. Elizabeth ate her salad and prayed that the lunch would conclude quickly.

Elizabeth knew she would swallow her pride and do things on their terms. It's how she had always done it and why she was still hanging in there at the firm. And there were worse people to be tethered to than Kenny. If he got it, he got it. But that wasn't going to happen. She was better.

She had to relax. She should put some time into planning the weekend with the girls.

*Heather really shouldn't have cancelled*, thought Elizabeth. Sure, Heather operated at a whole different level now than her four old friends, but she should be careful. She was getting so famous now that the four of them might be the only women who would still treat her like a normal person. To them, she would always be a small-town girl from Oconomowoc, Wisconsin, one of a group of five former residents of the left hall of the second floor of the Choates dormitory.

The five of them—Heather, Elizabeth, Carmen, Martha, and Sara—had been a unit since that first day of college more than twenty years ago. The next years brought new cities, jobs, marriage, and children, all of which conspired to push them apart. Somehow, they managed to remain good friends despite the fact that their lives had unfolded very differently. To be fair, some of them were closer than others. Carmen and Martha had always had an especially close bond. But they continued over the years to find time to be all together as a group.

After more than two decades of friendship, they probably knew each other better than their own spouses knew them, and certainly better than their own children knew them. Women's lives are funny like that. It becomes so easy to forget that girl you were at eighteen. The girl who was ready to set the world on fire, without a glimmer of the compromise and disappointment that was to come. If you are lucky enough to have just one friend to remind you of that girl, you might manage to hold on to a piece of her.

Elizabeth didn't want to forget that part of herself, so she worked hard to stay in touch with her four old friends. Those old friendships felt even more important to her now because she had chosen a profession—law—that seemed to be unique in its ability to wear down a person's confidence and passion. And today was no exception.

In any case, this was the year all the girls were turning forty, and Elizabeth had hoped they could do something extra special to commemorate the occasion—but not a repeat of the Vegas debacle when they had turned thirty (Carmen's idea, of course). It had taken her a week to recover from that particular event. No, they should come up with something more dignified for this milestone.

Maybe she could get Carmen to help. But she knew Carmen would probably come up with an excuse as to why she didn't have time. She had a lot of excuses to choose from. She ran her Gold Coast neighborhood association, entertained frequently for her husband Mark's colleagues and clients, had been the PTA president from the second her daughter had started formal schooling, and was now managing the renovation of her and Mark's new vacation home in Lake Geneva. Carmen had the firm belief that she was at least as busy as the other four of them. Elizabeth was dubious (really, unless you had worked in a big job like Elizabeth's, you had no idea how demanding they were), but Carmen was her friend, so she tried to be respectful on the point.

No, whatever her argument, this year's planner had to be Carmen. Elizabeth and Sara were always buried at work, and Martha was days away from giving birth. So it had to be Carmen.

As she finished her salad, Elizabeth's thoughts turned back to Heather's e-mail. It was typical that just as Elizabeth was about to get ahead a step, Heather was "transforming" her career. That's how it always had gone in their friendship. One small step for Elizabeth, one leap forward for Heather.

She would have to ask Heather what she was up to when they saw each other next. Or, more likely, when they e-mailed each other next, since Heather didn't seem to have time for old friends anymore.

Elizabeth wished that she and Heather had stayed as close as Carmen and Martha over the years. But she and Heather both had grueling jobs. She told herself it was just different. And some days she believed that.

# CARMEN

Carmen was finally meeting Martha for lunch. Martha had been in Milwaukee just a few months since Robert had moved them and their two boys from Boston so that he could spend the year at Children's Hospital for his newest cancer study. Carmen was delighted that Martha was only an hour drive away now. It had taken all of her patience to wait a few months for this visit to give Martha a chance to settle in.

Carmen and Martha were more than just friends; they were each other's person. In so many ways they were opposites, cold, uptight Martha and fiery Carmen, but the chemistry had worked from the start. For more than twenty years, they shared the puts and takes of their lives, sometimes in person, but more often in daily calls or texts. Strung together, they were a diary of the mundane, hilarious, disappointing, and occasionally even sublime business of marriage and motherhood. And now, after Martha's big move, they could talk in person whenever they wanted to. It was a game changer for their friendship, and the timing felt perfect to Carmen, especially since she had just become an empty nester when her only daughter, Avery, went off to college last September.

Well, it would be perfect timing unless Martha messed it all up. In the last year or so, Martha had been making noises about wanting to go back to work after her baby was born. Carmen had already decided that she wasn't going to let that happen—and this lunch was an intervention.

Carmen knew she had to be subtle. Best not to launch into the importance of being home straight away. Carmen suspected that Martha secretly sided with Heather, Elizabeth, and Sara, who thought that working was an essential part of staying whole and happy. To Carmen, staying at home was a job in and of itself. And it certainly wasn't a mistake, as Heather had said to Martha at that disaster of a dinner in Chicago several years ago (what a pretentious bitch Heather had been that night). And then there was what happened to Martha after Jack was born and she was trying to work and juggle everything all alone. If Carmen had not intervened then, things would be very different indeed. Carmen hoped she would not have to bring that part up.

Carmen had found a cozy table in the corner and sat waiting for Martha, twirling her wild brown curls that framed a still unlined heart-shaped face. After a few minutes, she saw her old friend waddling in. Carmen couldn't help but giggle. Martha's five-foot-nine frame was skinny absolutely all over save for what looked like a pumpkin hiding under her tunic. That poor girl.

As she carefully lowered herself into the chair, Martha glared at Carmen and said, "Yeah, yeah, go ahead and laugh. Enjoy!"

"Hey, at least your perfect blond ponytail still looks great," Carmen teased. "So how's the rental?"

Exhaling loudly and twisting around looking for a comfortable position that didn't exist, Martha said, "You know, it's actually pretty nice. The houses here are so much bigger for the money than in Boston. Five bedrooms, Sub-Zero fridge, lake view, the works, all for under seven figures. Robert is excited about the school. It's called the University School. I wanted to try public school. Some of the northern suburban school districts like Shorewood and Whitefish Bay are supposed to be really good. That's what Elizabeth says anyway. But Robert thinks we're better off in the bigger house farther north where there are lower taxes so we can afford a private school. I didn't want to fight about it, since the boys are so young. Who knows how long we'll be here anyway."

"Martha, you wouldn't know the first thing about a public

education." Carmen laughed. A little more seriously, she asked, "Are things going better for the boys at school?"

"They seem okay, I guess. I found out that Bobby's first-grade class had three other new kids this year, so that's not too bad. I think the school gets a lot of executive types who are coming and going. But he told me that some of the kids are mean. So, you know, it's a process. The kids in Jack's 4K still don't seem to know where the bathroom is, so he's good," Martha joked, but then, her mood changing, she crossed her hands on the table and sighed. "I know it's hard to move schools for Bobby, but I mean, what was I supposed to do? Have the baby by myself in Boston in March in one of those polar vortex snowstorms? I'm not sure Robert really thought about how hard it would be on us to move. You know, the snow here might actually be worse than Boston, which I didn't think was possible. How do you even put a baby in a car seat in the snow nine months pregnant?"

Martha shifted again in search of the elusive comfortable position. "Robert tries to help, but he has this knack for being physically present but mentally disengaged when he's with the family. I shouldn't complain about him, but sometimes I get so tired, Carmen."

Carmen reached across the table and squeezed Martha's hand. "Hey, you're allowed to complain. You are raising two little kids going on three, and with Robert's schedule, you're basically doing it as a single mom in a city where you know like two people. It's impossible and you're doing great. And think how lucky you are. I would have killed for another kid or three."

Martha squeezed Carmen's hand back, and a quiet moment passed between them.

Trying not to let the sadness creep up, Carmen said, "And how's my good friend Evelyn?"

Smiling again, Martha said, "Oh, Carmen, you should hear my mom talk to her friends. Even with all their fancy educations, I don't think any of them could locate Wisconsin on a map if they tried. Robert told her that the position at Children's might only be for a year, so she's calling it his 'ex-pat' assignment. I mean, really, like Wisconsin's another country."

Carmen grinned, remembering the first day she met Evelyn. It was move-in day at Dartmouth. Her dorm was called the Choates. She had no idea how to pronounce it, and she wasn't going to try until she heard it come out of someone else's mouth. She was a long way from Texas, and she was determined not to make rookie mistakes.

As she and her parents walked into her new room, they had been greeted by three people who collectively looked well, pastel, for lack of a better word. The dad had been wearing pink pants, and the mom had been wearing a cotton shift dress with an unappealing floral motif that wasn't doing her emaciated frame any favors. Carmen did like the mom's canvas tote, though. It screamed, *I belong here*, Carmen had thought. Behind her parents, a pale, rail-thin girl with stick-straight long, blond hair (kind of the color of a wheat field, Carmen had thought) sat on one of the two twin beds in the room surrounded by her matching monogrammed luggage (the same canvas as the mom's tote, of course). She looked kind of miserable, Carmen remembered thinking.

"Hello, dear," the mom had said. "You must be Martha's roommate! How exciting that she gets to learn about your culture!"

*Great*, Carmen had thought. *Here we go again.* To her credit, the girl reddened a bit and opened her mouth to object, but before she could get a word out, Carmen's father had lunged forward and boomed, "I guess you mean Texas culture! Hey, we're all Americans, right?" Pink pants flinched at the volume and took a quick step back.

"Oh, of course," the mom had stammered while she looked back and forth in confusion at Carmen's very white father and very not-white mother. Not knowing what to do, she shook hands with Carmen's father while taking in his cowboy boots.

Carmen had immediately known that quietly blending in would not be in the cards that day. She remembered thinking it was going to be a long four years as she watched her parents pull away. But she had been wrong. It had turned out to be an amazing four years. She and Martha might have been from different worlds, but they were the same where it counted. After a few months they were as thick as thieves, and Martha was her official tour guide for all things East Coast. They also got friendly with the girls across the hall—Heather and Elizabeth—both girls from the Midwest. A fifth girl who lived on their floor, Sara, a third midwesterner, quickly joined their band, a victim of a bad roommate match.

After those four years, Carmen had forgotten what it felt like to be an outsider. She was just Carmen.

A waitress came over for their drink orders, and Martha asked for a triple espresso.

"Good God, you never change. That much caffeine all at once is really not good for you or the baby," said Carmen, feeling a little alarm bell go off in her mind. "She'll have a water too," she instructed the waitress.

"So," said Carmen carefully, "what have you decided about work? I know that you had planned to go back when Jack started 4K, but with the baby, don't you think it makes sense to give it a few more years? I mean, what's the rush?"

*Be gentle*, Carmen reminded herself. But she knew she had to remind Martha of how hard the mom job really was. Especially as the kids got older. Martha's oldest, Bobby, was only in first grade, and the job didn't get any easier. Of all of Martha's friends, Carmen was the only one that had been a full-time stay-at-home mom all these years. Even if she hadn't ever had an outside job, as her mom friends used to say, Carmen had worked her ass off since graduating from Dartmouth almost twenty years ago. Playground monitor. PTA president. Manager of her daughter's sometimes grueling dance schedule. Head of the local Gold Coast community association (and chair of the beautification and historical preservation subcommittee). It really irritated her over the years when Heather, Sara, or Elizabeth insinuated that she must have all the time in the world. They had no idea how much work volunteering and full-on mothering with no help really was. And even though Carmen sometimes longed for the exciting job she had missed out on, she would remind herself that the working moms she knew at Avery's school always seemed exhausted, and though they might show up for the occasional field trip or concert, they were never fully part of things.

In any case, this was her chance to convince Martha to make the right decision, not just for the sake of her kids, but also for the sake of her health and sanity. And maybe if Martha didn't go back to work, Carmen could see more of her, which would make life a little less lonely. But Martha had been programmed from birth by her uptight Boston clan to be a world-beater, and Carmen knew she was going to have to dig in if she wanted to win the argument.

Carmen continued, "So, I was thinking that we should make some summer plans, you and me. Lake Geneva is gorgeous in the summer, and I'd love to have you come down for a while. The house won't be totally finished, but close enough. It would be like glamping."

"Maybe," said Martha slowly, avoiding Carmen's gaze. "I'm actually planning to get a summer nanny so I can get back to work. If I can get something going, I could keep her in the fall or maybe just put the baby in day care. Anyway, I don't know how things are going to go."

Carmen couldn't hold it in any longer. "Look, you know what I think. I know your parents, and certainly Heather, and probably Elizabeth and Sara, too, think continuing staying home is a mistake for you," replied Carmen as calmly as she could. "Don't forget that Heather and Elizabeth have huge amounts of help at home. We all know Phil is doing all the dirty work. Or at least he has to coordinate the army of people they have raising their kids and keeping their house in order. And don't forget that Elizabeth has William. You and I don't have a William. And Sara, well, I think that's really good evidence for my argument right there. I'm worried one of these days she is going to drive her Odyssey right over a cliff because she's so stressed and distracted."

"That's not fair, Carmen," scolded Martha. "Sara is a really good mom. You can figure out both parents working. People do it all the time."

"Maybe, but four kids and both parents working is actually just too much. You remember when Sara moved from New York to my neck of the woods and she blew off every invitation from me to do stuff, right? I mean, I get that she's busy, but there's busy and then there's no-life busy. C'mon, Martha. I know you. Is the Sara life really the life you want? Just because you *can* do something doesn't mean you should, you know."

Carmen was on a roll. "Please just enjoy that baby. It will be your last one. Seriously, what's a few more years? It's not like you need the money or anything. And we'll have fun—I promise. It will be just like the good old days."

"I've been home over three years now. It's already been too long. And besides, when my boys are in school in the fall, we'll have time to do stuff. Doctors get time off, you know," countered Martha.

"Listen, you put your baby in day care, you'll have hand, foot, and mouth disease within the month," Carmen teased, taking a different tack and hoping Martha would relent.

But Martha wasn't having it. "Carmen, you know I love being home with the boys. But I miss medicine so much. I worked so hard for it, and I really thought that I could do both. I don't think it's fair that I have to bear the burden of making sure the children Robert and I created are getting everything they need.

Really, we are both doctors and both parents. Why is this my burden alone?" Martha's eyes welled up a little, and she looked away in embarrassment.

"I know," said Carmen softly, "I really do get it. I never asked Mark to lift a finger, but my situation was always different. Look, if working is what you want, you should do it. I love you and will support you no matter what, you know that. But Robert is not going to be a different guy. So I would quit being disappointed on that score. You have to do what's right for you and what's right for the family. Don't you think just focusing on the mom job will give you the most happiness in the long run? I see those exhausted working moms all the time, and they look miserable."

"I guess," said Martha slowly, "but there's nothing like doing a job you were trained to do and doing it well."

"Martha, don't forget what happened the last time," Carmen reminded her gently. Carmen remembered getting the text from Martha and rushing to Boston to take care of her boys while Martha locked herself away in her bedroom and slept. Robert had been in Europe on another one of his work trips. "Anxiety," the doctor had said. "Your friend just needs some time to rest." Martha had sworn Carmen to secrecy and decided not even to tell Robert. And it had stayed their secret since.

"Carmen, I'm better now, and I can handle it this time. And I don't want to talk about it again. You promised we wouldn't talk about it," said Martha quietly as she stared down at her hands, which she was kneading in her lap.

After a pause, Martha continued, "Anyway, I have a call scheduled for Friday with an old med school classmate who might be able to get me a position at a local clinic he runs. I owe it to myself to look into it. Carmen, do you ever think about how weird it is that we started out so ambitious and driven in college, and now here we are not working? I don't know, I feel like if women like us can't get this figured out, then nobody can, you know what I mean? We started out with every advantage. Especially me."

Carmen didn't know what to say to that, so she decided to say nothing for the time being. She was clearly losing the battle. And Martha was going down that old, bad road again. This would not be the last conversation they would have, vowed Carmen.

After a prolonged silence, Martha made an attempt to change the subject. "So what's the plan for our girls' weekend?"

"Well, Heather has already bailed," said Carmen dramatically, trying to put her concern to the side and rolling her eyes for good measure. "No surprise there. She's working on some secret project."

"You know, I'm not sure I care that she's not coming," said Martha matter-of-factly. "Ever since she was so judgy at that dinner after Jack was born, well, let's just say I've had trouble enjoying her company."

"This is what I've been saying for years," agreed Carmen.

"But Elizabeth and Heather are kind of a package deal, aren't they?" Martha sighed.

"And Heather does pony up the free stuff. Do you remember when she sent us all those e-readers preloaded with hundreds of books? Not bad," Carmen conceded. "So we should consider that."

The waitress returned with their drinks.

"Is Mark excited for the new house in Lake Geneva?" asked Martha.

"You know, he said he would get up from the city more, but he's so busy," said Carmen.

"Hmmm. Well, I hope he appreciates all the effort you are going to," said Martha with suspicion.

"I'm sure he does," responded Carmen brightly. "But, well, it's hard sometimes—"

Suddenly, Martha interjected, "Oh God, I have to go to the bathroom, again! When will this be over?"

Carmen laughed and watched her friend negotiate her way to the bathroom at the back of the café. Carmen had been about to admit that things with Mark weren't so great. It was the one area that she never wanted to discuss with Martha, though, because she just couldn't face the truth herself, and talking to Martha about it would make it real.

And if she and Mark could just get pregnant it could be different. No, it *would* be different. He would stop making excuses for why he couldn't get up to Lake Geneva from the city. And if there was something there, well, it couldn't compete with what she could give him—loyalty, family, a shared history.

By the time Martha came back from the bathroom, talk of Mark was forgotten, and the girls filled the rest of their lunch talking about house stuff, both of them happy to avoid deeper conversation.

# MARTHA

A few days had passed since Martha met Carmen for lunch, but the conversation had stuck with her. As she sat in the stiff, narrow, and unyielding chair outside the office of the head of the lower school where Bobby and Jack were enrolled, waiting for her appointment, she considered whether Carmen was right.

Martha really did enjoy being able to be there for so many things she would have otherwise missed. It was the small things at the strangest times. And mostly in the car, it seemed. Maybe on the way to school when they wanted just one more hug before starting their day. Or, even more likely, on the way back when they forgot she was there and spilled their secrets to each other with no apparent filter.

But being a doctor was more than just getting up and going to a job. It was being the person who solved the puzzle and helped set someone else's life back on the right course. It was time for her to get back that part of who she was. And this time she would do things differently. She wouldn't let it all fall apart again.

As she decided that she would move ahead with her call tomorrow with her old classmate, she heard the office assistant call her name.

"Mrs. West, the dean will see you now."

Martha rose from the chair and walked into the dean's office, quickly locating the widest available seat.

"Please sit down and make yourself comfortable, assuming, of course, that remains a possibility for you at this stage," the dean said wryly.

Martha smiled and said, "Not really, but I'll give it a chance."

"When are you expecting the new arrival?" the dean asked pleasantly.

"Any day now," replied Martha with a tired smile.

"Excellent. Well, I won't beat around the bush given your condition. I'm sure a rest would do you good. I called you and your husband in to discuss a serious matter."

"Yes, I'm sorry Robert was unable to make it. His work at the hospital makes it very difficult for him to get away," Martha interjected apologetically, annoyed that she was yet again in the position to have to make excuses for him.

"Well, if we don't make some progress, I will want him to participate in future discussions. It's important in our community that both parents are part of the process."

"Of course," replied Martha, wondering what could be such an enormous problem at the first-grade level that it required both Robert and her to attend a future meeting.

"I assume the issue is in the first-grade classroom," prompted Martha, wanting to get this over with and find a place to get ice cream. She was hungry and tired.

"Actually, this is a more global concern," replied the dean in a serious tone. "Our staff have observed some ongoing issues with both the boys. In the case of Bobby, we have witnessed a number of instances of aggression toward the other children. There was one instance in which he pulled the hair of another classmate and two reports of shouting on the playground. These sorts of behaviors are not the kind that are acceptable in our community. While they haven't risen to the level that would require immediate action, we wanted to inform you of our findings so that you can be part of the solution moving forward."

"I'm sure that a part of that is the stress of the move," said Martha, vowing to read Bobby the riot act when she got home. "Robert and I will address it, of course. You mentioned that there are issues with both boys?"

"Yes, with Jack, the staff informs me that he has had a number of accidents requiring the staff to be pulled away from learning activities to assist him. As you know, our policy is that all 4K community members must be fully toilet trained. I appreciate that accidents happen, but more than a few accidents indicate a failure to be fully trained. And, as you know, the accidents are, shall we say, often so catastrophic that we can't simply clean him up here at school, necessitating an immediate parent pickup."

Martha felt her cheeks go hot with embarrassment. "Yes, I know Jack has had some issues in that department. I think the change has been hard on him as well."

"Agreed. And we will give you every opportunity to adjust more fully. It's only been nine weeks after all. But I must advise that with the arrival of a new baby, we often find this can create additional difficulties. I have an excellent consultant if you are interested." The dean began rummaging around in her desk. "She's available to speak with you tomorrow if you are available."

"Actually, I have an interview tomorrow," Martha blurted out.

"Yes, I imagine you are still looking for all sorts of help. You know, we produce a list of recommended service providers for a wide variety of needs, from household help to doctors, tutors, and coaches. I'll ask Glenda to e-mail it to you," said the dean.

"No, actually, I am interviewing to get a job as a doctor in a local clinic run by an old classmate."

The dean looked confused.

"But won't you be taking care of the new baby for some time?" she asked.

"Maybe for a few weeks, but I'd really like to get back to work. I'm a doctor," said Martha lamely.

"Is there a financial consideration? We can certainly talk with your family about our financial aid options."

"No, no, we don't need the money," Martha replied, with growing embarrassment at this entire exchange. "I miss being a doctor, and I'm excited to return to the profession."

"I see," said the dean, although it was clear that she didn't see. "I do hope you take into consideration the needs of your boys and the issues we covered as you make your decisions. Perhaps you could delay that degree of change until things are settled." Rising from her chair, she continued, "Well, that's enough of that. Good day. My door is always open."

Having properly shamed Martha, the dean motioned her out.

*Well, there you go*, thought Martha. *Women who think men are the problem really are missing the boat because no one is less kind to women than other women, regardless of the circumstances. We truly can't win. And shame is the weapon of choice. The dean would have never told Robert not to go to work.*

It made her remember again that day she had been so angry with Heather, the moment that she had never fully forgiven, if she was being honest.

It had happened right after Jack was born. Heather had started her family and had just been recruited to her big executive job at FLASH. Elizabeth had made partner at her law firm, but she hadn't started trying for a baby yet. Sara was on baby number three and was working at her in-house lawyer job. And Carmen was home with Avery, probably busier than any of them with her various school and community commitments.

That year they had decided to meet for their annual girls' weekend in Chicago, where Carmen and Sara were living.

Martha was excited to tell her friends about her choice to stay home full-time. She didn't tell them the whole story, of course. Only Carmen knew about all of it. But she thought they would be happy for her, and, selfishly, she was trying to be okay with her decision, and their approval would have gone a long way toward that cause.

Heather had insisted that they go to the Four Seasons and that she pay. They all objected. The stress of keeping up with the Joneses was making everyone feel relatively poor, and they expected Heather was no exception . . . until she told them what her pay package was going to be at FLASH. When they heard the eye-popping sum, they couldn't say yes fast enough.

Heather had booked them into the biggest suite in the place. For her money, Martha would have stayed in the room the whole weekend, luxuriating in the enormous white-and-gray marble tub, but Heather had insisted that they all get dressed up to celebrate her and Elizabeth's promotions. They went to dinner at one of those great Chicago restaurants where an individual cut of steak was enough to feed the whole table.

Martha still had a picture of the five of them at that dinner in a moving box somewhere. Everyone looked so happy and full of life in the picture, with their glasses raised in a toast.

The dinner went as it always did. They told stories about the old days—skating on Occum Pond, building the ice sculpture on the Green, dancing around the bonfire at Homecoming. The conversation would inevitably turn to gossip about mutual acquaintances. Everything had been going swimmingly until Martha shared her news.

Sara had said flatly, "Good for you—parenthood is exhausting, and you can always go back."

Elizabeth hadn't crossed the motherhood bridge yet, but she apparently felt compelled to point out that when the women at her firm left, they never, ever returned. "But if that's what you want, Martha, good for you," she had said.

"Do I have to be the asshole here?" Heather had exclaimed with exaggerated exasperation. "Martha, you are making a big mistake. Huge. If you leave now, you'll never go back. You worked so hard to become a doctor. You went to Harvard, for Christ's sake. And you're great at what you do. What are you thinking? Just hire more help!"

Carmen had immediately interjected, "Heather, it's extraordinary that you think you know what's best for everyone when you barely have time to hear about what's really going on in all of our lives," but she stopped short when Martha shot her a look that said, *Shut it, Carmen.*

The girls moved on to happier topics, but Martha couldn't shake off Heather's comments, and she did her best to hide her hurt. Carmen was right—Heather didn't know all the facts, but she knew enough to wound. Martha intended to enjoy staying home regardless of all the reasons for being there, but she did feel some shame that she couldn't do it all on her own, at least not right then.

On the way back to the hotel, Carmen took her arm and whispered, "Heather's a bitch. You are going to love being home with your baby. And don't forget, this is what you need to do right now. It's not a knock on you. No one can do it all alone. Not even Martha Adams. And of course you can go back when you're ready. Elizabeth doesn't know anything about the medical field. You're good."

Martha didn't look forward to talking to Heather much after that weekend. It was ironic. She should have had more in common with Heather after Bobby was born—she was in the motherhood club now! But she felt more distant from her than ever. It was so easy to stop talking every week. Then every month. And then one day they weren't talking much at all. Martha didn't avoid her per se, but she didn't seek her out either. They were together on their girls' weekends a few times in the intervening years, but Heather didn't ever seem to perceive the rift she had created in their relationship. Martha never pushed the issue because Heather had always been Elizabeth's closest friend and Martha didn't want to hurt Elizabeth, who didn't have many other friends outside their group. Besides, Elizabeth was a genuinely good person and didn't deserve it.

*Things change*, Martha thought as she walked out of the school and climbed behind the wheel of her car to drive back home. Dartmouth felt like a lifetime ago.

At the end of the day, it didn't matter what the dean or Heather or anyone thought. She couldn't go back to work if the boys were in trouble.

It was all very disappointing but somehow felt inevitable at the same time. It would be too much, again.

Of their entire group, Sara was the only one who had managed to figure out how to work and mother with another working spouse, although Sara didn't feel like a good data point. She seemed to relish living on the edge of disaster. Martha didn't want to live like that.

But Sara did. She wanted it all. And then she wanted to double it.

# SARA

Sara always ate lunch at her desk and always while she was multitasking. As she raised a forkful of cobb salad, her phone rang.

"Sara Beck," she said in her serious lawyer voice as she smoothed back her long brown hair, which was possibly infused with vomit. She really had no idea. She had thrown it into a bun on her way into work. Her worn navy suit jacket had probably been hit too. Whatever. After she was back to her usual size ten, she planned to throw out the size twelves (okay, some fourteens too) and maternity items for good. Maybe she would burn them.

"Scott Beck," came back a deep, teasing voice.

"I'm busy, Scott," chided Sara.

"Busier than taking care of a pukey baby?" Scott tossed back.

"And I'm eating lunch," said Sara.

"Well, lucky you! I'm cleaning lunch up off the floor, and I'm taking a vacation day!" Scott retorted.

"Okay, I'm putting down my fork," Sara conceded with a sigh.

"I just wanted to be sure that you can pick up the kids from aftercare and soccer. And probably pick up dinner."

Sara tried to control her annoyance. To be fair, Scott was taking his turn with the baby today. Not that it would matter. Even though they had been taking turns staying home when the kids got sick, Sara had missed almost six days in the first quarter alone because of a family strep outbreak, which she couldn't seem to halt even after replacing every last toothbrush three times (total cost—fifty-four dollars). If she kept at it, her boss would give her that sad look he got when he thought she wasn't performing up to her potential.

"You got it, honey. I have to get back to work. Love you," she replied in the most positive tone she could muster.

She needed to do better and be kinder to her husband, Sara reminded herself. Since she and Scott had gone for baby number four, the very little time they had together had evaporated. Like ships passing in the night, her friends would say. *Not exactly*, thought Sara, *More like exhausted shift workers forced to put in overtime without extra pay.* And when she was tired, Sara was snappish at best.

Sara's work friend Katherine came into Sara's cube to chat. Katherine was more than a decade younger than Sara and back from maternity leave from her first baby. She was finding it hard to keep her energy up throughout the day because the baby barely slept. Sara was also happy to lend a sympathetic ear or just chat for a while to help Katherine keep it together. To be fair, it helped them both keep it together.

"I'm tired," said Katherine.

"Same," agreed Sara.

"Hey, what's going on with your fancy friend in California?"

"Heather Hall?"

"Do you have other fancy friends I don't know about?" asked Katherine.

"No, she's pretty much it, sorry," Sara said with a laugh. "Let's consult my favorite guilty pleasure, Facebook, shall we?" She turned to her computer. "You know, my friends and I barely hear from Heather anymore. She's gone, like, supernova."

Sara clicked over to Heather's page, and there was her old friend. Well, technically, not a "friend" on Facebook. Heather only had "followers" at this point.

There she was. Heather Hall, Global COO of FLASH, the leading internet-based clearinghouse for, well, everything on Earth. She looked so perfect in her profile picture. Perfect maroon dress and cardigan set off by her perfect blond bob and blue eyes. Her cover banner featured three perfectly turned-out blond children posed along the perfectly blue ocean.

Yeah, Sara was jealous. Definitely jealous.

"What does her husband do anyway?"

"He invests," replied Sara.

"That's nonsense," said Katherine.

"One hundred percent," Sara agreed, laughing. "Stars, they're not just like you and me."

"What do you think it takes to be a Heather? She clearly has all the help in the world. But there has to be something special there, right? If we all could just focus one hundred percent on ourselves, do you think we could be Heathers too? Do you ever think about it?" asked Katherine.

*You have no idea, Katherine,* Sara wanted to reply. Sara often wondered what her life would look like if she hadn't been so eager to start a family with Scott in her twenties. At the time she'd made that decision, she really thought she had what it took to come back to her firm and make it work after her first baby was born. But she didn't. She had been so young then. She hadn't learned yet that when you leave a place and come back, even just months later, it's never going to be just the same as it was before. The place will have changed, and, more importantly, you will have changed. The rewards and benefits that had seemed so enticing were—how could she describe it?—*flatter,* perhaps.

"Nope," Sara said to Katherine. "Heather is just one of those one-in-a-million people."

"Well, good for her. Just thinking about that life makes me more exhausted. But it does look amazing on social media, I'll give her that. Hey, I think I'll go for a Starbucks. Want one?"

"No, I'm good," replied Sara as she watched Katherine trail out of her cube.

As Sara sat alone, she reflected on whether she might have become a Heather if things had been different. In truth, she believed all four of her old friends were wildly talented. But life, for lack of a better word, had happened to all of them.

In Sara's case, she had traded the exciting big firm life for marriage to the guy who had shown up to fix her computer on her first day, a less demanding attorney job at a local company, and four babies. So not Heather's life, but, truly, not bad.

*Speak of the devil*, she thought as the phone rang and she saw it was Scott calling again.

"What is it, Scott?" she asked, taking care to sound light and pleasant.

"I think the baby needs to go to the doctor."

"Okay, what are the symptoms?"

"So, basically he won't stop crying. And more puking."

"A lot of puke?"

"Well, no, but the dry heaving makes me want to puke."

"Nope. It's a virus. You just have to deal with it."

"Sara, you know I really don't do bodily fluids. Can you just work from home or something, please? I need a break. I've been at this for like five hours since you left."

Sara bit her tongue. *Mmmkay. Five whole hours. Daylight hours at that.*

"Yes, I'll come home," she replied, "but Scott, we still need to pick up the kids."

"I thought you could give me a few hours off, then pick the kids up, and maybe get dinner while you're at it."

She wanted to reply, *Sure, Scott, I'll just do everything.*

Instead she said simply, "Sure, Scott," trying not to use a sarcastic tone. She just wasn't up for another round of The Fight today.

The Fight was always about the same thing—who was doing more, especially more of the shit work: dirty diapers, food prep, food service, food cleanup, cleanup in general, day care coordination, soccer driving, registrations, private lessons, doctor appointments, parent-teacher conferences, and on and on. The list was endless.

The Fight was in reality an ongoing war with no winner and enormous collateral damage. The worst effect of The Fight was that neither of them could ever fully relax and enjoy their precious little time off. If Sara was watching TV with a glass of wine, Scott would assume that she was slacking off on something that he would have to do instead. And vice versa. When Scott watched football every Saturday in the fall, Sara looked around the house suspiciously thinking that he must be ignoring some of his chores. Sometimes she ran the vacuum during a big game just to be spiteful. He would retaliate by making a big mess of his "hands-off" space, just to make her squirm. Sara also suspected that he often worked late just so he didn't have to hear about all the things he wasn't doing right. And on and on The Fight went.

Sometimes it was just easier to give in, and today was one of those days.

As she sighed and turned her attention back to her computer, she got a group text from Elizabeth:

Ladies, this is your official save the date: Carmel, June 1. Heather's out, but her new cottage is in! Carmen, please be the planner! Pretty please?

Aw, Heather was out. Too bad. She knew their little group of five had its tensions, but it wouldn't be the same without Heather. Sara was well aware that Martha and Carmen had their issues with Heather, but Sara kind of admired her. She could be difficult, sure, but look at what she had done with her life. It was amazing, really. And Heather had always shared her success with her old friends. When they had all gotten together in Chicago, Heather had put them up at the Four Seasons. Sara had really enjoyed that weekend, even though Martha had gotten bent out of shape when Heather tried to encourage her to stick with her career. Maybe Carmen and Martha were just pea green. Understandable.

Sara responded to Elizabeth's text:

Of course, I'm in. But I can't plan it, you guys. I plead temporary insanity. Ha! Get it, it's a lawyer joke!

# HEATHER

**From Heather Hall's Twitter**

**Heather Hall** @therealheatherhall · March 5

Mark your calendars for September 1 #projectlaunch #whatsholdingyouback

← Reply  ↔ Retweet  ♥ Favorite  ⋯ More

# ELIZABETH

After the awkward lunch at Harbor House, Elizabeth spent the rest of the week grinding away as usual. Today was Friday, though, and she didn't want to spend even one more minute thinking about the office. She needed a little fun and was going to book a surprise vacation for her and William at the end of the month.

Maybe Paris. Whatever the destination, she had already lined up William's parents to take care of George. She needed the break and couldn't wait to tell William. And Paris would be a great place to get pregnant.

She was clicking around the Air France website when she heard a familiar—and unwelcome—sound coming through her office door.

"Hey there," Kenny called.

Elizabeth grimaced and swiveled towards the door. "Hey, Kenny, what's up?" she asked.

"Well, I was thinking we should get a weekly meeting on the schedule. You know, make sure I'm up to speed and all. Hey, we don't want to disappoint Joe."

"Sure, Kenny," Elizabeth replied tightly. Couldn't he wait at least a week before trying to take over her job? "Why don't you speak with my assistant on your way out? Let's start with monthly and see how it goes."

"Sounds good," Kenny said as he slowly eased his way out of her door.

Elizabeth was going to have to keep her eye on him.

# CARMEN

It was the first Friday of the month. That meant Carmen was driving down to the city to see her new fertility specialist, Dr. Lee.

Dr. Lee's office was on the seventy-third floor. She parked and made her way through to the clinic.

"Good morning, Mrs. Jones!" enthused the receptionist. "Please sign in on the iPad and take a seat. Dr. Lee will be with you shortly. The client satisfaction coordinator is at his desk to the left and will be pleased to meet your every need."

*Right*, thought Carmen, *every need except the most basic one. The need for another baby.*

The really frustrating thing was that she was in a group for which no one felt much pity. She already had a baby. She wasn't childless. And Mark had provided an exceptional quality of life for her and Avery. The relationship wasn't always great (when Mark managed to find time for it at all), but she wasn't divorced. And that was something, she supposed.

"Mrs. Jones, your turn," a young nurse announced.

Carmen was escorted to a beautifully appointed room in the back of the clinic with an acupuncture table at the center. The young nurse took her vitals, reviewed her journal, made some notes, and prepared her for the procedure.

Fifteen minutes later, the needles were sliding in.

"Good afternoon, Carmen," said Dr. Lee. "How have you been in the last month?"

"The same," Carmen said. "I've been following your instructions. But I can't say that anything is different."

"It takes time. And patience. And belief. This process is all about faith. Now try to relax. I'll be back in twenty minutes. And no phones." He looked suspiciously at her purse.

Carmen just smiled in response, electing to keep her thoughts about Dr. Lee's time and faith to herself. It was her strongly held suspicion that for Dr. Lee it was all about the cold hard cash. But she was desperate. And desperate women did desperate things, like treat their body as if it were a pin cushion. She wasn't sure that any of this would do a thing. But she was willing to give it a try.

None of the doctors had been able to explain why she couldn't have another baby. Mark had been tested years ago and passed with flying colors. And all of her tests had come back clean. So there was really no explanation. Mark refused to do IUI or IVF or anything else that was on the infertility menu. So Carmen was left with Dr. Lee. But she had socked away some money in the household account and quietly frozen her eggs ten years ago, just in case she really did run out of time.

As Carmen lay on the table and tried to relax, she heard her phone buzz.

*Shit.*

Trying not to move, she reached her arm down to the floor and felt for her purse. She managed to locate her phone and lifted it above her head to put it on speaker. She couldn't put it next to her face without hitting one of the needles. It was Martha.

"I'm with Dr. Lee, and I can't really talk," she whispered into the receiver.

"But I really need to talk, please?" begged Martha.

"Okay, fine, but be quiet," hissed Carmen.

As Carmen tried to hold the phone aloft, she listened to Martha's entire story about the boys, and the dean, and pulling hair, and potty training.

When Martha finally took a breath, Carmen replied, "So we agree then it makes sense to wait a little on the job, right?"

"Yes, I guess," answered Martha. "I'm just disappointed. You understand."

"Of course I understand," said Carmen softly. "Don't you remember the day I decided to keep Avery? I mean, that was a pretty fucking huge compromise. But it was also my best moment in a lot of ways."

"Absolutely, I remember," said Martha. "You were so strong, Carmen. I still can't believe Mark didn't stay back in Hanover for our senior year. I mean, come on. You were pregnant and alone."

"Martha, that's not fair, he needed to be successful at the bank, and New York was too far of a commute. Look, I graduated and we got married, so what else could I have asked for? I wasn't exactly the love of his life. As you will remember, Mark was supposed to be the fun senior frat guy. But we've made the best of it, and I can't complain. And I wasn't alone. I had you guys."

But Carmen hadn't had them, not really. Avery was born in New York shortly after the girls graduated. None of them were able to visit her in the hospital. Elizabeth and Sara had already gone back home to get ready for law school in the fall. Martha was gearing up for med school. Everyone had big plans. Everyone except for Carmen. It had been a hard, lonely time.

"I don't know, Carmen. I still say he could have done better. But you're right, Mark did the right thing in the end. And I know you love him, Carmen. I just think you deserve perfect happiness," said Martha.

"Well, maybe these treatments will finally do some good," said Carmen, not wanting to get into a conversation about Mark with Martha. Maybe she should talk to her friend, though, about what was going on with Mark. Martha was probably the only one that knew *almost* the whole truth. That Carmen's marriage to Mark was one of compromise. That Carmen had pushed away her disappointment and concentrated on Avery's success and her own plans for a bigger family that she could pour all her energy and love into. That even there she had failed because her plan for a big, busy family with Mark had not materialized. That maybe her mom had been right all those years ago on her graduation weekend.

It had been a disaster of a weekend. Carmen hadn't told her parents about the pregnancy (much less the marriage) until a few weeks before graduation weekend. She hadn't been showing at Christmas break and had fabricated a reason not to come home over spring break. Her parents also hadn't even met Mark. The only thing they thought they knew for sure about him was that he didn't care enough about their daughter to show up for her graduation. Carmen assured them that Mark had been a stand-up guy and that they had married a few months before, but that seemed to make her mother even sadder.

At the end of the graduation weekend, she had planned to meet her parents for breakfast at Lou's. Before the food even hit the table, her parents asked her if she would consider coming home and raising the baby there instead of going to New York, "which was no place for a human, much less a baby." They were concerned that Mark's family would never accept a half-Hispanic wife or even a quarter-Hispanic daughter. Carmen told them that they were being ridiculous—this wasn't 1965, and it wasn't Texas. But they weren't convinced and thought she should get a quick divorce, cut her losses, and start over in Texas.

That idea seemed ridiculous to Carmen, but her mother insisted, "You'll see, honey. Time will tell. He's not the man for you. And you will be so lonely by yourself in a tiny apartment with a baby and no help. And your poor baby. What will come of her?"

Carmen had hated it when her mom turned out to be right, at least about the alone part. She might have nailed Mark, time would tell, but she had been very wrong about Avery. On that score, the proof was in the pudding. Avery was in her first year at her mother's alma mater. And things would be different for Avery.

"Martha," Carmen continued, "I've been thinking that maybe I should stop trying for a baby."

"What do you mean?" asked Martha. "You're still young. Don't give up. That's not you."

"I just wonder if maybe I'm still trying to make something work that's not meant to be."

"Carmen, I'm going to need to go," interjected Martha suddenly.

"Oh, okay," said Carmen, disappointed that she wasn't going to get a chance to talk about Mark now that she had gotten up the courage to broach the topic. But this was always Martha's way. Always something happening. "I'll call you later I guess."

"Yeah, no, Carmen, I'm going to need you to come to the hospital. Like right now. My water just broke."

"Yes!" screamed Carmen with excitement. "We're having a baby!" She sat up abruptly and starting pulling the needles out of her arms.

At the noise, Dr. Lee burst back into the room.

"What are you doing?" he demanded, fixing a glare on the cell phone in Carmen's left hand.

"We are having a baby! Like right now!" she shouted as she pulled out the last of the needles and pushed past him out the door.

As she exited the office, she heard Dr. Lee ask the receptionist to make a referral for her to a psychiatrist.

As she rushed back to her car, Carmen clicked open her phone to make a note to call Dr. Lee back and explain. She noticed a text from Elizabeth and Sara.

**Elizabeth**: Ladies, this is your official save the date: Carmel, June 1. Heather's out, but her new cottage is in! Carmen, please be the planner! Pretty please?

**Sara**: Of course, I'm in. But I can't plan it, you guys. I plead temporary insanity. Ha! Get it, it's a lawyer joke!

Of course they wanted her to plan the weekend. Some things never change. She texted back:

Fine. But you fancy lawyers are ponying up for the booze.
Also, get your shit together and get over to the hospital.
We're having a baby!!! No excuses, Sara!

# MARTHA

"You've got this, honey—one more push!" encouraged the petite blond nurse who was so young that Martha doubted she had yet experienced the pleasure of being anchored to a bed by an IV and paralyzed from the waist down.

The OB at the foot of the bed wasn't Martha's regular doctor. This baby was coming early—and quickly—and her new Wisconsin OB wasn't able to get there on time.

And Robert was going to miss it. Again.

He had been traveling when Bobby was born a few weeks earlier than expected. All of their doctor friends had assured them that first babies were always late. Nope.

He'd also missed Jack's birth because he had a presentation scheduled the same day Martha went into labor, and he just couldn't cancel. Hundreds of doctors had come to hear him speak about his research.

So here she was again, alone in labor for the third time. Goddammit, she should have just stayed in Boston. At least her mom and dad would be around. The only thing currently keeping her company was the neighboring cornfield. *No, that's not entirely accurate*, she reminded herself. She was here in labor with this doctor who was a stranger to her and her new "friend," Tiffany, the teenage nurse. She couldn't be sure, but she thought Tiffany had a tiny *T* tattoo on the back of her neck. At least she hoped it was a just a *T*.

In Robert's defense, Martha's baby was almost three weeks early this time, and Robert had thought he would have time for a quick business trip. He had left on Wednesday and promised to be back by the end of the day Friday. Several hours too late, it turned out.

Martha heard a commotion at the door. Maybe he had made it after all. But then she heard, "I *am* family, Tiffany, is it?" and she knew everything was going to be okay.

Carmen rushed in, grabbed Martha's hand, turned to the OB, and demanded, "Are we doing this now or what?"

Martha sighed and gave one more push. And then she heard her baby cry.

"It's a girl!" Tiffany proclaimed as she hovered over the OB's shoulder.

"It's a girl!" screamed Carmen.

"Carmen, please don't scream," said Martha, but she didn't really mean it. A girl. If she weren't so tired, she would scream it herself.

As Carmen pulled out her phone for pictures, Tiffany took the baby to be weighed and cleaned up. "She's a beautiful little thing! Just five pounds even!"

*That's small*, thought Martha, with quiet worry.

"Tiffany, let me know if you need anything else," said the OB brusquely as he headed for the door. "And please inform all our guests about the visiting policies," he said as he shot Carmen a dirty look.

*Shitty bedside manner*, thought Martha. *I never treated a patient like that.*

After a few minutes, the nurse brought the baby over to Martha, and Martha's worry evaporated as she got the first glimpse of her daughter. Tiffany gently placed the baby on Martha's chest, and just then the cloud outside the hospital window passed, and the late afternoon sunlight burst into the room. Martha stared into her daughter's blue eyes and stroked her hand over the little tuft of pale hair on her crown. Finally, a baby that looked like her. The boys both had darker hair and eyes like Robert.

This was her baby.

She and Robert had been talking about names for the last

month or two. Martha was adamant that the baby's name, boy or girl, include her maiden name, Adams, to honor her side of the family. She only had a sister, and she knew her parents had some lingering sadness that the Adams name was not going to be brought forth into the next generation. This was her chance to fix that, if only a little bit, and in a great sort of feminist way. Robert had agreed to the idea if it was limited to the baby's middle name, but he'd insisted the first name should be Irish to represent his side of the family.

*But Robert isn't here, is he?* thought Martha.

"Her name is Lucy Adams West," she announced to Tiffany and Carmen.

"What a beautiful name!" Tiffany responded. "I'll go get her bassinet—be right back!" Carmen followed her out, making a series of demands beginning with a Diet Coke and chocolate cake for Martha.

Martha and Lucy were alone in the room.

"Hi, baby," whispered Martha as she pulled her new baby close. "Your name is Lucy. Mommy picked it just for you. It was my grandmother Adams's name. It means the bringer of light. My little ray of sunshine."

Martha heard another voice outside her room, and she knew that she had more company.

"We are basically sisters, so I don't think that rule would apply to me, Tiffany." Elizabeth was here too.

Life was going to be good in Milwaukee.

# SARA

Sara was trying to wrap things up for the week. She had gotten a text from Carmen that Martha had gone to the hospital. If it weren't for Carmen's texts, Sara and the rest of her friends would probably have no idea what was going on. It was funny. Since Martha had moved and Carmen had taken up her weekend home project, it felt like college all over again. Carmen had always been the town crier.

It was three o'clock, and Sara wanted to pick up the train to go up to Milwaukee and see Martha. Maybe if she was lucky, the baby would already be born. She knew this would seriously impair her credit with Scott for purposes of The Fight, but it would be worth it just for the newborn smell alone.

It was a Friday near the end of the quarter, and she should have known better.

She was putting the final touches on one of her long-term projects when the phone rang.

"Sara Beck," she said curtly.

"Oh, thank God I found you," the voice on the other end of the line said. "I have a contract emergency. If we don't get this fixed, my numbers for the quarter are really going to be screwed. Please. You gotta help me. My back's against the wall here."

Sales guys. They always thought everything was an emergency. And it almost never was one. She sighed and reserved the last available conference room on the other side of the building. At least she would get her steps in. Her journey to size ten was that of ten thousand steps per day.

This "emergency" turned out to be particularly ridiculous. The client's procurement office wanted a full rundown of her company's corporate structure to make sure that they were signing with the "right" entity. It was a load of nonsense, but what their clients wanted, their clients got. She spent the next hour going through the organizational chart with the sales guy.

She was wrapping up The Stupidest Client Call Ever when she saw that she had gotten four IMs from the department's paralegal, Lisa.

"Sara, just a kind reminder that our filing deadline for the 8-k is 5:30 Eastern time (4:30 CST)."

"Sara, it's 3:30. Please approve the language, and I'll file."

"Sara, where are you? We have only one hour left to file, and I really prefer not to cut it close. PLEASE ADVISE."

"Half hour left. I'm coming to find you!"

As Sara read the last message, Lisa rushed into her conference room.

"I know, I know—sorry, let's go!" Sara said in a rush.

Sara had picked the farthest conference room from the department. The pair ran back as fast as they could and made it back to Lisa's desk in record time. It was 4:09.

Sara grabbed the filing and started a final check. After six long, silent minutes, she said, "Good to go. Let's file it. And, Lisa, so sorry for the drama. Won't happen again."

It was now 4:15. *Plenty of time*, thought Sara. She slumped in her chair at her cube and tried to catch her breath. She still wasn't quite recovered.

"Done!" Lisa called from her own cubicle a few minutes later.

Sara clicked onto the SEC website, and that's when she saw it. Her company had just made a filing with the SEC announcing the hiring of their new CFO. But they had uploaded the wrong file, announcing the company's first choice, who had politely declined their offer, instead of their second choice, who had enthusiastically accepted.

*Fuck me*, Sara thought.

# HEATHER

**From Heather Hall's Twitter**

**Heather Hall** @therealheatherhall · March 6

A goal without a plan is just a wish #favoritequotes
#AntoinedeSaintExupery #Frenchwisdom

← Reply   ↔ Retweet   ♥ Favorite   ··· More

# ELIZABETH

*TGIF*, thought Elizabeth as she pulled her BMW 3 Series into the drive of her center-entrance brick colonial on one of the most desirable streets in Whitefish Bay.

She and William had moved into the house about ten years ago, right before William's family sold their business. The house had never even gone on the market. It was a classic. A perfectly maintained, five-bedroom colonial within a few blocks of the elementary school and Klode Park. The holy grail of Whitefish Bay real estate.

Everything about it was perfect, she thought as she looked at her home, now surrounded by mounds of snow that wouldn't be melting for a while. Perfect except for one thing. The house was still too empty. But she was working on that.

As she walked through the back door, she could smell something fantastic emanating from the kitchen. Spaghetti Bolognese. That meant William was in a good mood. It was one of his favorite dishes to cook and it smelled like it was done, so William was probably halfway into a martini and almost ready to serve.

"Hi, babe!" William called from the kitchen. "What should I pour for you?"

"Just a glass of red would be perfect," Elizabeth called back as she went upstairs to slip out of her work clothes and find George.

A few minutes later, they were all seated around the table. George was already happily digging into his meal.

"William, I have a wonderful surprise for you," began Elizabeth as she placed a kiss on George's forehead.

"Oh, yeah, what's that, babe?" replied William, only half

paying attention because he was trying to help George keep the spaghetti from escaping off his plate.

"I got tickets for us to go to Paris at the end of the month!" Elizabeth announced. "Remember that great place we stayed for our honeymoon? I thought since it's almost our fifteen-year anniversary, it would be fun to go back! I know our actual anniversary isn't until August, but I thought that we could start celebrating now. Work has been a grind, and, well, we really need to reconnect . . ."

As her voice trailed off, William smiled and said, "I'm sorry. Did you say you booked it already?"

"Um, yes. I did," replied Elizabeth. "I wanted it to be a surprise and all ready to go. It's not like you have anything else going on other than George. And I have that covered! Your parents and sister are willing to take him."

William did not look happy, Elizabeth thought.

An awkward silence passed between them, and then William broke it.

"Elizabeth, you know I love the idea of getting away, but did you think to ask me first?" William said with more than a little irritation.

"I just thought that whatever you had going on could be shifted around. And I know you could use a break from the baby stuff, right?" asked Elizabeth tentatively.

"Well, it can't just be shifted around with no notice," William answered with now-apparent irritation. "And it really bothers me that you think it can. You're not the only one with a schedule. For your information, some of my buddies and I were planning a March Madness party. I think they've already taken off work. I was even considering having it here so George could participate."

"I'm sorry—you were planning for the baby to participate in a day of eating hot chicken wings, drinking beer, and watching basketball? I don't know what to say to that." Elizabeth laughed.

"You should say that you are going to find another weekend for our getaway. And you should consider whether it's a good idea to treat me like one of your associates you can just boss around and whose plans you override whenever you feel like it. The fact that none of this crosses your mind is really a problem. And it also really pisses me off that you are laughing about it."

William's tone took Elizabeth by surprise, and she immediately felt her anger flair.

"Jesus Christ, William. You're talking to me like I'm some kind of thoughtless asshole. Excuse me for trying to schedule a week of fun for us. I'll just go back where you want me—sitting at my desk, working hard, while you boys have all the fun."

"Elizabeth, that's not the point, and you know it. Look, I'm sorry if I snapped. Being with a three-year-old all day isn't easy," William said, reaching out for her arm.

"I get that," Elizabeth said as she flinched away, "but my needs should come first sometimes. Look, if we don't start having a lot more sex, we are never going to have another baby!"

William's face stiffened, and he turned away from her. Elizabeth responded by picking up the bottle of red and going to hide upstairs in their study.

*Shit.* The baby thing was starting to ruin her life.

But she couldn't help it. Elizabeth had recently moved George out of the nursery into his big boy bed. And now the nursery sat empty, mocking her. This was the part of her life that no one got to see, a very private pain, the one thing coloring her otherwise wonderful life. Things that used to bring her pure joy —a walk in the park when it was bursting with color, a dinner out with her family or friends, even presents at Christmas—were now laced with regret and longing for another child. The more she tried to repress those sad feelings, the more they seemed to bubble to the surface. It may not have been rational, but it was very real.

Elizabeth was a little ashamed of her pain. She understood

on a deep level that no one would ever feel sorry for her. *Really,* they would think, *you have a big, lucrative job, a supportive husband, a healthy child, and a community of friends.* But knowing all that didn't change how Elizabeth felt. It was what it was. She desperately wanted a second child, and she was starting to worry as she watched forty come and go in February that this might be the one thing that she could not achieve.

Maybe she should have taken Heather's lead and done a little more aggressive family planning. *No, that isn't fair,* she reminded herself. She was actually a pretty good planner, but some things you can't plan for. After William's family business was sold, she became the sole breadwinner overnight while William tried out a bunch of new things, none of which panned out. She remembered lying in bed that night thinking, *Okay, it's all on me now. You got this.* So she put off motherhood for the time being and set her mind to becoming partner. She'd made it by thirty-five, and they immediately started trying. William Jr. (whom they immediately christened "George") was born two years later. And William wanted to stay home with George. So Elizabeth put aside any fantasy of staying home or going part-time and simply went back to work. It had been surprisingly easy and drama-free.

George was three now . . . and Elizabeth was forty. She and William had been trying unsuccessfully for a second baby as soon as they could after George was born.

And William never considered going back to work. He loved being at home, and she didn't have the heart to force the issue. Well, that, and she loved having him at home. Being a parent was a joy for her in part because she wasn't responsible for the day-to-day drudgery, and she didn't have to worry about outsourcing it properly either. She was free to concentrate on herself and her career from the moment she woke up to the moment she came home. And, though it was challenging, she liked working, being part of the world outside the house, which wasn't a small thing.

As she sat on the bed in frustration, it took her about three minutes to admit to herself that she was being unfair. William was working *really* hard. In fact, there was no harder job than caring for a three-year-old. William was right. She should have asked first about the trip or at least not assumed he was free. And the sex thing, well, the first rule of fight club was never to talk about fight club. She went back downstairs to apologize.

She ran into William as she exited the study. He must have just put George to bed.

"William, I'm sorry," started Elizabeth.

"If you want to work on having another baby, you don't have to take me to Paris, you know," said William as he pulled Elizabeth into his arms. He was so easy to forgive.

"But—" Elizabeth countered.

"You need to learn when to shut up, counselor," William whispered as he put a hand over her mouth and pushed her against the wall, pinning her arms above her head. She felt his mouth on her neck as he slid his hands under her T-shirt. Elizabeth made a contented noise.

"You better be quiet or you'll wake up George," William breathed into her ear.

Minutes later, she was shaking with pleasure and slumping against the wall. Elizabeth had gone from angry to frustrated to aroused in less than five minutes. William always did this to her, every time, since their first time together.

"Ready for your dinner now?" William teased as he kissed her tenderly. "Or did you want another round of dessert?"

*This guy is too good to me*, Elizabeth thought. *I should be careful what I say. He might decide someday that he doesn't want to take it from me anymore.* William was the kind of person who couldn't be dissuaded once he had made up his mind. There wouldn't be a fight, just a quiet end. *No*, thought Elizabeth, *I'm not ever going to let that happen to us. I'm going to figure my shit out and be happy.*

# CARMEN

At another dinner table, Carmen and Mark were enjoying the filet mignon with capers that Carmen had prepared, along with scratch chocolate cake for dessert.

*This is really nice*, Carmen thought. *Just the two of us.* She had tried to set a romantic mood. Candles. Real linen. She had even pulled out their wedding china. Technically, it was bought three years after the wedding, but who was counting.

After eating quietly for a while, Mark started the conversation.

"This is delicious, Carmen. Really good."

"Thanks, honey," replied Carmen as she tried to adjust her shirt to show off her décolletage and to hold her neck at its most flattering angle. "How was your week?"

"To tell you the truth, it's really been rough. I might have to stay down in Chicago next week and through the weekend."

"Really, again? I was thinking we should plan a getaway. We really haven't gone anywhere good since we bought the house. Maybe something romantic?"

"Not going to happen, Carmen. I'll make it up to you later this year, okay? Promise."

Carmen felt her stomach drop and tried not to get upset. Another chance to get pregnant out the window.

"Sure, of course," she heard herself say for what seemed like the thousandth time in their marriage, a union that made her a little smaller and a little quieter every day.

They silently finished the rest of meal, and Mark excused himself to go work.

Carmen sighed and was about to start on the dishes when

she heard a buzz. It was Mark's phone. He must have forgotten to take it with him into his home office.

She grabbed the phone and reflexively looked down. He had gotten a text from a "Nicole." It said, "Make it quick, buddy." She remembered that he had a Nicole on his deal team. Apparently, he made her work all hours too. Why couldn't he have picked a different profession? Or, more likely, he was fucking her. She walked to the study to return his phone to him.

She was going to have to up her game.

She moved around his desk and slid herself in front of him.

"Carmen, I'm busy." He sighed.

"C'mon, it only takes a few minutes," Carmen said as she started to unbutton her shirt.

He considered for a moment and then pulled her to him.

As they fell into their old routine, Carmen's thoughts went elsewhere. They always did, really. Maybe it would be different if he were a better kisser. That hadn't been something high on her list when she was looking for a fun time at college. But he was here and he was with her. That was all that mattered, she told herself. But deep down, she knew better.

# MARTHA

It was almost midnight when Robert burst into Martha's hospital room. A good half-day late. To his credit, he looked anguished.

"God. I'm so sorry. My flight was delayed. How are you? How is she?" Robert asked, and his eyes seemed to plead with her for forgiveness.

*Lucky for him, I'm not one of those women who doesn't get it,* thought Martha. She may have been disappointed as a wife, but as a fellow doctor, she understood why Robert worked as hard as he did.

"Take a breath." Martha smiled. "I'm fine. She's fine. Everything is just fine."

Robert grabbed the chart at the foot of Martha's bed and began scanning.

"Hey, Doctor, the patients are over here," said Martha, waving to him from her hospital bed. She shouldn't bother, she thought, knowing full well Robert wouldn't be satisfied until he had read through her entire chart front to back, and Lucy's as well. Again, it was both irritating and reassuring.

"I see you named her Lucy," he said after a few minutes without looking up from the chart as he continued to read. "Fair enough, given the circumstances, I guess."

Martha just smiled innocently.

"Her weight is low, but not bad given how early she was. Good thing she wasn't a boy. Girls are generally healthier in these situations, if I remember correctly from my OB-GYN rotation. Hey, I'm going to go find the attending and just double-check on everything." And with that, Robert strode out of the room, acting more like the doctor than the father.

He had forgotten to hold Lucy.

# SARA

Sunday was supposed to be a day of rest. *I'll get right on that*, Sara thought, *right after I finish paying the bills*. They had gotten take-out today, so at least she didn't have dishes on top of it.

Sara was sitting at a little writing desk crammed in a corner of the crowded living room with her laptop and a large glass of red wine. The desk wobbled as she tried to speed through the process; it hadn't quite been put together right. She and Scott had ordered it from IKEA and decided to assemble it together. Their relationship had survived the ordeal, but that would be the last time they attempted a team assembly of Scandinavian furniture.

At the moment, Sara was looking at the cable bill, which struck her as outrageously large, especially because they also now subscribed to at least three streaming services.

"Scott," Sara said as she clicked through the bill. "Do you really need all the channels we are subscribing to? Do you even watch that sports plus stuff?"

"Yes, Sara. You ask me that every month, and the answer is never going to be different," Scott replied from another corner of the room, where he was lying on the couch with a beer and probably watching one of those exact sports channels.

"It just seems like we are really overpaying for television when we barely watch it."

"Well, cancel HBO then. And the Netflix and Hulu while you're at it."

"No. Those are my things. And those are like forty bucks a month. The sports stuff is what's killing us."

"Or you could quit buying clothes," Scott countered.

"Sure, I'll just wear yoga pants to work. I'm sure they won't mind," Sara snipped right back.

"Sara, you need to back off. We are doing fine. And it's good to have stuff to cut if things get rough, right?"

"I guess," said Sara. "I just would really like to be saving more for retirement and for the kids' college."

"To be honest, if I have to choose between college football and college education, it's not a contest," Scott teased.

"Clearly," replied Sara sarcastically.

Sara sighed and turned to Scott.

"I just feel nervous, Scott. We're almost forty, and we have this huge mortgage. And the day care bill. And all this other shit," Sara said as she waved her hand at the laptop. Although Sara acknowledged mentally that sometimes the only thing standing between her and the abyss was Netflix, noise-canceling headphones, and a glass of red wine.

"Sara, the day care isn't forever, we've paid off your student loans, and we could sell the house if we needed to. The school district is so good here that we're not going to lose money. Really, you need to relax. Finish your wine."

"But what if one of us loses our job?"

"Then we'll figure it out. And I really think that's a pretty remote possibility."

"I don't. Remember how annoyed my boss was when I told him I couldn't travel for that big deal?"

"Sara, that was years ago now. Plus, he was clueless. He probably didn't even remember you were pregnant. You're way too sensitive. Guys say dumb shit all the time. Move on."

"I guess," said Sara as she turned back to the bills, but she wasn't convinced. She had a good relationship with her boss, but he still brought that stupid trip up years later, as if he thought, deep down, he couldn't really count on her. It was infuriating, really. She had missed so much kid stuff demonstrating her commitment to her job. She had been late. She had gone days without doling out hugs. And then she had drawn a necessary and reasonable boundary. Apparently that's all it had taken to negate all her previous sacrifices. It made her feel insecure.

At least Scott was doing well at work. He always took the initiative to keep his skills current—the IT guy who was always teaching all the other IT guys how to do their job. He was the whole package—super smart and played well with others. No matter what happened with her job, she could count on Scott to be the anchor for their family.

*Count your blessings, not your pennies*, Sara reminded herself as she pulled down the screen of her laptop. And she would try. If everything didn't feel so fragile, it might have been easier.

# JUNE

# HEATHER

**From**: Heather Hall <HHall@flash.com>
**Sent**: Sun. 5/31 4:00 p.m.
**To**: Elizabeth Smith <ESmith@gmail.com>
Carmen Jones <MrsMarkJones@yahoo.com>
Martha Adams West <MAW@gmail.com>
Sara Beck <Sara.Beck@bigcompany.com>
**Subject**: Exciting news

I'm so glad you guys are heading to Carmel. I wish I could be there. Trust me, it's for a good cause! My agent would kill me if I gave away too much before the September launch of my new project . . . but . . . I can tell you that I've written a book! I can't tell you much more now, but it's very special. We are working out the final details on the marketing plan. I don't think it gives away too much to say that I've written something that I think will help women everywhere. You guys will be very excited, I promise.

Love and kisses,

Heather

# ELIZABETH

*Carmel-by-the-Sea is heaven*, Elizabeth thought as she walked by herself along the beach. There was no other word for it. Ocean air. The faint smell of salt and seaweed. Ever temperate, even in June, which seemed kind of magical in California, where every other city seemed to blister in the summer. Just the right number of high-end shops and restaurants. Every building and corner perfectly appointed with an almost English countryside touch.

And it was her favorite part of the day: eight o'clock, before anyone was up. The morning fog still hung over the coastline. Elizabeth knew it would burn off by the afternoon, and she wanted to get at least five miles in while it was still cool. She needed the exercise to keep her stress at bay, even on vacation. She knew that the minute she checked her e-mail back at the cottage there would be at least three "emergency" e-mails from Kenny. He really didn't know what to do with himself when she was gone.

She walked along the coast, enjoying the feeling of her bare feet digging into the sand as the waves crashed over them, leaving a bubbly froth in their wake. *Nature's pedicure*, she thought with a smile. As she continued down the beach, she felt a little sad that Heather wasn't by her side on the walk. It wasn't going to be the same without her, but she was still glad to be here, with or without her old friend.

The girls had argued for a full week about whether they should take this trip together without Heather. Elizabeth felt like they should do the right thing and reschedule for a weekend after Heather was done with her big project. Sara seemed to agree with her. Carmen thought they should just go, and it was stupid to argue.

At the bitter end, it was Martha who had made the decision for them.

"If Heather wants to assuage her guilt for bailing on us, who are we to say no? I know we always said we wouldn't leave anyone behind, but it's just this one time. And if we skip, it might be another year before we all have a date that works for everyone. Maybe longer. Look, this mommy could use a break from her baby. And Robert really needs to take a week of paternity leave. He has barely touched Lucy since she was born because he's so busy. I'm going, and you guys are coming with me," Martha had argued.

"Yes!" Carmen had texted back with excitement.

Noting that Sara didn't seem too eager to weigh in and fight for a delay (she probably wanted the relatively cheap mini-vacation), Elizabeth had relented. "Fine, you guys win."

So here they were in Carmel for their annual girls' weekend.

Heather's largesse had not disappointed. Most of the homes in Carmel were quaint one-story cottages surrounded by little French gardens, tiny gazebos, or some other charming décor in miniature. Elizabeth thought it looked like a luxury Smurf village. If you were lucky enough to own a cottage in the golden triangle, the beach was only minutes away on foot.

Heather's "cottage" didn't fit with this scheme. It was an enormous, newly built, five-bedroom right on the ocean with a view of Pebble Beach. Definitely not a cottage. The stunning exterior of the home and the views were matched by an equally eye-catching interior. Heather had told Elizabeth that she had hired a famous West Coast designer to create an environmentally conscious, clean interior. "Clean" was Heather-code for "no expense spared" and lots and lots of white. Over the years, Heather had developed a definite anal streak. *She must not let her children visit*, Elizabeth had first thought when she walked into the sea of white. Heather had also stocked the house with all their favorites: Diet Coke, La Croix, champagne, and the movie they rewatched together every year—*Heathers* (what else?).

Elizabeth had walked as far as she could go before the beach gave way to craggy black rock. It was time to turn back, read her e-mail, and fix whatever stupid thing Kenny had likely done.

Elizabeth decided she should try and call her old friend. *I mean, what could she be doing this early on a weekend?*

She dialed the number and it picked up immediately: "Hi, you've reached me, but this phone is for outgoing use only. E-mail me and I will do my best to return!"

Elizabeth hit "end" and sighed. Heather could call her, but she couldn't call Heather. Things sure had changed.

# CARMEN

Carmen had slept until ten. She didn't want to leave her five-hundred-thread-count, Egyptian-cotton paradise. But she was hungry. She would see if Martha wanted to go to breakfast.

Elizabeth and Sara had carved out at least four hours every morning to work, so she wouldn't bother to ask them. Sad, really. She and Martha had found this perfect little breakfast spot with an outdoor fire pit. It was strange to think a fire pit would be nice on a California morning in June, but Carmel was cool in the mornings, and the fire was the perfect complement to a big plate of eggs and fruit—with a mimosa, of course. Why would you prefer work to that?

She hoisted herself out of bed and padded down to the kitchen to look for Martha. She found her sitting on one of the stools at the enormous white granite island. Martha was on the phone.

As she got closer, she noticed Martha's face was pinched. Her head seemed to be hanging a bit too. These were both bad signs, she knew from experience.

As she got closer, Martha hung her head even lower and visibly slumped in the chair. That was an even worse sign. That girl maintained perfect posture twenty-four seven due to whatever torture her mother had inflicted on her during Martha's formative years.

Carmen froze and waited for Martha to wrap up her conversation.

After a couple of awkward minutes, Martha hung up and turned to Carmen.

Her eyes were filled with tears, the worst sign of all. Martha was not a crier, and Carmen was pretty sure that she was one of the few people on Earth who had witnessed Martha actually giving in to tears.

"Martha, what is it?" asked Carmen carefully, not knowing whether to touch her. "Whatever it is, we'll fix it."

"No, Carmen, we won't," whispered Martha. "She's gone."

# MARTHA

"Lucy's gone," Martha continued as she stood up. She walked past Carmen and out of the kitchen as quickly as she could. She needed to be alone in her room, safely behind closed doors.

After shutting the bedroom door behind her, Martha stood there with her back to the door for several minutes, too shocked to move.

She heard Carmen's voice from outside the door.

"I'm here, and I'm not leaving."

As she listened to her friend's voice, the tears came, hot and heavy. Time seemed to melt away. She might have been there for seconds or minutes. She wasn't sure.

"Martha, let me in. I'm going to stand here until you open the door, so you might as well open it now."

Martha turned and opened the door. When she saw her friend's concerned face, she rushed into her arms and let out a terrible sound.

As Carmen held Martha, the story came out over Martha's sobs.

"How could this happen to us, Carmen? I mean, we're doctors. This doesn't happen to doctors."

"Of course it does, Martha. Don't be silly. This happens to everyone, and it's not your fault," Carmen said as she held her best friend tight.

"If I had been there, Carmen, this wouldn't have happened. I would have sensed it. I know it. I should have never left her alone."

"Well, that's also silly. She was with her father. And I would bet my life that not one thing would have been different if you had been there. It's not your fault, and it's not Robert's fault either. That was his only daughter, Martha. And he will need you now."

"He doesn't need anyone," Martha said angrily as she pushed Carmen away.

"Martha, don't take this out on him. This is horrible enough as it is," Carmen said gently as she reached for Martha's hand.

"I know." Martha sighed and ignored Carmen's hand, instead sitting down and covering her face. "I don't mean it, not really. I'm just so sad, Carmen. And angry. Fuck. I don't know what to feel."

Martha was now rocking back and forth and continued, "He said she had been great all morning. He put her down for her nap and did a little work. He thought she had been sleeping too long, so he went to check on her. He said that he knew immediately that she was gone. That he had done everything he could. The paramedics too. He just kept saying, 'I couldn't save her.'"

"Because he couldn't, Martha. Nobody could. This was God's decision today," Carmen assured her gently as she sat down next to her.

Martha uncovered her eyes and fixed Carmen with an angry glare. "Carmen, you know what I think about God, and he didn't do himself any favors today with me."

"And you know what I think, Martha. Some things are just outside our control and part of his plan. God loves all of us, but his plan is bigger than any of us."

"Well, his plan sucks and so does he," said Martha with anger. At the thought of the finality of Lucy's death, her limp little body being carried out of their home, Martha felt a searing pain across her forehead and a different, equally awful pain in her chest. *This must be how the family feels when the doctor gives them the terrible news*, she thought. It had been unimaginable to her before now.

"Maybe if I had done something differently," continued

Martha. "You know, God is probably punishing me because I wasn't excited about the pregnancy at first."

"I don't think that's how it works," replied Carmen.

"Robert said that there would be a brief investigation but that it would probably be over before I'm back. He said he wasn't worried because it was textbook SIDS, and they would update him when the death certificate was complete. He sounded so cold and clinical, Carmen."

"Martha, being mad at Robert or yourself or God isn't going to do you any good. Shit happens, and it's no one's fault. Be angry and hurt, but please don't take it out on the people you love or the person I love. I'm here for you, and we are going to get through this, just like we always do."

Martha looked at Carmen in total misery. "But Lucy is my baby girl, Carmen." Then she paused. "Was." And as she turned away from her best friend and thought about the face of her perfect little girl again, the pain returned to her head and her chest. Martha put her head in her hands and curled herself into a ball. She wanted to make herself as small as possible and to squeeze away the pain that felt like it was swallowing her whole.

# SARA

Sara was in the kitchen digging through the fridge for her third Diet Coke when Carmen found her.

"Why can't those stupid sales guys leave me alone?" Sara whined to Carmen as she was shoving the contents of the fridge around in her search for the coldest can of her favorite beverage. "I mean, really, they need to give it up and let me have a vacation."

"Sara, you need to come sit down at the table. We need to talk. Something terrible has happened," said Carmen as calmly as she could.

"You guys need to leave me alone for a couple more hours. I'm really busy," Sara started to say as she turned toward Carmen, but she stopped talking when she saw Carmen's face. She knew that look. Something was very wrong.

And then Carmen told her the awful news.

"Oh God, Carmen. That's my worst fear, losing one of my babies. Is it terrible that I feel relieved it's not me? All I've done since we left on this trip is complain about how hard it is to have four kids. Isn't it awful that it takes something like this to appreciate what we have?"

"No, it's just human," replied Carmen sadly.

# Heather

Elizabeth, I got your text. Terrible news. Please let me know when the service will be. I will try to get there, but it may not happen. You understand. And e-mail me so my assistant can pick it up. I don't really text, too busy. Also, congrats to you. It's so weird how everything happens at the same time, no? H

# ELIZABETH

Martha and Carmen had been barricaded in Martha's room for several hours, understandably, while Elizabeth and Sara worked out the logistics of getting them all home as quickly as possible. It wasn't much, but it was what they were able to do for now. As the day wore on, Elizabeth felt increasingly sick and restless, so she decided to take another walk and call William.

She started down one of the cobblestone paths, walking slowly because she felt unsteady on her feet. The phone rang almost five times before William picked up.

"Hi, babe! How's the high society life treating you?" he teased. "Don't worry, I'm not jealous. I'm planning my turn."

"Hi, honey. Well, Carmel is one of the most beautiful places I've ever been," she started softly, "but, William, something really awful happened today."

"Let me guess, you guys ran out of champagne. Tragedy!" William laughed.

"No, it actually *is* a real tragedy," she continued, a little more sharply than she intended. "Is George close enough to hear us?"

"No, he's glued to his new iPad. I know you thought he was too young for it, but he was kind of sad you were gone, so I caved and took him to the Apple store. You can be mad at me when you get home. I did do the parental controls right I think."

"Oh, William, I don't care about that. Really, I'm just so grateful to have George. And you."

"Okay, you sound weird. What's the bad news? Does Joe want you to move to the new Beijing office or something?"

"No. I wish it were something stupid like that," Elizabeth replied. After a pause she said as evenly as she could, "Martha

74

lost Lucy today, William. They think it was SIDS. She just slipped away during her nap. The investigators are probably at her house right now."

"Oh, shit," breathed William into the phone. "What should I do? Do you want me to go up to their house to see if Robert's okay?"

"I have no idea what to do," said Elizabeth. "Robert might be there, or maybe he is at work? I have no idea. To be honest, I think I've actually spoken to Robert maybe twice in my whole life, and both of those times it was more like talking at him than to him. He's always working. I wouldn't have any idea how to approach him."

"You know I'd do whatever you asked me to do, but I barely know the guy either. I'll at least call up there and see what I can find out. You guys flying home tomorrow?"

"Yes," Elizabeth replied sadly. "I think they are going to try for Friday for the service. William, can you please get my favorite black suit from the cleaners?"

"Sure thing," William said, and then he paused. "Hey, did you tell the girls your news? Three months. Past the danger zone."

"Don't jinx it. And no, it's still a secret. Well, I did tell Heather, but I was waiting to tell the girls tonight over dinner. Obviously, I can't do that now. It can wait. I've got to go, honey. See you tomorrow."

As Elizabeth walked back up the cobblestone path, she couldn't help but smile thinking about the life growing inside her, the joy of which could not be dulled even by her friend's terrible pain. Elizabeth knew exactly when this baby had been conceived. The first week of March. Probably spaghetti bolognese night. She could still feel William's hot breath on her neck and his hands gripping the small of her back. And all that love had become a baby. After so much waiting and pain, she finally felt complete.

But now the unimaginable had happened. And Elizabeth needed to be 100 percent focused on getting one of her closest friends through what would probably be one of the most difficult days of her life.

# CARMEN

"Why the fuck did she choose a church across from an elementary school?" said Carmen to Elizabeth as they stood outside the Episcopal church.

The funeral had been planned for ten, but Carmen had gotten there before eight to be absolutely sure she was there when Martha arrived. She had stood outside the church and watched as hundreds of happy kids walked to school with their colorful backpacks bobbing up and down. It was their last week before summer vacation, and their faces shone with the anticipation of the coming freedom. Thankfully, all the children were tucked away in their classrooms long before Martha and her family arrived.

She and Elizabeth were now waiting for their friend.

"It's fine, Carmen. Pull it together," replied Elizabeth tightly. "And try not to swear in front of Evelyn."

"I personally think Evelyn had something to do with the church selection. Martha's not even religious," Carmen complained.

"It doesn't matter. Let's get this done. Look, they're here now," said Elizabeth.

Martha and Robert's car pulled up, and Robert deftly parked, swiftly exited, and walked right past Carmen into the church with barely a glance in her direction.

Elizabeth and Carmen exchanged a glance, and Carmen said, "You know men. They have no earthly idea what to do in these situations. Well, except William. He really helped pull things together."

"Yes, he's always clutch," replied Elizabeth with a sad smile.

It took a little longer for Martha to exit the vehicle. Carmen walked over, opened the door, and held out her hand. Martha looked like she was trying to be brave, but she didn't reject Carmen's offer and let Carmen walk her into the church.

Martha's parents were not far behind. As they approached the church, they looked a little dazed and distinctly out of their element. This wasn't their church in Boston, and their people weren't there to support them.

Carmen heard them say to Elizabeth, "Did Carmen get our note?" and she heard Elizabeth reply, "Yes, and she asked me to coordinate everything."

*Bless*, thought Carmen.

Carmen had actually agreed with Evelyn's position that it would have made more sense to have the funeral back in Boston. The family even had a lovely plot in one of Boston's oldest cemeteries. But Robert had insisted that they do something simple and local. Martha was too exhausted and in too much pain to fight him. So here they were in a new city and a practically unknown church next to a bustling elementary school. Nothing was right about it, thought Carmen.

A few minutes later, Carmen and Elizabeth took their places in the pew behind Robert and Martha, who sat next to each almost like strangers.

As the time of the service approached, a remarkable number of mourners began to stream in. What must have been every nurse and half of the doctors Robert worked with showed up at the service. There were even a few patients who were participating in his research study. Those families hugged him and thanked him profusely for everything he had done for them.

Carmen whispered to Elizabeth, "Robert's people love him. Who knew?"

"Where's Mark?" asked Elizabeth.

Carmen flinched and answered, "He feels so bad, but he just couldn't make it. He's out of town this whole week and couldn't get his flight changed fast enough."

"Huh," replied Elizabeth in a tone that suggested she wasn't convinced.

"Frankly, it's easier without him," said Carmen dismissively. "The only person I care about right now is Martha, and this way I can concentrate on her one hundred percent."

"That's a good point," agreed Elizabeth.

The service was swift and sad, and there was a great deal of open weeping when the tiny casket was carried out by Robert, Martha's father, William (who had been drafted at the last minute and, of course, played the role perfectly), and one of Robert's work colleagues. Some of Robert's patients must have had children who had been gravely ill. Carmen imagined that the whole thing was too terribly close to home for those families.

As they walked out of the church, Carmen said to Elizabeth, "Thanks again for having the reception at your home."

"Of course. It was the least we could do," replied Elizabeth, again looking so sad. "See you at the cemetery."

# MARTHA

The graveside service was over and everyone had gone over to Elizabeth's house save her and Carmen. They stood next to the small pile of fresh dirt surrounded by the beautiful June grass that covered the rest of the cemetery.

"Carmen, I'm losing them both," said Martha.

"Don't be ridiculous," replied Carmen. "Men deal with their grief differently."

"I suppose. He's barely spoken to me, Carmen. Honestly, I would prefer if Robert would scream at me. Or hit me even. Anything but this deafening silence."

Martha continued, "And my mother hasn't even cried. You know what she said, Carmen? She said, 'Well, at least you can go back to work like you were planning.' I mean, what? Why on earth is she thinking about my career at a time like this?"

"Martha, we established your mother's limitations a long time ago. She loves you and wants to make it better as quickly as possible. But she's totally lacking empathy."

"I'm allowed to be sad. I'm allowed to be broken."

"Of course you are."

Carmen fished in her purse for a bottle of pills. "I brought something for you, if you need it. For the anxiety. It's what the doctor prescribed the last time."

"No, Carmen, I don't want to take these again. It's not like last time. I can handle this. Those pills make me feel like I don't care about anything."

"Martha, there's no harm in getting a little help. And you can just take them for a few days. Just to get through this. There's no nobility in pain. And no one needs to know. You have two other babies. They need you."

"I'll think about it," Martha said as she tucked the bottle in her pocket.

Martha didn't know what she would have done without her friends.

Elizabeth had taken on her most frustrating problem, corralling her parents who were trying to control everything that was happening. Martha had picked a church where she thought her mom would be comfortable, but she sensed that it didn't make a difference in the end.

Sara had volunteered to take Bobby and Jack for a few days. Martha had been more than happy to agree and had felt enormous relief as she saw them drive away to the Dells for a long weekend. Sara and Scott were amazing parents, and she knew the boys were going to have a great time enjoying the water park. When the weekend was over and all her guests gone, particularly her parents, she would talk to her boys about Lucy in her own way.

Then there was William, who had outdone himself, and cooked Martha and Robert a week's worth of meals in addition to hosting the reception tonight.

And, of course, Carmen. The one person who was there for her, without judgment, no matter what.

"I love you, Carmen," said Martha as she reached out her hand for Carmen's.

"I love you too," replied Carmen, grabbing Martha's hand and giving it a hard squeeze.

As they walked back to Carmen's car, Martha said, "Heather sent a beautiful altar piece. Elizabeth said she had a commitment she couldn't break so she couldn't make it. Not that I expect everyone to come."

"Please," said Carmen.

"I'm sure it was important," insisted Martha. "Be nice, Carmen."

"Fine," said Carmen, "but I can't think of any reason that would have prevented me from being here."

# SARA

Sara was sitting at one of the indoor water park's highly sought-after poolside tables with Mikey. Scott was in the water with Martha's two boys and their other three children.

Sara was ashamed to admit that she had been profoundly relieved that she didn't have to attend the funeral. She was pretty confident that she would not have been able to hold it together, which would have been terrible.

Sara actually thought about her children dying a lot. She didn't know if it was normal or not, but it had been like that since the beginning.

When Tommy was born, she remembered waking at night and wondering if he was dead in his crib because he should have been crying by that time. Her next thought was always that it would be useless to check because if he were, in fact, dead, checking him wouldn't make a difference, better to sleep another twenty minutes and then plan the funeral. After about five minutes these morose thoughts would inevitably be interrupted by a very much alive baby ready for his next feeding. Dark and twisted stuff. That is what sleep deprivation does to you, she guessed. In retrospect, she had probably had a touch of postpartum depression. It seemed just too lucky to have four really healthy, smart kids. She was always waiting for the other shoe to drop.

Scott was at the top of the giant fort, aiming a water cannon squarely at the pack of their five charges, who were squealing and pretending to run away from him. Sara waved him back to the table because a giant pizza was being delivered to them from the snack shack. She didn't know if it was the chlorine or the exhaustion, but the pizza tasted delicious.

The wet, straggly wave of kids made their way to the table and shoved in the pizza as fast as they could. Minutes later, they left a pile of wet towels and soggy paper plates in their wake as they headed off to the nearby wave pool to float and digest. Sara and Scott were left with the mess and a sleeping baby.

"You are my hero, honey," Sara said to Scott as she covered Mikey with a couple towels while keeping an eye on the five kids in the pool. She hoped he would manage to take a nap, unlikely as it was.

"I know the reason we're here is horrible, but I'm actually having fun. Sure beats the awful vibe at work," Scott replied.

"What do you mean? I thought work was going really well?" Sara asked.

"Well, look, we haven't had much time to catch up. And I didn't want to worry you. There have been some changes at work. I don't think I'm at risk, but I'm not one hundred percent certain about that."

"At risk? What are you talking about? You're practically running the place. Half of your people wouldn't know what to do without you there."

"That's just it. There have been mistakes. And we haven't done a good job with some of our new processes. I really thought they would give us some time to work out the kinks in the new systems, but they may have run out of patience. Our time might be up. I've heard from a few people who should be in the know that they're considering whether to outsource a big chunk of our work. If that actually happens, a lot of people are going to lose their jobs, but they will need some people to stay behind. I'm pretty sure I'll be one of those. But no guarantee, I guess."

"Holy shit, Scott. Why didn't you talk to me about this earlier?" sputtered Sara, feeling her insecurity that always lingered below the surface start to rise.

"Settle down, you'll wake the baby. It hasn't exactly been easy to get your attention lately, you know." Then Scott added quickly, "I know it hasn't been easy for you to get mine, either. Me telling you then or now wouldn't have made a difference anyway. I can't control this, and I have no idea if and when it's going down. The only reason I'm talking to you about it at all is that I just don't want us to make any big financial decisions until I know what's going on."

"This is what I've been saying, Scott! This is why we need to cut a bunch of stuff out of our budget and have like an eighteen-month emergency fund! Did I not tell you?"

"Don't panic. It will most likely turn out to be nothing. We can probably start looking at houses next spring after this cloud has passed. It may just be gossip or some demented way of making us work harder. This is a tough enough weekend without piling on more worry."

"All right," said Sara reluctantly as she picked up the last remaining slice of pizza. It had gotten cold. "But we are going to keep talking about this," she said to his back as he headed into the wave pool to be with the kids.

*Goddammit, it was stupid to think his job was totally secure*, she thought. *We both are at the mercy of our bosses.*

# HEATHER

**From Heather Hall's Twitter**

**Heather Hall** @therealheatherhall · June 5

Tough week—a good friend's going through a bad time, and I'm not able to be there for her, but this important work must go on— we are just a few months away from launch #makeplansnotmistakes

← Reply   ↔ Retweet   ♥ Favorite   ••• More

# ELIZABETH

*William is really a mensch*, thought Elizabeth as she watched him moving among their guests with his oven mitts and a tray of hot appetizers. Their house was at capacity with friends and neighbors who wanted to comfort Robert and Martha. Which was ironic, of course, because Robert and Martha were two of the most introverted people she knew. This had to be pure torture for them.

*The worst part*, she thought, *is that everyone always has a way of making someone else's loss about them.* In just the first hour, she heard the following snippets:

"I know just how you feel, honey. When I lost my cat, I wasn't right for weeks. Months even."

"You must feel terrible that it happened when you were on vacation. I can't imagine. Maybe if you hadn't gone . . ."

"To think that you and Robert are doctors. I guess it's true that this really can happen to anyone. Honestly, I always thought SIDS was something that happened when drunken mothers rolled over on their babies. Robert doesn't drink much, does he?"

"You really should get pregnant again right away, you know. That will help you put Lucy to rest."

People were incredible in their lack of tact. Elizabeth had her own selfish thoughts and feelings, but she knew better than to verbalize them. In fact, she thought that she had done a remarkable job of covering up her own private pain.

The timing of it all had been just terrible.

It had happened on the flight she, Carmen, and Martha had taken back to Milwaukee from Carmel.

She hadn't felt well all morning but had chalked it up to the stress of the day. After the plane had taken off and they were at altitude, she realized all the water she had been drinking that morning had caught up with her. She turned to Carmen and Martha and said, "Be right back."

Martha had responded with a pained smile and looked back out the window. Elizabeth knew Martha was shut down and understood that was the only way Martha would make it through the long day of travel. She didn't know how she would survive it, personally.

Elizabeth made her way down the aisle and into the cramped restroom. It smelled like it hadn't been cleaned recently, and she shifted to breathing through her nose. Vowing to get out of there as quickly as possible, she pushed down her jeans—and that's when she saw it.

The blood.

She gasped with a horrible realization of why she hadn't been feeling well. It wasn't the stress at all. She had thought she was out of the danger zone. The end of the first trimester. But it was happening, again.

A loud knock came through the door as Elizabeth's world was crashing down around her.

"C'mon, lady! There's a line here!"

*Shit, shit*, she said to herself as she struggled to control her emotions, bracing herself with outstretched arms in the cramped bathroom.

"C'mon, lady, we don't have all day," she heard as she held back her tears.

*Get it together, Elizabeth*, she told herself. She had forgotten to keep breathing through her mouth and was now also overwhelmed with nausea as her emotions and the foul smells mixed together. *Your friend needs you.*

But pain was pain, and Elizabeth was struggling to feel her way past hers, no matter what had happened to Martha.

Elizabeth wiped her eyes, took a deep breath, and unlocked the bathroom door.

The waiting passenger shoved her aside as he entered the bathroom.

"Took you long enough, lady."

Elizabeth resisted the urge to punch the asshole in his generous gut.

As she made her way back down the aisle and to her seat next to Martha and Carmen, Elizabeth fought with her emotions.

Martha had her headphones on and was looking out the window, seemingly oblivious, which was a blessing. Carmen sat protectively next to her and didn't really notice Elizabeth as she sat back down. Elizabeth put on her headphones and closed her eyes, counting the minutes until they would touch down in Milwaukee.

Thankfully, the worst of it from a physical perspective didn't come until she was home, and that part was finished by the time of the funeral. So, physically, she was sufficiently recovered to attend. Emotionally, of course, she was nowhere near whole, and she knew that William would be a wreck, too, in his own quiet way.

Elizabeth wondered how William processed these things. Like her, he had been so excited, thinking this time would be different.

She flashed back to the day they had first found out, a few weeks before her trip.

It had been a Thursday, the day of the week that Elizabeth typically started craving a big glass of wine. But her period had been a few weeks late, so she thought that maybe she should check before pouring herself the standard Thursday night glass and a half.

Her period was often erratic, so she figured this would be just one more waste of yet another pregnancy test. But she had been wrong. Minutes later she was looking down in amazement at two pink lines. She screamed down the stairs for William, and he materialized within seconds in the doorframe, with a look of worry on his face.

"What is it? Are you okay?" he asked.

Elizabeth said nothing, just handed him the stick. And then she watched the joy spread across his face.

"It's early, please don't be too excited," warned Elizabeth, but she couldn't help smiling herself as William wrapped her in a one of his signature bear hugs.

Every day of the next two months was spent hoping and holding their breath a little.

By the time the trip to Carmel came around, Elizabeth had started to breathe easy and decided she was safe. So she told Heather and planned how she was going to tell the others.

And then came the series of tragic events. Lucy. The discovery on the plane. The even more painful conversation with William later that day.

It actually wasn't much of a conversation. In the end, William hadn't been able to say anything. He had just given her a hug and lingered much longer than he usually would. He had opened his mouth as if there was something he wanted to say, but then his head had dropped and he turned away and started cooking for the funeral.

It was a terrible loss for him. Unfairly, she felt like it was even worse for her. After all, she had to go through the physical and emotional part of it. And she couldn't share her pain with her friends.

She suspected that everyone would think that Elizabeth's loss was nowhere close to the same magnitude as Martha's, but for her it was the same. However, there was a hierarchy to grief, and, in that order, the loss of a child clearly outranked a miscarriage. So Elizabeth and William were alone with their pain.

After ushering the last of the guests out the front door, Elizabeth threw herself into washing dishes and reorganizing the first floor.

"Hey," she heard William say as he hugged her from behind while she stood scrubbing at the sink. "Let me finish."

"No, this makes me feel better," she replied. "You know cleaning is my therapy."

"Yes, I know I'm the luckiest guy on the planet," he teased.

"Really, do you feel that way?" Elizabeth asked as she turned into his hug. "Because I feel like I keep letting you down, William. I'm so sorry." And with that, her face crumpled and the tears started to flow.

"Of course you haven't. Don't be silly. C'mon. We're living the dream," he replied, but Elizabeth could tell that his voice was laced with the same sadness she felt.

If only it were that easy. It might be myopic and selfish, but her dream had always been the three kids, the white picket fence, and the stable, professional job to support it all. She wanted sibling rivalry and crazy schedules and a broken vase because the kids were playing ball in the house. If William hadn't beaten her to it, she might have even enjoyed being at home.

"You know, we can still adopt, Elizabeth," William said softly, interrupting her thoughts.

"William, you know how I feel about that. I want to be excited about it, but I'm just not there yet. I want a child of my own."

"Okay. But don't get in your own way, Elizabeth," he replied.

Elizabeth had a friend who had recently adopted from China, and she'd had a really good experience. But she knew in her heart that she just wasn't there yet. She still wanted to try for her own biological child. She wasn't ready to give up on her dream yet.

# CARMEN

June in Lake Geneva was stunning, Carmen thought as she stood in her kitchen making breakfast. The kitchen was situated to provide sweeping views of the sparkling lake through its oversized bay windows. She had to admit that Mark had been right. Having this home was really wonderful. It was nice to finally be in a quiet, expansive space after the drama of the trip to Carmel and then all the awful events following it.

It was already well into Avery's summer break, and she hadn't even had time to properly welcome her home from college. Avery had gotten home just as Carmen was leaving for Carmel. "Don't worry, Mom," she'd said, "I need to sleep for like a week anyway. Go have fun, and we'll catch up when you get back."

Just as she was beginning to wonder whether Avery had left her bedroom since Carmen had last seen her, she heard a familiar shuffling. Carmen's pancakes worked every time.

"Hey, Mom," Avery said with a sheepish smile.

"Hi, sweetie," Carmen replied. "Come sit down. I have a stack of your favorite—blueberry pancakes."

"That sounds amazing, Mom, thanks. I literally can't get enough to eat. And I've been so tired," Avery replied with a sigh as she padded into the kitchen in her oversized men's plaid pajamas.

Avery had grown into a gorgeous woman. Light brown hair like her dad's, green eyes like her mom's, and skin that had just a hint of a tan, which Carmen knew would be interpreted by her classmates as a souvenir of a weekend someplace warm and expensive. And unlike her mother, she was fairly tall like Mark and had the long, lean limbs of the dancer that she was.

Avery gracefully slid onto one of the stools along the granite island in the center of the kitchen, pulled her long brown hair into a messy bun at the nape of her neck, and began to dig in. Carmen enjoyed the silence as she watched Avery make quick work of the pancakes.

After a few minutes, Avery put her fork down and said, "Mom, I need to talk to you about something. I'm really nervous about it, so I hope you'll just let me say what I have to say before you respond. And if you don't want to say anything, that's fine too. Please just be thoughtful before you respond."

*Holy shit*, thought Carmen. *She's pregnant. Just like I was.*

She flashed back to that breakfast at Lou's all those years ago. She could still see the disappointment on her parents' faces. *Oh God, I'm going to have to tell them about Avery too.* She suspected her mom was holding out hope for seeing her granddaughter in a white dress someday. She was going to be devastated again.

"Honey, if you want to keep the baby, I'm here for you one hundred percent. And if you want to do something else, we'll take care of it. I support your choice, whatever it is," Carmen said a bit too stridently as she grabbed Avery and gave her a big hug. Her eyes had started to water, and she didn't want Avery to notice.

"Um, Mom, what are you talking about?" Avery laughed. "I'm not pregnant. And I might be insulted."

"You're not? Oh, thank God, honey!" Carmen exhaled. "Well, then, what is it? Whatever it is, it can't be worse than being pregnant."

"Well, I hope you won't think that, Mom," said Avery, suddenly serious. "I'm gay."

Carmen froze and furiously processed the information. Gay? That was out of left field. Had Avery's girlfriends in high school been *girlfriends*? Were the ones that had slept over at her house so many times girlfriends or friends who were girls? Did she have a girlfriend now? Was she safe? God, she was out of her depth.

And then she knew exactly what to say.

"Honey, I love you. And I will love whoever you love."

A look of relief washed over Avery's face, and her shoulders visibly relaxed. "Thanks, Mom," she said.

"You know, lesbians have babies all the time," Carmen pointed out. "Just because you are gay doesn't mean I don't want grandchildren."

"Good grief, Mom." Avery laughed again. "I don't even have a girlfriend yet. And to save you the pain of asking, I haven't had sex yet either."

"Then are you sure you're gay?" asked Carmen. "There's nothing wrong with a little experimentation, you know, just to be sure. As long as you're safe. I wasn't always married to your dad, you know."

"Gross, Mom," replied Avery, wrinkling her nose in disgust. "Yes, I'm sure I'm gay. And I want to save that other stuff for marriage anyway. Or at least for the person I'm in a serious relationship with. All right, Mom, that's all I can handle today. I want to go for a run now."

Unable to fully let her off the hook, Carmen said, "Honey, I don't think I've ever been prouder of you. One more thing, though—you are going to need to assure your grandmother that there is still a chance for a white dress."

"I can handle that, I guess," Avery said with a chuckle. "But, really, please don't get too ahead of yourself. And I love you, Mom." With that, she sprinted away to slip into her running clothes.

*Amazing how life can shift so fast and with no warning*, thought Carmen as she cleaned up Avery's dishes. But this wasn't a bad shift. Carmen was going to have to get together with her girlfriends and figure this gay thing out. Did they have a good lesbian friend? She wasn't sure. But the important thing was that Avery was happy and successful. No, this was just a twist in the road. Life was good.

*Now, if I can just get lucky and have one more baby.* Why wouldn't God give another child to someone who was so obviously rocking it with her first? Maybe she should just stop with Dr. Lee and really try to relax and be happy. As Avery was opening the front door to leave for her run, Carmen saw Mark walking through it. *That's strange*, she thought. *He's made it up here really early. I hope he's not sick. No*, she chided herself. *This is an omen. Change is in the air today.*

Mark walked into the kitchen and sat down on the very stool Avery had just vacated. *Customer number two*, thought Carmen.

"Carmen, we need to talk," he started.

"That's so funny. Your daughter just said the same thing to me thirty minutes ago."

"We can talk about Avery later," Mark said impatiently. "Right now, I need to talk to you about something else. Sit down please."

"All right, shoot," said Carmen as she sat down on the stool next to him, reminding herself to talk to him later about Avery's disclosure.

"You know we didn't exactly get the most traditional of starts, Carmen."

"No, but we certainly built something great." Carmen smiled, wondering if this was going to be the conversation when they could finally be real and have it out. *I've got this*, she thought. *I'm going to ask for what I need.*

"Yes, in some ways we did," Mark pressed on. "I did the right thing, and I'm proud of what I did all those years ago. But Avery is grown now and through her first year of college. It's time for me to be happy."

"Actually, I couldn't agree more. I know things aren't the way they are supposed to be. Let's fix it," said Carmen in an upbeat voice.

"Carmen, you're not hearing me. I'm not happy and I'm done. This isn't about you. You've been a great wife."

*Been,* heard Carmen. *Past tense.*

Mark continued, "You will get your fair share. I won't be a jerk. You can have this house, and I have set up accounts for your retirement and everything else you'll need."

Carmen just sat there staring at him, her brow knit.

"Carmen, you knew we weren't the love of each other's life when we got married. We were thrown together, and we made the best of it. It's my turn to find out what else is out there for me."

"Hold up. Mark, I know you have probably been running around. I forgive you, okay? Don't you want to give us a real chance? For Avery at least?" asked Carmen.

"There aren't any other women, Carmen," said Mark coldly. "That isn't what this is about."

"Really? How about Nicole then? If you would be honest with me, maybe we have a chance to move forward," Carmen spat at him, losing control of her emotions.

"Actually, no." Mark laughed. "She's a little young for me. And she's just a work colleague. But there is another colleague of mine I am interested in dating. She's five years older than me, if you can believe that. Never had kids and doesn't want them. She says she's at the point that she wants to travel and enjoy life. And I want to do that with her if she'll give me a chance. Look, I didn't want to cheat on you, Carmen. I haven't. I wanted to do the right thing and divorce before I start something with someone else. I've always done the right thing, and I'm not going to stop now."

*She's forty-five,* thought Carmen. *Christ.*

"I don't know what to say," said Carmen slowly. She couldn't process all of it fast enough. She could feel the tears welling in her eyes. Anger was right behind them. If he didn't want to try, then what was the point?

"You don't have to say anything. I have given you full control over the household account. There's enough money to keep things going for the rest of the year. My attorney will be in touch with the full financial pack in a few months. Like I said, fifty-fifty, fair and square. I am going to pack up a few things today and take them to my apartment."

"Mark, wait, please, let's take time to think before you do this," pleaded Carmen. "I think everything would be different for us if we could have another baby. Don't give up yet."

"Carmen, you still aren't listening. And for God's sake, please stop talking about another baby. You've been on it for years. Look, even if that's what I wanted too—which it's not, by the way—it's never going to happen," Mark said sharply.

"You don't know that. This could be our year," replied Carmen, desperation in her voice.

"No, it won't be. It will never be. I can't father children, Carmen," said Mark.

"Um, well, you obviously can, since we have Avery," said Carmen testily, her mood quickly shifting from desperation to anger.

"Carmen, I got a vasectomy after Avery."

Carmen was stunned into silence. And then she felt a cold fury. Everything suddenly made sense. Brutal, horrible sense. All those tests and worry and obsession for all those years. For nothing.

"Why on earth would you have done that to yourself?" she yelled at him. "Didn't you want more children? What is wrong with you?"

"I knew that if we didn't have more children, I would have my life back at forty," said Mark softly.

He had been planning this from day one. Her mom had been right all along.

"Congratulations, I guess. You are free now!" shouted Carmen, her voice shaking with anger as she struggled to process how she could have missed this all along.

Mark turned to leave the kitchen and go upstairs. "Mark, just out of curiosity," Carmen yelled after him, "if you had a vasectomy, why didn't those early tests show that? And why wouldn't the doctors tell me?"

Mark turned around and replied coldly, "Because I asked them not to. And they respected that confidentiality. And, by the way, you never asked."

*No*, thought Carmen. *That couldn't be true.* She flashed back to that first doctor. He had told her that she had no problems and that "someday she could get pregnant." He had never said Mark was the problem.

Mark was right—she hadn't asked. She had based everything that came after that on the faulty assumption that she was the problem. *Stupid woman*, she thought.

She felt a well of anger surge and grabbed for the nearest plate.

"If you think you have done the right thing for the last twenty years or that you are doing it now, you are deluding yourself!" Carmen screamed, and flung the plate at his head. It missed and struck the wall, smashing into hundreds of shards. "And just because you haven't had your dick in anyone else doesn't mean you're not a cheater!"

"Goodbye, Carmen. I didn't want to end things like this," said Mark sadly. "Tell Avery I will be calling her soon. And please don't smash the good stuff."

"Come back and fight, you coward!" screamed Carmen. But it was too late. He was already walking out the front door.

And as he pulled the door shut, Mark closed the book on the last twenty years of her life. Just like that.

# MARTHA

Martha had been in pajamas since the funeral, which had been weeks ago.

Robert was still not talking to her much, but he had at least figured out a day camp for the boys and had been dropping them off on the way to work and leaving early to get them on the way home. Her friends commented on how loving he was being by giving Martha some space and time to process her grief. It wasn't love, Martha thought; it was fear. She bet that it was his greatest hope that she would snap out of it in a couple days, and then they could move on as if nothing had happened. If it were up to him, they would probably not talk about Lucy ever again. In this way, her mother and Robert were peas in a pod.

The last time she heard Robert say Lucy's name was when they had talked to the boys after the pair came home from their water park adventure. Bobby understood right away. He had a friend who had recently lost a parent to cancer. They were not sure about Jack. He understood that Lucy was not there right now but kept asking when she was coming back.

Martha had tried to talk to Robert about it all later, but he had brushed her off and said that talking about "it" would just make things worse. *It.* So Martha had taken up residence on the couch with her old sketchpad and pencils; she didn't have the heart for anything else. It was a bit of a rebellion, and she wondered when Robert would fight back.

"Honey," Robert said with feigned enthusiasm, "your boys are all home. I brought takeout."

"Okay," Martha answered. "Why don't you bring me mine over here."

"No, we're eating at the table like a normal family. Let's go," replied Robert with a bit of edge in his voice.

*Maybe enough is enough*, thought Martha. *Talking won't bring Lucy back anyway.* She got up off the couch, resolving to pull it together, at least for the kids. Robert was right about that.

After the boys finished their food (Jack at least, Bobby just picked at his), Martha and Robert sat alone at the dining room table.

"I know the timing is terrible, Martha, but I have to make a choice about my September schedule," said Robert.

"What choice?" asked Martha.

"Well, the medical college has actually offered me a permanent position and a grant to continue my research."

"That's great," said Martha. "Take it. Maybe I can start house hunting."

"Well, there is also an opportunity in California. Something entirely new. I'm really excited about it," Robert said, and started sketching out the details.

She could see Robert's mouth moving, but she stopped hearing the words after he said "California."

"No," she interrupted flatly. "Enough. Just no."

"Look, I know you've been thrown by what happened, but life goes on," Robert insisted. "That sounds terrible, but please, you know what I mean. We have other children. We have each other. We need to go back to living."

"I said no, Robert. I know you think this is about what just happened, but the truth is that life wasn't exactly perfect before Lucy died. I was lonely. You never saw the boys. I didn't have a prayer of getting back to work, any kind of work. And now you want to make it worse. If you think I can do another move right now after what happened, you need to have your emotion chip checked. You take the offer here and find a way to be home a lot more. The boys need you. I need you." Her voice cracked on the last words.

"But this may not come around again—" Robert started to argue, seemingly oblivious to her pain.

"Robert, listen to yourself. Enough," said Martha, and she left the table and stalked off to the bedroom.

Martha heard her cell ring and decided to answer it when she saw it was Carmen.

"Martha, I know that you are in a horrible place, but I need you. Mark left me," said Carmen in a rush.

"Well, shit," replied Martha.

# SARA

"That's what I'm saying, Katherine. I've redone the budget six ways from Sunday. It doesn't matter. Even with no dinners out, no new clothes, no subscriptions, we can't make it on my salary alone. Unless we move, we're screwed if Scott actually loses his job."

"Then move. It's not the end of the world. I know you love your fancy school district, but it will work out, really," replied Katherine as the company's COO strolled into Sara's cube.

He was a very tall, impeccably dressed man with the kind of bland good looks and domineering presence that made everyone assume he was a bright, competent, natural leader. Which he wasn't. They never were. This guy's particular brand of awful was that he was an uninspired penny-pincher. A lot of Sara's colleagues said he was trying to shrink the company to greatness. It would be funny if it weren't so depressingly true.

"Sara, right? Great to meet you!" he said enthusiastically, and extended his perfectly manicured hand toward her.

Sara grabbed the wrinkled, slightly too small suit jacket on the back of her chair and tried to shrug it on discreetly as she rose to shake his hand. She hoped he wouldn't notice her jagged nails.

"And who are you, young lady?" he asked as he turned to Katherine.

"Katherine Baker. I've actually been a lawyer here for twelve years."

"Right, right. Well, you look young. Take it as a compliment. It's good to meet you too. Would you excuse us? I have a pressing issue for Sara."

"Of course," Katherine said as she exited Sara's cube and flashed Sara a thumbs-up of support.

"Good afternoon, Mr. Rose," Sara said. "What can I do for you?"

"Your boss told me you would be the perfect person for this job I need done. Stat. We are trying something new this year. It's called zero budgeting. Heard of it?"

*Yes*, Sara thought, *it's something so old that the rest of the world has already decided it's ineffective.* Instead she said, "Yes, I believe I saw an article in *HBR* about that." She left out that the article was probably from the last century.

"Right, good. So you can probably guess what I'm going to ask you to do. For every headquarters service function, I'd like to track down every expense and consider whether we can drop it. You know, start from zero."

"Of course, I'm happy to help, but wouldn't one of the accounting staff be more suited for this? We only have seven working attorneys on the headquarters team here, and we're pretty full up at the moment."

"What do you mean, full up? You attorneys are always sandbagging—no one is busier than sales and operations," he said with a dismissive wave of his hand. He continued in a more serious tone, "I need the numbers absolutely no later than September one. We aren't exactly hitting the cover off the ball, so you need to find me some fat." And with that he walked out.

*There goes July*, thought Sara. *And probably August too.* She looked down at her household budget numbers and resigned herself to her fate. *Look on the bright side*, she told herself, *maybe I can use this exercise as an excuse to figure out if I am underpaid.*

# SEPTEMBER

# Heather

**From Heather Hall's Twitter**

**Heather Hall** @therealheatherhall · September 1

Download The Four BIG Mistakes of Women Who Will Never Lead or Win #todayistheday #makeplansnotmistakes #HERstory

← Reply   ↔ Retweet   ♥ Favorite   ··· More

# ELIZABETH

Elizabeth was not big into Twitter, but she did get alerts for Heather's tweets. *Good for Heather*, she thought as she saw that her book launch had happened on target. She laughed at the title. She felt a little sorry for Heather's one-percenter, Silicon Valley friends whose "mistakes" were featured in the book. How embarrassing, but probably some voyeuristic fun. Elizabeth hoped to get to it this weekend.

"Ms. Smith! I'm here, should I wait outside?" came an enthusiastic voice.

*Right*, thought Elizabeth. It was September, and the new class of associates had arrived. She was assigned a "Blake" as her mentee. Millennials had some really weird names. There was also a "Chase" and a "MacKensie." Together, they sounded like an overpriced accounting firm.

"Come on in, Blake," called Elizabeth.

"Thank you for taking the time to meet with me, Ms. Smith," Blake said as she floated into the room. If she'd had on normal shoes, she would have been about five feet seven, but she was closer to five feet ten with her three-inch patent leather red stilettos. The shoes made Elizabeth wince. She had to concede, however, that Blake's black pantsuit was beautiful and perfectly tailored.

"Please, call me Elizabeth," insisted Elizabeth warmly. "Those are some shoes, Blake."

"Oh, these." Blake laughed. "I know the red is a little bright, but I read that wearing a sexy shoe tells the boys that you are confident and not afraid to take chances, but in your own uniquely feminine way. And if I'm doing something, I like to go all in, if you know what I mean."

"Of course," said Elizabeth, as she thought, *If your goal is to go all in on looking like a stripper*. She conceded that the thought was mean and a little unfair. Instead she said, "Just be sure you have something more comfortable at your desk. You will find that you are in for many late nights your first year."

"I've got no problem with that," said Blake. "But I assume you got my memo on my preferred work environment?"

"Sorry, no, I haven't seen that," replied Elizabeth, suppressing a laugh.

"That's weird. I texted you a heads-up. Kenny gave me your number. Well, anyway, I want to be sure that I have some ability right away to work remotely so I can keep my balance."

"Typically, we allow flexible work arrangements after you have been here a few years and learned the ropes," explained Elizabeth, trying to keep her face as composed as possible. She really hoped Blake would try this routine on Joe. "And I prefer e-mail, not text, for work."

"Oh, right, got it. No problem. I might need to keep a yoga mat here then!" she replied with a wink.

Was Blake flirting with her as well? Interesting strategy.

"Blake, maybe we should talk a little bit about what you can expect this year in terms of the actual work."

"That sounds good, but I want to add one thing to the agenda," said Blake, suddenly looking serious.

*Wow*, thought Elizabeth. *This girl is a piece of work.*

Blake continued, "I would like to brainstorm my master plan with you."

"Your what?" asked Elizabeth. This time she couldn't hide her amusement.

"My master plan. I've been thinking about it ever since I started following Heather Hall a few years ago. She's so amazing."

"Yes, she's had a remarkable life," Elizabeth agreed with a little smile.

"You were really lucky to know her," said Blake. "I saw her posts on your Facebook."

"Did you?" asked Elizabeth, wondering how Blake could see her Facebook. She made a mental note to change her privacy settings. "Well, this meeting is about you, not my old friends."

"She has a new book out today. Did you know that?"

"I did actually," Elizabeth replied. At least she was up to speed on this point.

"Well, I was offered the chance to review it in advance. Actually, I volunteered on her website. All I had to do was post a review on FLASH today. Anyway, the book is really great. But I guess we should be talking about me, right? Listen, Elizabeth, I want to be like Heather. No offense. I mean, your career is great, don't get me wrong, but I want to take mine to the next level. To get there, you have to architect your life right at the start, like Heather says, and avoid the four key mistakes. I'm trying to make a master plan that will do that," gushed Blake.

Elizabeth just sat there, unable to bring herself to interrupt Blake. This stuff was too good.

"For starters, I want to be sure I'm in a position to have my first baby soon like Heather recommends. I'm sure you agree."

"Are you thinking about having a baby this year?" Elizabeth finally interjected with surprise. "It's possible, of course, but you won't be eligible for the full maternity leave until you have been with us a year."

"Oh God, no!" Blake laughed. "I'm not even married yet. Actually, I don't have the guy picked yet at all. I am not totally clear on the right guy to marry. You know, it's really important that he sign off on the master plan. But I don't want to marry a loser either who just wants to glom on. It's definitely a problem."

"Blake, I would strongly recommend you focus on being successful here for now," said Elizabeth. "Marriage and motherhood will happen when they happen. And you might want to consider that your perfect man may want to have a say in the master plan."

"I thought you might say that," replied Blake. "But let's be real. More than anyone, you know the importance of planning. I mean, after what happened to you. Everyone knows. After the book, I mean. Anyway, I think if you pick the right guy, he won't ruin your plan. That is Heather's whole point, really. We have to take total control of our lives and not let the boys boss us around."

"Blake, what on earth are you talking about?" asked Elizabeth with confusion.

"Well, I know that Heather was talking about you in her book. I mean, she used your initial, 'E,' but it's so obvious. And she basically confirmed it in her Facebook post today. I would have probably figured it out anyway."

Elizabeth's mind was racing. What had Heather written? Did Heather really write about her?

"Anyway, congrats on the baby. When are you due? It was probably hard to get pregnant again, right? You passed thirty-five at least five years ago. I'm not a stalker or anything. I just saw on your firm profile when you graduated law school. Anyway, so happy for you!"

"Blake, where exactly did you get the idea I was pregnant?"

Blake was looking at her like she was stupid.

"It was in Heather's post today—didn't you see it on your wall? Because you and I are friends, I saw it right away this morning. Don't you get a notification from Facebook when something new goes up? I can help you change your settings to fix that."

Good God. She had to end this conversation fast and get Blake out of her office. Preferably off her team if she could manage it. Blake appeared to be good at basic arithmetic. Maybe she could get her transferred to the tax team.

"Blake, you are misinformed. I'm not pregnant. And even if I was, it's not something you and I would be discussing. In fact, you may find that providing fewer personal details at work will be advantageous as your career progresses," said Elizabeth in an attempt to get control back over the conversation.

"I totally disagree! My generation is going to be totally open and authentic," countered Blake with oblivious enthusiasm.

"Okay, Blake, it sounds like you have everything figured out," said Elizabeth curtly, needing to make this conversation be over *now*. "Please let me know if there is anything else I can do to help you."

"Unless you can get me a lunch date with Heather personally, I think I'm set for now." Blake laughed as she crushed Elizabeth's new carpet with her red stilettos on her way out. "Actually, I don't really need Heather when I have my mom. She's amazing. She's more of my friend than my mom. She's always gone to bat for me my whole life, know what I mean? No matter what I do, she's always in my corner. I hope I can have as good a relationship with you as I have with her!"

Elizabeth made a mental note to expect a call from Blake's mom after her first performance evaluation.

Elizabeth did her best to remain cool as Blake exited and then turned quickly to her computer. Where should she start? Blake had said something about a Facebook post today on Elizabeth's wall. She clicked open her profile and started scanning. Okay, it looked like Heather had shared one of her own posts with Elizabeth.

**From Elizabeth Smith's Facebook Timeline**

**Heather Hall shared FLASH's post**

September 1 at 2:12 a.m. · San Francisco

Hi world! I'm sure you haven't missed the release of my book since you are my closest family and friends. But just in case you are living under a rock, please don't forget to read (and recommend!) my New York Times bestselling book, The Four BIG Mistakes of Women Who Will Never Lead or Win! (we debuted at number 5!). Special thanks for the inspiration from <u>Elizabeth Smith</u>, <u>Carmen Jones</u>, <u>Martha Adams West</u>, and <u>Sara Beck</u>. Your stories are helping women around the world navigate through the choppy waters of life!

*Like   Comment   Share*

Your friend Blake Spears and 4,712 other people like this post.

**Jane Smith** Elizabeth, dear, is this your old friend from college? How nice that she remembers you! I'm going to order this for my book club—I have a famous daughter!

*Okay*, thought Elizabeth, *so far, so good*. But then she saw the note just below it.

**Heather Hall -> Elizabeth Smith**
September 1 at 2:14 a.m. · San Francisco

Hi, lady! So look, I know that your "story" isn't quite right because you did finally get the family you wanted! The book was already set when you told me about the baby in June. I didn't want to say anything because that would ruin the surprise! I hope it's OK I'm putting this note here—I'm sure you must be showing by now, I mean considering how big you got with William. And you really should do more updates on your page! If I have time, you have time!

*Like   Comment   Share*

Your friend Blake Spears and 22 other people like this post.

**Blake Spears** Elizabeth! I didn't know you were pregnant —congrats. I'm so glad that you're my mentor!

**Jane Smith** Elizabeth, you're pregnant? Why is the
mother always the last to know these things? I'll call you
tonight.

*Oh my God. I never told Heather about the miscarriage*, thought
Elizabeth. How could she have forgotten? Martha's tragedy—
both of their tragedies—had swallowed her whole that week, and
by the next week she was head down at work again.

*Jesus.* This was officially a grade-A clusterfuck. Where to
start? Should she correct the record now at work before the damage spread? Or should she go home and read Heather's book
first? Why would Heather be writing about her anyway? Much
less talking about her pregnancy? She was going to have a word
with her old friend later today.

No, first she needed to quickly shut Blake up. Then her mom
(ugh). Then get out of here and figure out how to fix Facebook.

How did Blake get to be her friend anyway? Did Elizabeth
really say yes to that? She must have. Social media was a men-
ace. She clicked on Blake's profile and hit "unfriend" somewhat
violently.

She turned next to her e-mail to send Blake a note. She noticed a new message from Kenny and clicked it open to be sure it
wasn't an emergency.

Joe and I tried to call you, but you didn't answer. When
you were doing that mommy thing at your son's
preschool this morning (Don't be mad at Linda for
telling me), Grey Corp. called about the draft merger
document. When they couldn't find you they called Joe.
They needed someone to get on the phone with the
target right away. Sorry, had to be done. Look, the client
really likes you and wants you to stay on the account,
but the client agreed with my suggestion that I take the
lead in negotiations. Makes sense, especially since you

are pregnant. Congrats, by the way! Blake gave me the
heads-up. She said that you should be due around year-
end (BTW, you don't even look fat yet, so good on you).
Don't worry, I'll be on hand to bring our deal over the
finish line. We got your back!

*Motherfucker.* Project Greysteel was her deal. Now Kenny
was in the driver's seat because she had been away from her desk
during the only three hours she had taken as personal time in
months.

And it probably hadn't taken Kenny more than two minutes
to convince the client. Actually less than that. Just the time it
took for him to say, "Elizabeth's pregnant." It didn't matter that
it wasn't true. Even though she would make it clear that, no, she
wasn't pregnant, she knew whatever she said wouldn't matter—
the damage was already done. Joe wasn't going to go back and fix
it with the client (and accuse them of sexism?).

And the fact that the whole thing had gone down when she
was at George's preschool this morning really pissed her off too.
She was also going to have to have another talk with her assistant, Linda, about the confidentiality of her schedule. After
years of giving her a five-thousand-dollar gift card to Nordstrom
at Christmas, she expected a little more loyalty.

The worst of it was that Elizabeth didn't think her absence
had been worth it at all. Those three hours were not what she
would consider "quality time." They were a blur of cleaning tables, disinfecting toys, and cutting out shapes for some future art
project.

She couldn't let this stand, she thought. She picked up the
phone.

"Yep," Joe answered.

"Joe," she said, "I heard Kenny is taking over the deal."

"Elizabeth, I know, but it's what the client requested," he
gruffed suspiciously.

"Look, I think that happened because Kenny was misinformed that I am pregnant. I'm not," Elizabeth informed him calmly.

"Sure, sure," Joe said, and, after an awkward pause, added, "Look, we can't go back now. But this won't affect anything else. And you don't know that the pregnancy thing had anything to do with anything. Don't make negative assumptions. Anyway, can't change horses now. Gotta go. Big call coming in. Talk later."

As Joe hung up on her, Elizabeth sighed. This was a mess.

Elizabeth gathered up her things so that she could get the hell out of her office. She had a lunch date with Heather's book.

Elizabeth needed to get to the privacy of her own home. She sped there and locked herself away in the study to see what Heather had committed to paper (or the permanent digital record, as it was, since her book was available for download today, immediately, worldwide).

She started with the full description:

*This sure-to-be runaway hit is a must-have for all women looking to get ahead in a man's world. FLASH executive Heather Hall has been there, done that—and so have her closest friends. Drawing on all their collective experience, she reveals a distinctive set of mistakes women make that ultimately sabotage their careers—and their lives.*
*They are:*
*Mistake #1: Opting Out.*
*Mistake #2: Ramping Off.*
*Mistake #3: Half-Assing It.*
*Mistake #4: Ignoring the Fertility Cliff.*

She knew then with a sickening certainty that this book wasn't a send-up of the first-class problems of Heather's fancy friends. No, this was something very different.

She began to scan the book.

After about thirty minutes with the book, it was clear to Elizabeth that Heather had done something very, very bad.

Heather had the nerve to sum up each of her four best friends' journeys—every choice, every trade-off, every win, and every heartbreaking loss—under the heading of one of four "big" mistakes women make that sabotage their lives.

Elizabeth couldn't decide which of the chapters was the worst. Her bashing of "C" for leaving behind a world of opportunity to live with a man she was certain was unfaithful to her? Her criticism of "M" for giving up her medical career to be "just a mom"? Her scolding of "S" for struggling because she was overcommitted at home and undercommitted at work? Or was it her warning not to end up like her best friend, "E," unable to complete the family she wants because she planned badly?

Four mistakes. Nice and tidy. And devastating. Especially for Elizabeth. Her old roommate. The person Elizabeth thought would be there for her on the things that really mattered.

At least Heather had the decency to try to "anonymize" their names (well, at least until her incriminating Facebook posts). But Heather had not anonymized the facts, not even one little bit. Elizabeth's whole life was bloodlessly detailed right there in Heather's book under "Mistake Number Four." As Elizabeth read "her" section, she felt all her old insecurities, the ones she worked hard to keep safely below the surface, bubble up and threaten to overwhelm her.

By about one in the morning Elizabeth was satisfied that she had taken in everything that Heather had put out there. It was time to break the news to the others. They would not be likely to read Heather's book unprompted (Did Carmen or Sara read much at all these days?), and they needed to know what their friend had done.

She picked up her phone and started texting: DEFCON 5

# CARMEN

Carmen was in her car when she got Elizabeth's text. Carmen thought it had to do with the Christmas get-together they had been talking about. But then she saw it: DEFCON 5.

*That's dramatic, even for Elizabeth*, she thought.

After some back and forth, she realized that she would be forced to read Heather's stupid book if only to calm Elizabeth down. In short order, she downloaded the audio and was listening to her old friend's chirpy voice echoing inside her car.

*Let's start with Mistake Number One: <u>Opting Out</u>.*

*I'll be honest. I really hate writing about this particular mistake.*

*What can I say? This mistake is about women who take a spot at a good university and often professional school as well, and then, well, there's no nice way to say this, simply waste the enormous investment those institutions have made in them by quitting.*

*Sometimes these ladies get their "MRS" right out of the gate and never even get started. Sometimes they fold up their tent after only a couple years. So many of them throw in the towel the moment they get pregnant.*

*All the same, I'd say. And all such a waste.*

*My friend "C" was one who quit right out of the gate. In her defense, it wasn't premeditated—she accidentally got pregnant in college. But what a loss. C might be one of the very smartest people I know (and I work in Silicon Valley, so I know A LOT of smart people!). She was the top student in the economics department. She would have been going on to a great job and probably Harvard Business School after that if that was what she wanted.*

*She didn't plan a pregnancy, but it happened all the same. And it prevented her from getting the amazing start she deserved. I encouraged her to end the pregnancy. She was in college—much too young to bring a new life into the world! I'm not sure she's ever fully forgiven me for that. Especially because it turns out that her baby is still an only child, even after years and years of trying (Hey, maybe this will be her lucky year—ha!).*

*Also, it's my personal bet that Mr. C is a serial cheater. But you know what? She lives with it. Why? Because she doesn't have much of a choice (more on that later . . .).*

*But I digress. While C quit sooner than most, thousands of the most well-prepared women in America have joined her. They quit after college. After law school. After medical school. After a couple of years into what had been a promising start in a great company. National media outlets have heralded them the "Opt-Out Generation."*

*Let's get real. First, it's my sneaking suspicion that this is not a real "choice" for many of these ladies. It's an excuse for women who are struggling in their chosen field and don't want to do the work to get better. There, I've said it.*

*And the consequences of this choice are nothing less than disastrous. Let's start with the simple power dynamics. When a woman becomes a mere "Mrs." she becomes a dependent. No different than a child really. Her husband has all the power. If she's lucky, he loves and supports her without resentment. That will happen, statistically speaking, about half the time. For the other half, the numbers become grim, fast. Let me acquaint you with some more statistics . . .*

*I knew it*, Carmen thought. *Elizabeth should have listened to me all those years ago when I warned her about Heather. That cold calculation. That ambition.*

She didn't care anymore what Heather thought about her choice to have Avery. That ship had sailed a long, long time ago. But what she wrote about Mark, that was a different matter. Mark might be a bastard, but he was still Avery's dad. And Avery didn't need to read that shit about her dad. Or her mom, for that matter.

It was time to call the tribal council and vote Heather Hall off the island once and for all.

But first she had to deal with the bastard himself.

Carmen still couldn't believe how quickly almost twenty years of marriage could dissolve. And how little of him surrounded her now. To be fair, they hadn't had time to bring his stuff up to Lake Geneva. But he wasn't even in the places he should have been. Even the family pictures she had installed there were just of her and Avery—Mark had always been "working." He had never really been there. And he certainly wasn't going to be now.

A few days ago she had received the financial settlement Mark's attorney was proposing.

When the term sheet arrived, everything had looked good. She wasn't a lawyer, but she knew enough from her past education to understand how to read it. The hard part wasn't the legalese—it was that Carmen actually had no idea how much money they had. She had always managed expenses from a generously funded household account. She knew they had enough money for a really fancy house and nice vacations. But, at a high level, she didn't know exactly how wealthy they were.

As she looked over the terms, it seemed like things were going to go as planned—fifty-fifty. Twenty thousand dollars per month for spending. She got to keep the weekend house, as promised. The 401(k) plans would be split evenly, as well as all their deposits.

But then she'd spotted some odd language at the bottom of the sheet. It stated, "To the extent either party is the owner or beneficiary of any company or legal entity held separately in their own name, that party will retain their interest wholly in such entity with no expected or actual contribution to the other party."

*Huh*, she had thought. *That's weird.* Neither of them owned other companies or entities. That she knew of, anyway. Was Mark up to something sneaky?

Carmen had stewed about that provision for a while and finally decided that it was time to once and for all learn everything about the real Mark. She did a little checking and found a forensic investigator who specialized in situations like her own. He had agreed to meet her in his office downtown that afternoon.

As Carmen pulled into his building, she turned off chirpy Heather—she would get back to her later—and gathered her thoughts for the meeting.

Carmen had been in his waiting room for about five minutes when her new investigator, Paul Stark, came out to meet her.

She found herself looking at the best set of eyes she had ever seen. Kind, warm, green ones, and she could swear that they were smiling at her. And then she noticed his body. Not a gym body. The body of a guy that takes care of his own lawn and always volunteers to carry the heavy groceries. Carmen felt a little shiver run through her.

"Nice meeting you, Carmen," Paul said as he moved to shake her hand. "I shouldn't say this, but that husband of yours must be a real idiot." He laughed, revealing a welcoming smile.

His hands were big and a little rough. She felt a little current of electricity when he touched her shoulder, as well as an unfamiliar flutter in her stomach.

These were all feelings that Carmen thought grown women didn't have anymore.

The meeting with Paul went very well. Aside from her initial impression, he was clearly well suited to the job. When the meeting concluded, Carmen signed a retention agreement and got back in the car to go home. As she started the engine, her thoughts turned back to Heather. She couldn't wait to hear what Martha thought about all this.

# MARTHA

Martha tried to visit Lucy's grave once a week, but only during the school day so the boys wouldn't have to dwell on the sadness of her death. Now that they were finally back at school, they seemed to have moved on for the most part. Bobby had regained his lost appetite and was back to a healthy weight, and Jack had stopped asking Martha when Lucy was coming home.

In the end, Robert had quietly taken the extension in Milwaukee after their fight in June and actually started coming home more often as well. She wouldn't say she was happy, but she was better. They had never talked about it, but on some level Martha knew she might never be able to leave Wisconsin. This is where Lucy would be, forever. The idea of that was somewhat unimaginable, and she still couldn't really wrap her head around it. But there it was, and there it would remain.

As she made her way to the gravesite under a lovely oak, she saw a man standing near Lucy's grave. She realized with a start that it was Robert.

He must have come over on a break because he was still wearing scrubs under his barn jacket. He was standing with his hands at his sides and his head bent. Martha waited a short while before she walked over to meet him. She stood quietly next to him for a few minutes and then decided that today was the day they were going to have a real talk about what had happened to them both.

"Robert, I didn't know you were planning to visit."

"I wasn't really. But I missed her. I was the last person she saw, you know. The very last one. And I couldn't save her." His voice broke a little, and he looked away, embarrassed.

"Robert, I'm so sorry. That must have been awful for you.

But no one could have saved her. Please believe that I don't blame you."

Martha reached for Robert's hand and tried to hold tight, but he dropped her hand as he seemed to lean away from her.

"Martha, I know that, I do. But it will always stick with me. I couldn't save my own baby. I've lost patients before, and it was painful. But this. It's something else. I can't even put it into words. But I know it's something that I will be carrying around for the rest of my life." He sighed, bowed his head, and stuffed his hands deep into his pockets.

"And I'm the mom who didn't want her."

"That's ridiculous, Martha. Of course you did."

"After she was born, I did. But I also kind of resented her at first. You know I was thinking about trying to go back to work before I got pregnant with her. Maybe this was my punishment for being so conflicted about the whole thing."

"This wasn't anyone's fault," said Robert as he finally took his hands out of his pockets and reached for Martha's hand. "And we can't change it. But we can change how we are now. I love you, Martha. I want to be better. For you. And for the boys. I'm trying to be home more. I'm doing my best—I really am."

"I know you are. I appreciate it, I do." Martha paused and took a deep breath. Now was her moment. "But Robert, I need more. I want to get back into the world. I can't just sit at home while you and the boys are at work and school. I think I want to practice medicine again. But it can't be like before. Robert, do you remember that business trip you took after Jack was born when Carmen came to visit?"

"Not really," he replied.

"The one after which I decided to quit at the clinic and stay home."

"Oh, okay, yes, I sort of remember."

"Well, a lot more happened that weekend than I ever told you."

"Okay."

"Robert, I pretty much had a full-on anxiety attack. I didn't feel like I could leave our bedroom for several days. If Carmen hadn't rescued me, I don't know what would have happened. I was trying so hard to do it all. Practice medicine. Breastfeed Jack exclusively. Run the house. You know, everything. I lost it, Robert."

"Martha, why didn't you say something?"

"I don't know. I was embarrassed, I guess. I felt ashamed that I couldn't handle it all."

"Martha, I'm so sorry. What can I do differently this time?"

"Well, for one, I need you to help me more. Especially if I want to try to go back to work. To be honest, I'm not sure anymore that's what I want, but I need the option to try. And I don't want to live in fear that you are going to take a job somewhere else and I'll have to give up my thing, whatever it ends up being. I need something real and permanent."

Martha looked down at her feet, worried that Robert would go back to his old ways and disappoint her again. And then he surprised her.

"Okay, let's fix it," Robert replied, and squeezed her hand. "I might not always have the right words or do the right thing, but I will always, always, be on your side. No matter what. I hope you know that. I love my work, but I love you more. If it seems like I take things for granted, it's because I don't worry about us, ever. You were home for me right from the beginning, Martha. That's never going to change." Robert pulled Martha into his arms and held her as tightly as he ever had.

Martha knew at that moment that they were going to make it. She was going to plan a life here in Wisconsin. She would have roots here. All of them would, including Lucy.

As she and Robert parted and she walked back to her car, Martha made a note that September in Wisconsin was so much more beautiful than she had expected. It wasn't New Hampshire perfect, but that same fall smell was there, and the colors of the leaves hinted that a beautiful display was coming in a few weeks. Maybe she would take pictures and send them to her mother; without some compelling evidence, she wouldn't believe that Wisconsin's fall rivaled New England's.

Martha decided then and there that it was time to get on with the business of being happy.

As it turned out, that sentiment lasted less than a half an hour.

As she climbed behind the wheel and grabbed her phone to check her messages, she saw an alert that Heather had posted something with her name on it on Facebook. *Weird.* And there was a text from Carmen that said, "CALL ME!" and another group text from the girls that started with "DEFCON 5." She decided to start with the Facebook post.

Minutes later, she had downloaded the book and sat in total silence at the cemetery reading in her car.

It didn't take Martha very long to figure out what she was reading. And she had no trouble identifying "her" mistake —"Mistake Number Two." As she read Heather's cruel words, she felt a cold fury building inside herself:

*Mistake #2: Ramping Off.*

*You will tell yourself that you will just take a few months off. And then you will go back to work and realize how hard it is to do both.*

*And they will show you a "ramp."*

*Maybe it's part-time. Maybe it's a temporary leave. Maybe it's "We understand, and there's a spot for you when you come back."*

*I'm here to tell you that if you get off on one of those exit ramps, you may never get back on the highway. And if you manage to find your way back? The cars you were traveling along with? They are miles down the road. You will never catch up, no matter how fast you drive.*

*Never.*

*I have a friend. Let's call her "M." She's a doctor, and so is her husband. Well, was. Only one of them is practicing now because M took one of those off-ramps. Maybe she will get back on someday. I doubt it, but we'll see. But I can tell you this much. While she's at home saving yogurt lids or box tops or whatever for the PTA, he gets to save something else.*

*He gets to save lives . . .*

Martha dialed her best friend.

"What a fucking bitch," Carmen answered.

"Beyond," agreed Martha. "You know, I don't care what Ms. High-and-Mighty has to say about stay-at-home moms. I mean, whatever. And she has no idea what is really going on behind closed doors between Robert and me. Her analysis is just simplistic and stupid. What I just can't process, Carmen, is that while Heather was spending time getting ready to launch a book picking us over, I was putting my baby in the ground. How on earth could she have justified missing a funeral for *that*? Carmen, I think I'm done with Heather for good."

"I get that," said Carmen. "It really is unforgivable."

"I just don't see myself ever getting past this. And I shouldn't have to. Heather doesn't have an entitlement to my friendship. You know I don't like to cut people out of my life, Carmen, but Heather's not family, and some people don't deserve a second chance."

"Elizabeth and Sara are probably going to defend her."

"Well, they need to think long and hard about that. Enough's enough."

# SARA

Sara would be the last of the four to figure out what was going on that day.

It was the end of the workday, but she had one meeting left. Today was the day she would be discussing her expense study findings with the COO.

Sara had never fancied herself a businessperson, but she was beginning to wonder if she had missed her calling. She had spent the last few months interviewing department heads to understand their cost structure. She had found the fat and was excited to pass it on to the new COO and get back to her regular legal work. Just as Sara had gotten her things ready for the meeting, she saw the texts from Elizabeth and jumped into the conversation:

Hey! Some of us have to work, Carmen. Be nice.

After the back and forth she decided she would have to check out the book at her first opportunity. Elizabeth seemed pretty upset, which was really out of character for her. As she reluctantly put down her phone, she realized she had no more time and had to get right down to Mr. Rose's office.

"Sara! My secret weapon," Mr. Rose said as he met her at his door. "Come on in. I have such great news for you. First pick a chair. And keep in mind that whatever chair you pick tells me everything I need to know about you!"

The four chairs were arranged in a circle facing one another. After a moment of panic, she decided on the chair facing east, and he seemed to nod his approval. *Good God*, Sara thought. *This guy really is all hat and no cattle, as Carmen would say.*

"Sara, you've nailed it. I knew we had a number of overlapping and repetitive things going on. I was surprised at how many items you flagged, I have to say. But we can do more here. What's your experience with outsourcing?"

*Um*, thought Sara, *I have had the "experience" of discovering it might be killing my husband's job.*

"Well, Mr. Rose, none. I'm a lawyer."

"As a company, we are behind on this. You have proven that we have a ton of potential here. Let's take it to the next level."

*Oh crap*, Sara thought. *What have I done?*

"Well, I think that might be simplifying things a bit," she said. "There is still an element of judgment in many somewhat repetitive processes."

"Of course. Hey, I'm not talking about using robots. These will still be humans."

"I understand. I hope you are able to meet your goals, of course. Were there any other questions about my conclusions?"

"I'm not in the details. But you will be. I'd like you to come work for me as a VP. Whatever you are making—double it. But expect to spend some significant time in India for training and process development. Maybe the Philippines. And you have to take early calls because of the time differences."

"Mr. Rose, that's all very flattering, but I'm an attorney. I like to practice law. And I also have four children, so my schedule is not incredibly flexible."

"Hey, I'm a feminist. I don't care how many kids you have. And I don't care when you work. As long as the work gets done, I'm happy. Any eighty hours, you know what I mean? Do it. Don't do it. Your choice. But the offer expires Friday. After that, I'll find someone else. And trust me—there is always someone else," he said as he rose with a wink and moved to shake her hand, signaling that the meeting was over.

Sara shook his hand and left, bewildered at her predicament.

She went back to her desk with her head in a jumble. She decided to take a break and sort through her personal e-mails. At the top of the list was a reminder to pay the AmEx bill. It was over seven thousand dollars this month because, in addition to the typical three thousand dollars of regular expenses, there were the annual soccer registration fees (another three) and the twelve pairs of back-to-school shoes (four sets of everyday shoes, gym shoes, and winter boots).

"Hey, friend," Katherine said as she breezed into Sara's cube. "How did the meeting go?"

"Well, it's not what I expected. He offered me a job, Katherine."

"No shit. Better pay."

"Like crazy better pay."

"Take it! What do you have to lose?"

"Well, it's not really a law job per se. But if Scott actually loses his job, we'd be covered. But I was told it's extensive travel. Or maybe it was extreme travel. Like India. And more hours."

"Well, what if you did it for just a year or two and banked the cash?"

"Maybe," said Sara. "I just don't want to work those long hours. It's why I left the firm in the first place."

"I get that. Well, look, it's nice to be asked anyway. So, hey, I saw your friend pop up on Twitter. I think she published a new book or something. Do you know what it's about?"

"No, I don't downshift that fast." Sara laughed. "I'll probably order it today, though. I think it's something about career mistakes or something. Maybe I can learn something. I hope it has some dishy stories about some of her famous friends."

"Right?" said Katherine. "Well, I gotta get back to it."

Sara didn't feel like working, so she decided to download the book and read it furtively on her phone.

As she settled into her chair and began to read, she suddenly came to a terrible realization.

This was not just any book. And it wasn't dishing dirt on Heather's famous friends. It was about them.

What had Heather done?

A crushing wave of anxiety hit Sara as she thought about all the conversations about work and life and, well, everything, she had shared with her friends over the years.

Sara thought about all the stories she had told Heather about the law firm (not great). And her company (really, really not great). The "woman" stuff. The pathological narcissism of senior leaders. The sheer meanness. She thought Heather had understood that those stories went deep down into the vault, only to be opened upon pain of death. Sometimes you had to eat your little pile of shit in the workplace, and it was the job of a good girlfriend to let you bitch about it and commiserate. But never, never tell.

She felt the bile begin to rise in her throat.

Would this book hurt her career or her relationships with her work colleagues? She suspected that there would be consequences, and she wouldn't necessarily see them coming. It's not like her former colleagues were going to pick up the phone and scold her for her criticism. That's not how those people operated. They would have their revenge in due time. Like when she needed a letter of recommendation. Or a favor for a friend.

What about Tommy? He was almost thirteen. His friends' moms might read it too.

*Okay. Calm down, Sara, one thing at a time*, she told herself, trying to quell the rising nausea. She had to assess the actual damage and then she would let herself freak out.

Sara zeroed in on "her" section right away—Mistake Number Three, "Half-Assing It."

*You haven't quit. You haven't ramped off.*

*Good for you.*

*But let's not forget—half effort will equal half results. If women want to lead and win, they have to be willing to put in the blood, sweat, and tears that are always, always required.*

*I look around the room at the executive retreats I often attend. And I think about the boardrooms of the Fortune 500.*

*Not a lot of women.*

*Why?*

*Because they aren't willing to put in the extra effort. To look for the promotion. To go for the raise.*

*I understand the desire to have time for family, I do. But ladies, here's the secret—once you make it to the top, you can actually achieve the balance you are trying to strike! You just have to work hard NOW to get it. Yes, sacrifice might be required, but the alternatives are not good ones.*

*So go for it. Or you can just plod along like my friend "S," doing everything half-assed and badly. If she would just dig in and make it to the next level at work, she would find that she has the time and resources to enjoy her four children.*

Sara felt her anxiety drain away as she finished her section. *Well, Heather's book is certainly unkind,* she thought. *But she didn't say anything that would hurt me at work. God, it could have been so much worse. Hell, maybe she's right. I did bite off more than I can chew.*

Sara breathed a sigh of relief and gathered up her things to go home.

The traffic was light, and she was home way ahead of schedule. As she pulled into the drive, she noticed Scott was already home too. Early for him as well. *Great,* thought Sara, *maybe he already has dinner going.* The adrenaline of the afternoon had not quite worn off yet, and Sara was hopeful that she could just crack open a bottle of wine and couch.

She pushed the front door open, stepped over the ever-present pile of backpacks and shoes, and went over to sort the mail. Right on top she saw a folder labeled "Beck, Scott, Separation Agreement."

She knew instantly that she would have to get her immunizations for India.

# HEATHER

**From**: Heather Hall <HHall@flash.com>
**Sent**: Thurs. 9/5 7:15 a.m.
**To**: Elizabeth Smith <ESmith@gmail.com>
Carmen Jones <MrsMarkJones@yahoo.com>
Martha Adams West <MAW@gmail.com>
Sara Beck <Sara.Beck@bigcompany.com>
**Subject**: So what do you think?

By now, I hope you've made the time to read my book (If I have the time to write it, you guys certainly have the time to read it!). I can't thank you enough for the inspiration you gave me. Your stories are helping women everywhere. I am hearing from so many young people; they are so engaged! Finally, someone has given them the road map for success! Look, I know I covered some sensitive topics, but I also know how giving all of you guys are and that you wouldn't mind.

We always said we would tell our stories someday, didn't we? And you know what? Keeping things secret is one of the big obstacles to progress. Look at all the terrible things that have happened because people didn't speak their truth. It's our job to tell each other's stories so that we can pave the way for real, lasting change in society.

I know I said not to write, but I've changed my mind. I'd love to know what you think.

Love and kisses,

Heather

# ELIZABETH

Elizabeth had taken the day off to formulate her game plan at work. What a mess Heather had made! She had read Heather's e-mail this morning, and she couldn't believe that Heather had taken the position that it was *her* job to tell her friends' "truths." Somewhere along the line, she had neglected to realize that every woman's story belongs to her, and her alone.

Elizabeth decided to spend some time alone on her porch with her favorite coffee cup. It was her thinking place when life overwhelmed her. As she sat there considering how to handle her situation, she tried to remember what she had loved about Heather in the first place.

Well, for starters, if it hadn't been for Heather, she wouldn't have met William, so that was something.

She had been in her last year of law school at Columbia and, too late, found out that her parents were going on vacation over Thanksgiving, so she had no place to go. She was planning to just hunker down and study, but Heather insisted that she come with her back to Wisconsin. Heather had always been generous like that.

She remembered getting off the tiny plane and being amazed at just how green and clean Wisconsin was, particularly compared with the grime and smell of Manhattan that she had grown accustomed to. After experiencing a Thanksgiving right out of a Norman Rockwell painting in Heather's hometown of Oconomowoc, she'd driven her rented sedan back down to Milwaukee to fly back to school. But when she arrived at her departure gate, she'd discovered her flight had been canceled due to inclement weather in the New York area. *Oh well*, she had thought. *One more night here.* She'd plopped down into one of the seats in the waiting area and started asking around about a decent, cheap hotel nearby (it seemed too far to go back to Heather's in Oconomowoc).

"Looking for a place to stay?" a young man sitting next to her had asked.

"Yep," Elizabeth had replied, and she found herself looking at a guy with sandy blond hair and bright blue eyes who held himself with the confidence of a guy who might have been the high school quarterback.

And now they were celebrating their fifteenth anniversary.

Maybe Heather was right that she could have planned things better, but it was in the past. Who knows, it might have been just as hard for her in the earlier years. But she would never know. And that was the tough part. Living with the thought of what might have been. She needed to start thinking beyond the baby thing, though. Maybe she would put some effort into figuring out her next steps in her career for a change. She had spent most of her time at the firm with her chin tucked down, working at top speed, so that she hadn't really considered whether there was a way to approach the job to make it a little more enjoyable. It seemed kind of impossible, but maybe there was a way.

"Babe, can we get takeout tonight? I'm beat, and George and I just want to watch college football," called a voice from inside.

"You got it," replied Elizabeth with a smile, thinking, *Sure, George wants to watch football.*

*Oh, Heather,* she thought, turning back to her predicament. Elizabeth was angry, she was, but it was always hard for her to stay mad at Heather for long. Heather might have been distant since she became famous, but Heather had been from the beginning a good and loyal friend to Elizabeth.

Elizabeth would never forget the day she decided that Heather would be a forever friend. It was fall of their sophomore year, and the girls had decided to give sorority rush a go. It was the second round, and they had just been given a list of the houses that were interested in them. They had decided that they weren't going to go to the next round unless they all got invited back to the same houses on this round. They all agreed that they would be happy to be in any four of the six houses, and they also hoped that they would be together, or at least only split in two, which seemed to be good odds.

They had met at the Hop to open their bid envelopes.

"Yes! All four!" exclaimed Carmen.

"Same," Martha said with a smile.

"Me three," chimed in Sara happily.

Elizabeth opened her envelope and saw only one sorority listed. And it wasn't one of the four they all had liked. It was the one that you got invited to no matter what. She was embarrassed to admit it, but she wasn't really excited to pledge there.

"I didn't get any of the ones we liked," she said sadly. "I'm sorry, you guys. I guess I'm just not good at a party."

"Whatever, we'll just all drop out," replied Carmen, but she didn't seem very enthusiastic about the prospect.

Heather opened her envelope quickly and said, "Well, I just got the same as Elizabeth. Listen, you guys go ahead and keep going. Elizabeth and I can drop together. No big deal."

"Are you sure?" asked Carmen, failing to hide her hope.

"Of course," said Heather with a dismissive wave. "It's ridiculous to think we will all be together for this kind of stuff anyway. Go have fun. Just make sure we get invited to all the good parties."

After lunch, Heather and Elizabeth found their bikes and took off together toward Baker Library and their next classes. As they parted ways on the Green, something dropped out of Heather's backpack. Elizabeth rode over to pick it up, intending to give whatever it was back to Heather the next time she saw her.

Elizabeth realized as she picked it up that it was Heather's bid card. And right there, clear as day, was a list of the *four* sororities that had invited Heather back. Elizabeth had never told Heather she knew and certainly didn't tell anyone else either, but it was one of those things that she would never forget.

Sorority rush seemed like a trivial thing now that they were adults, but back then it wasn't. It had been a big deal for all of them, especially Heather, who was beautiful and bright, but didn't have the social connections of someone like Martha.

Yes, Elizabeth still hoped for a happy ending. After the girls punished Heather, maybe they could all figure out a way to forgive her.

And just as Elizabeth started to really settle into that thought, her cell phone buzzed.

# CARMEN

"We need to cut her off once and for all," said Carmen sharply to Elizabeth. "A group of five has always been too many anyway. We should have done this years ago."

"I kind of feel the same way," said Elizabeth, "but part of me thinks it might be better to take the high road. Don't you think?"

"Really, like I did with Mark? Look where that got me. At least I'm finally ready to move on."

"Of course you are!" replied Elizabeth kindly. "That asshole didn't deserve you. Not for a second."

"I appreciate that, but I don't want to be angry with him. I just want my fair share of the money, and I want to start a new life. But this isn't about me—it's about *her*."

"Carmen, I think we need to move on. It doesn't matter what she thinks. It actually doesn't matter what any of us think. Your own opinion about your life is the only one that matters, right?"

"But Elizabeth, she exposed you at work."

"Yes, that was bad, but it's also fixable. It's not enough to ruin a lifelong friendship over."

"You always take her side, you know. You two stick together every time," Carmen accused.

"Okay, that's not fair, and you know it."

"Maybe not," Carmen conceded. "Look, I get what you're saying about the high road, but you were always too much of an apologist for her Elizabeth. On Friday we need to have a serious group discussion about how we're going to handle this situation."

"All right, I'll play." Elizabeth sighed. "But let's be reasonable. How would she feel if she knew we were all getting together and talking about her behind her back?"

Carmen laughed incredulously. "You're kidding, right?"

# MARTHA

Heather was dead to her. Period.

But Martha still had the rest of her friends. And she was going to hold on tight because Milwaukee was going to be her home. She had decided that she wanted to live in Whitefish Bay near Elizabeth and send her boys to the public schools there; Robert owed her that at least. She had called Sara on the off chance that she might want to go see some available houses.

The whole situation with Heather made Martha want to improve her relationship with Sara and Elizabeth, too, and now she had the time to do it. Sara almost always said no to requests for get-togethers due to her distance and never-ending to-do list, but this time Martha was pleasantly surprised because she had said yes—and on a Thursday to boot! Martha had arranged to pick her up at the train station downtown.

Sara was one of the first passengers off the train. She gave Martha a big hug.

"A day off! I really needed this—thanks so much for calling! My life is crazy, and I really could use a friend to talk to." But then Sara paused and looked stricken. "Shit. I'm sorry. You probably don't need to hear about my problems after what you went through. How are you feeling?"

"Actually, I feel really good for the first time in a long time," replied Martha with a smile. "But let's not talk about me. Please. That would be so nice. Let's spend the whole day on Sara and houses."

"Okay, you asked for it." And with that, Sara grabbed Martha's hand and pulled her out the terminal door.

# SARA

They were on their third house on Lake Drive when Sara decided to tell Martha everything. Scott's job elimination. Her job offer. The money.

Sara knew Martha was exceedingly uncomfortable talking about money, but she also knew Martha was really her only choice. Carmen and Elizabeth would tell her to stay put in her current job and then try to offer her a loan or some other financial help while Scott got back on his feet. That was not what she wanted. She owed it to herself and her family to weigh the pros and cons of the COO's offer. She needed to talk it out with someone who would give it to her straight and help her arrive at the right decision. And whatever she and Scott did, she didn't want it to involve taking financial assistance from her friends. Martha's WASPy upbringing would never allow her to loan money to friends. So Martha it was.

They were inspecting a beautiful home done in an Italian Renaissance style while the realtor waited downstairs.

"Martha, something happened at work," Sara began casually.

"Oh, yeah, what's that?" said Martha distractedly as she systematically inspected the large master bathroom, turning on the water and peeking under the sink.

"I got a job offer," replied Sara.

Martha straightened up immediately and turned to Sara. "Wait, I thought your general counsel plans to be there at least five more years."

"He does. The offer isn't really for a legal job. Remember that budgeting project I told you about? Well, it actually went pretty well. I think the COO was really surprised at what I came up with. Anyway, he wants to promote me to VP and have me basically implement a bunch of my ideas."

"So you wouldn't be practicing law then?" Martha pressed as they walked out of the bathroom into the master bedroom. Martha paused to run her hand along the beautifully carved bannister that ran along the upstairs hall.

"Well, technically no. But I would be making twice my salary."

"Yes, but won't that take you off the track to be a general counsel someday?" Martha asked as she opened the closet door in the master suite to peek inside.

"I don't know, maybe. I guess it might. But maybe it's a plus?" Sara knew she wasn't selling Martha on the idea. She wasn't even selling herself.

"Well, I don't think you should ever take a new job just because it pays more."

An awkward silence passed as the pair walked out of the master bedroom and toward the rest of the rooms on the second floor.

"What if your husband just got laid off?" said Sara quietly. "Would that fact change your mind?"

Martha stopped and turned to face Sara. "What? When did that happen?"

"It literally just happened. Nobody knows, and I'm still processing it. I really thought his job was rock solid. They gave him severance through the end of the year, so we aren't in trouble yet. But we will be soon if he can't find something else quickly."

"Scott will land somewhere," Martha assured her. "Everyone in his industry must know he's terrific."

"I don't think so, Martha. He told me he's thinking about his options, but he said that a bunch of companies have outsourced the bulk of their IT to India or wherever. Nobody's hiring, no matter how good you are. There are just too many people out there looking at the same jobs. Scott might be out of luck. He's talking about getting a temporary job until he finds something permanent, but it wouldn't be stable. Our family can't handle that. We kind of live paycheck to paycheck as it is."

"You do not," chided Martha. "Please don't tell me an attorney and an IT professional can't make ends meet."

"Of course we can, I mean, at a really baseline level. And look, I know we are blessed compared to what others have. We are not going to starve, obviously. But you know what I mean. We're on track for retirement and college and everything. But what's left after the mortgage, the savings, and all the kid expenses is really pitiful. We have to think long and hard about even a long weekend trip."

"My dear, you did choose to have four children," Martha reminded her in her best physician's tone.

"I get that. But I never thought it would be like this. I'm an attorney. Money is not supposed to be my problem."

"It won't be if you take the new job, right?"

"It's definitely much more than Scott and I made together."

"Well, sounds like you know what you want to do. So go do it."

"I want that kind of high-level work and authority, and everything that goes along with it, but there is a big downside. Apparently I have to do some significant travel to India and maybe other places too."

"I agree, that's a big downside. India's beautiful, but you have a baby at home. Do you really think Scott can handle that? There is always another way. I'm sure you can find things to cut."

"Well, I think Scott will have a decent amount of time on his hands for the foreseeable future, so yes, he can do it. And I don't want to downsize or move to a bigger house in a crappy school district. We had the kids, and we owe them the best shot we can give."

"All right. But I hope you are considering that it will make it tough for him to look for work when he has four kids on his hands. And what about you? Can you stand not being the one to take your baby to the pediatrician? Or be there for the band concert? Or watch the big game?"

"I don't know," said Sara quietly. "I guess we are going to find out. I made a dinner reservation to talk to Scott tonight."

The girls' phones buzzed simultaneously. They had a group text from Carmen: *Get a babysitter for Friday night. We are going out.*

"She is really pissed about the book," Sara said with a laugh. "She's kind of being a drama queen. It wasn't all that bad."

"What planet are you on?" Martha snapped back, surprising Sara. "You get that she was working on the promotional plan for her book when she skipped Lucy's funeral, right?"

"Oh, I guess I hadn't thought about that," said Sara quietly. "I'm sorry. Martha, she's our oldest friend. I get that she went all mean girl on us, but I think we need to find a way to forgive her, right?"

"Yeah, no, we really don't, and I can't believe you think so."

"I'm so sorry . . ." replied Sara, surprised by Martha's anger.

"We are done talking about this," said Martha coldly. "Anyway, save it for Friday, like Carmen said."

Sara knew better than to say any more. Maybe they could vent on Friday and move on. They had to figure this out. They had been friends too long to just call it quits.

Anyway, Heather was not her top priority now. She had to settle things with Scott.

She headed back home to get ready for her dinner date with Scott. She went to the effort of dressing up for the occasion, and Scott reciprocated. Just a few hours later, they were seated at a quiet corner table, Sara in her favorite little black dress and Scott in his sport coat and bow tie.

Sara had picked a neighborhood spot known for its intimate and quiet ambiance.

Sara and Scott spent the first couple of courses talking about anything other than work. Sara knew that they had to start the probable fight, but she didn't want to ruin the evening. But there was a job to do, as there always was for them.

Sara launched the first missile.

"Scott, I've been thinking about it for a long time, and I think I should take it."

Scott looked up from his entrée and took a deep breath, looking sad and already a bit defeated. "Okay, but what about the travel?"

"I know, the travel will be hard, but I thought maybe you could pick up more at home since you have more time now."

A beat of silence passed between them.

Scott shifted uncomfortably in his seat and responded, "I don't think now's the time to worry about the house and kid stuff. Let's figure out our job situation and work from there."

"But the house and kid stuff is part of the job situation!" Sara argued, a little too stridently.

"Sara, I don't agree, but I don't think we need to go down that road tonight. Let's be practical. For now, I agree you should take the new job. But I'm not just walking away from the work world after what happened. This will be a temporary thing."

"Oh, I understand that, honey. I just thought that maybe you could do more stuff at home now when I'm ramping up in the new job, and then we could hire help when you go back full-time."

"Sara, lay off. Please. The stuff that needs to get done will get done, even if you get busier. And, for the record, I'm not exactly a slouch now. I'm already doing a lot. At least fifty percent."

"Scott, honey, you are not even within spitting distance of fifty percent."

"And here we go again."

"Scott, if me taking this job is going to work, you have to understand the kind of things that quietly happen every day that you give me absolutely no credit for."

"Like vacuuming when the floor is not dirty? Or folding the socks in pairs, just because that's the way you like it? Or going to two grocery stores because you have to have particular brands that taste the same as the other ones? Or, my favorite, throwing away my important shit because it looks ugly sitting on the table? Yeah, I'm not counting any of that toward your percentage. And if you want me to take over a bunch of stuff, we are doing it my way."

Sara was quiet. The truth was she wanted to do a lot of the stuff herself, especially the kid-related things, and do it her way. But she wasn't going to have time for a while. And she wasn't sure Scott would find another job anytime soon, so he might be in charge at home for a while, and that was something she didn't want to say out loud. His ego was bruised enough as it was. So instead she said, "Of course, I am totally fine with that."

"Sure you are," said Scott, still a little testy.

"Let's not fight, please," Sara pleaded. "You're right. This will be temporary, so it's not worth making a big deal over. However you want to get things done in the next few months while I'm figuring out my new job will be fine by me. But can I at least make a list with all the things that I usually do? And maybe some notes on process?"

"Uh-huh," said Scott with clear annoyance.

"Awesome! I'll make a spreadsheet in Google Drive with the to-dos, and you can just make a note of whether you are doing it and when it's done or whatever. And I'll do the same for the things I do."

"So I'm like your employee then?"

"No, this will just be a tool to help us keep on track."

Scott exhaled deeply and said, "Fine, let's give it a try. But Sara, you are treading on thin ice."

Sara ignored that and continued, "Great! Because if I take the job, the COO wants me to go to India in December. I'll get the sheet started right away."

# HEATHER

**From Heather Hall's Twitter**

**Heather Hall** @therealheatherhall · September 5

Register your book club at FLASH.com and receive a free Four
BIG Mistakes Conversation Guide #Makeplansnotmistakes

# ELIZABETH

*I really need to do something about my karma*, thought Elizabeth. In addition to having to deal with the whole "I'm not pregnant" fiasco, she was now stuck in her first-Friday-of-the-month general partner meeting. Today, they were discussing compensation practices. Being a partner wasn't as fun as she had imagined. What was the old law school saying? Oh yes, law school is a pie-eating contest, and the prize for winning is pie.

The group was seated around a pristine oval conference table in the new client center on the top floor.

The first item on the agenda was whether they would raise first year salaries another 10K to match New York. Everyone liked this idea because they fancied their firm as a national competitor to the big Manhattan firms. In the end, though, their fundamental midwestern thriftiness won out, and they decided not to match. *Blake is not going to be happy about that one*, Elizabeth thought with some satisfaction.

They ran through the rest of the agenda fairly quickly. As Elizabeth left the conference room, Joe pulled her aside.

"Hey, Elizabeth, do you have a second? Just wanted to give you a heads-up. The management committee has made its decision about department chair. Look, I'm sorry. They went with Kenny. Grey just loves him. We will find something else for you."

Elizabeth couldn't find the words. Fucking Facebook. Fucking Heather. The wrong little bit of information at the wrong time. Kenny hadn't lied about her, had he? He had repeated what was basically a public fact, at least for the day he needed to inflict a fatal blow to Elizabeth.

And she was extremely disappointed in Joe and the Old Man. Why hadn't they gone to bat for her?

She was trying to take the high road, she was. But now Heather had caused her to get screwed at work. And, if she were being completely honest with herself, she couldn't put Heather's cruel words about Mistake Number Four out of her mind:

*So you haven't opted out. You haven't ramped off. You have given it your all at work and effectively managed life's hiccups. Good for you! But, perhaps, in all your effort, you are making the last of the big mistakes. Like my friend "E," you might have ignored or conveniently "forgotten" about the fertility cliff at age thirty-five.*

*That's right, ladies. Thirty-five.*

*I know you had to get through school and get established. And find a man (or a partner).*

*And perform at work. Look, I know that it's tough because our peak fertility years correspond with the same time many of us are up for promotion.*

*Too bad.*

*The bottom line is that the work world is never going to change. It's up to us to change. To take charge of our fertility and not make Mistake #4. I want you to sit down and make a business plan. Yes, right NOW, before it's too late. Calculate how many children you want, and work backwards.*

*Tick tock, ladies.*

*Never forget—fortunes get spent and buildings crumble, but DNA is FOREVER.*

Elizabeth needed to talk to Carmen and tell her what had happened. And admit that Carmen might have been right. The high road wasn't too effective. And there should be consequences for Heather.

She pulled out her cell and started dialing.

# CARMEN

"How's the high road treating you?" Carmen asked as she answered her cell.

"Shit, actually," replied Elizabeth, before proceeding to tell Carmen what had happened at work.

"So you'll be on my side tonight then," said Carmen. "Good. That should make it unanimous."

A beat of silence passed between the two women. Finally, Carmen continued, "Elizabeth, I have something I want to propose to you. It's weird and awkward, but I need to do it. I've been thinking about it for a while and wanted to talk to you, but there hasn't really been a good time because of all this Heather crap."

"Okay, I'm kind of scared," Elizabeth responded with a laugh.

"Don't be. Reading Heather's book reminded me how badly you want a sibling for George. You and I have been talking a lot about women helping each other and being kind, and that doesn't just mean in the workplace. So you know how I froze those eggs of mine a while back? Well, I'm done with them. I don't want another child. I want to go get my MBA and maybe really go all-in on the career thing. I might be forty, but I look ten years younger than the rest of you, and I deserve a chance to be miserable in the work world too."

"Wow, that's a lot to process," said Elizabeth quietly. "I appreciate how generous your offer is, but doesn't it sound a little crazy?"

"Does it? It doesn't to me. We're forty. Let's throw away the rule book and just go for what we want. What do you have to lose? You want to be a parent again. So let's give you one more shot. Who gives a shit what people think? And, for the record, no one has to know it's my egg. C'mon, live on the wild side. You know you will have a much better shot with a younger egg than your own."

"Well, that's true. Our doctor thinks that I'm showing signs of premature ovarian failure, which explains why I've had so much trouble the last few years. The best shot for me is probably IVF with a donor egg."

"Alrighty then. That seals it. Let's do this."

"Fine, I'll think about it and see if I can get William on board," Elizabeth said, unable to stop her voice from breaking a little. Trying to pull herself together, she added, "I'm sorry. This is a happy moment, believe me. I just can't believe you want to do this for me. For us. Thank you, Carmen. I have to be honest, I wasn't excited about using a donor egg. I mean, it is like half your baby is a total stranger. This certainly fixes that problem."

A few moments of silence passed between them.

"So, I could use a little help with something myself," said Elizabeth.

"What's that?" asked Carmen.

"Since you are going to be getting your MBA, I'd like to pick your brain about a few business ideas I've been bouncing around. You know I'm frustrated with parts of how my firm runs things. And maybe I can change that."

"Deal," said Carmen. And as she hung up the phone, she mentally closed the book on the life of the old Carmen and opened the cover of a new, fresh volume. Nothing in recent memory had ever felt better.

# MARTHA

"Mom, Heather didn't write anything about my life that isn't true, and that everyone didn't already know for that matter. Honestly, who cares?" said Martha with exasperation. Of course, Martha cared mightily, but she wasn't going to give her mother the satisfaction of knowing that she was, in fact, very upset about Heather's book.

"Well, Bunny saw it on the Facebook, and she has been telling everyone at the club. It's very embarrassing. I really think you should rethink filing suit. In my day, no one would have ever dared to do that to an Adams. If you had made different friends in college, this all might have been avoided, you know."

*Here we go again*, thought Martha, rolling her eyes and vowing not to snap at her mother.

"Mom, I like the friends I have. If I wanted to mingle with your crowd, I would have stayed in Boston. I left town to do things my own way."

"You always did like to bring home pathetic stray animals and try to save them. Look, darling, all I'm trying to say is that your friends aren't like us. And they obviously think nothing of airing dirty laundry in public. Even my worst enemies wouldn't behave like that. There are just some things that are simply unacceptable in polite society."

"Mom, I'm sorry if this is embarrassing," Martha snapped. She took a deep breath and continued in a kinder tone. "Really, compared to what happened with Lucy, it's inconsequential, isn't it?"

"We don't need to discuss Lucy. It's in the past."

*Of course*, thought Martha. *Let's not talk about any of our pain and disappointment. That's always been so effective.* She considered arguing the point with her mom, but instead she said, "Okay, Mom. Tell Dad I said hello." And with that, she hung up and started to get ready to go out and meet her girlfriends for a drink.

She still couldn't believe that Sara hadn't understood how horrible it was that Heather had missed Lucy's funeral. She was glad she had been able to make her point before they all got together tonight. Otherwise, Sara would have found herself the odd man out.

# SARA

The girls decided to meet at one of the bars near the train station in downtown Milwaukee.

Sara was the last to arrive since she had the farthest to travel, and, as she entered the bar, she saw that her three friends were already nodding their heads in agreement.

"Well, we've already kicked Heather out of the group," said Carmen with a laugh. "Any objection?"

"Isn't that a little extreme?" asked Sara. "I mean, c'mon, guys. Let's not overreact here."

"Uh, no, it's not extreme," responded Carmen with an irritated frown. "Did you even read the book? I mean, I know you're too busy to ever go out with any of us and all, but I would have thought you could carve out some time for this one."

"Okay, that's kind of bitchy, Carmen," said Sara. "And I did read the book. Cover to cover. I get why you guys are upset, but let's try to put this in context. First, I think she's actually trying to help younger women learn from our mistakes. I mean, c'mon, aren't there things you wished you had done differently? I actually agreed with what she said about my choices. I think she has a point. It's been exhausting trying to do things the way Scott and I have been doing them. I'm going to take Heather's advice and outsource some stuff so I can give it my all in my new job."

"What new job?" asked Elizabeth.

"I'll tell you later. Let's finish this Heather stuff. All I'm saying is that we should admit that she might have written things that were uncomfortable to read, but they weren't secrets."

"They certainly were!" countered Carmen. "No one knew I thought Mark might be cheating. Which, by the way, he wasn't."

"Come on. He might not have technically cheated, but it's not a big secret that Mark is a douche," replied Sara.

"It was a secret from Avery," said Carmen hotly.

"And she did talk about my pregnancy, Sara," Elizabeth reminded her. "And I lost the chairmanship because of it."

"Be fair, Elizabeth. It was your fault for telling her you were pregnant and then forgetting to tell her you had lost the baby," said Sara.

"Well, if she had shown up at my baby's funeral, then Elizabeth might have had a chance. And Heather certainly knew I lost Lucy, didn't she?" asked Martha angrily. "And she couldn't break away from her low-class tell-all to attend the funeral."

"Martha, I get that you are angry about that choice, but Lucy's death really has nothing to do with Heather's book. I agree she should have come to the funeral, but her being there wouldn't have changed anything. And she did send those lovely flowers," Sara pointed out.

"Sara, I can't believe you actually think that's an equivalent," said Martha, looking incredulous.

"Of course it's not, that not what I meant," said Sara in frustration.

"Well, why don't you say what you do mean," replied Martha, crossing her arms.

"Martha," Elizabeth interjected, clearly trying to play the peacemaker, "I somewhat agree with Sara. It's not Heather's fault Lucy died. Personally, I think I got a pretty bad deal too. A miscarriage and a hit at work. But Heather is a good person. Remember sorority rush."

Martha looked at Elizabeth with disbelief. "Okay, I really hope you aren't suggesting that a dead baby and a missed promotion are the same thing."

"Of course I'm not saying that," said Elizabeth defensively.

"And sorority rush? What the hell are you talking about?"

"I never told you guys, but she actually got into all four

houses in the second round but pretended she had been rejected so we could drop together."

"Holy shit, Elizabeth. What an inconsequential nothing," Martha practically spat. "Grow up. You know, I think I want to go home. The fact that any of you think that what Heather wrote is worse than losing a child is unbelievable to me. I'm not sure that I want to be around you guys right now. And Elizabeth, did it ever occur to you that your 'hit' at work was actually just that Kenny won because he was better? You're such a narcissist." Martha quickly rose and headed for the door.

"Martha, please don't go—we're on your side!" Carmen yelled after her.

As Martha retreated, Carmen spun on the other two. "Look what you two did! Sara, you need to find a little time in your schedule to get a clue. And Elizabeth, I know your career is a big deal, but that wasn't exactly the best moment to make it about you. And sorority rush? What the fuck?"

"Back off, Carmen," said Elizabeth. "My life has kind of been sucking lately. I get that my situation is not the same as losing a child. But Martha is wrong," she continued defensively. "Me not getting chair had nothing to do with my performance. Heather screwed me, plain and simple. And you know what? Sorority rush was a big deal. When you and Martha got all those callbacks and I didn't, it was Heather who pretended she was rejected and stuck with me. You guys were happy to drop us both like a hot potato."

Elizabeth sighed and continued, "Look, I'll call Martha later and apologize. But not because you told me to, Carmen. You should too, Sara."

"What am I apologizing for?" exclaimed Sara. "I didn't do anything wrong! And Elizabeth, after everything Heather has done for you, I would think you could find a way to get past this. You know what, I'm going home too. I have a family of six to support on my own now, and I don't have time for this drama.

It's a long way home. You guys can have at Heather on your own."

"Fine, Elizabeth and I will stay and have another drink while I help her rehearse her apology," replied Carmen, to which Elizabeth rolled her eyes.

As she left the bar, Sara considered that the evening might be the end of their happy group. Maybe that was okay.

She bet that Elizabeth would forgive Heather. And she also bet that Martha and Carmen never would. She thought that this was partially because they were jealous. Sara thought that they always had been a little jealous of Heather, and Elizabeth and Sara, too, because of their professional success.

*It's easy to be friends when you're eighteen*, she thought. *Forty, not so much.* Maybe she needed to give up on the idea of having lifelong female friends, but whatever was going to happen among them in the long run, Sara had to ignore all of it right now and dig in at work. Her family's future depended on it.

# DECEMBER

# HEATHER

**From**: Heather Hall <HHall@flash.com>
**Sent**: Sun. 12/6 2:15 p.m.
**To**: Elizabeth Smith <ESmith@gmail.com>
Carmen Jones <MrsMarkJones@yahoo.com>
Martha Adams West <MAW@gmail.com>
Sara Beck <Sara.Beck@msn.com>
**Subject**: Gift idea!

Hi girls! I know we are all crazy busy over the holidays, but just want to drop you a note to let you know that if you would like to give my book as a holiday present, I can send you signed copies. Just let me know how many. Just you, though. I'm overwhelmed with requests.

Let's try to get together next year in Carmel. Maybe March? June? I miss you and really want to catch up. I know I've been a bad friend and haven't kept up with what's going on with you guys, but I'll make it up to you. Also, I kind of can't believe you are too busy to e-mail me your thoughts on the book—seriously, come on!

Kisses,

Heather

P.S. Elizabeth, you need to update your profile with pictures of the new baby!

# ELIZABETH

*Fall always has a way of evaporating before it even starts*, thought Elizabeth.

After the blowup at the bar, things had changed. Sara had returned to her busy life and new job. Martha had hunkered down in her house and basically ignored them all. Carmen and Elizabeth were the only ones who had kept the lines of communication open, although Elizabeth had been so busy in the fall that December had come faster than she ever remembered, and Christmas was just a couple of weeks away.

Elizabeth was wrapping presents on her Sunday off. Her cream-colored duvet was stacked with ribbons, paper, tape, and a possibly obscene number of presents. Elizabeth couldn't help reflecting on her year as she wrapped up a "make your own gin" kit for William. It had been an eventful one, for sure. First, of course, her sad loss. Then Heather's book and the ensuing embarrassment, just to magnify the pain. She had lost her window at work for a promotion to the next level, maybe, but she still had a great job, even if she had to watch Kenny enjoy the opportunity that should have been hers. But then there was the thing that she never saw coming—Carmen's offer.

She looked down, her hands lingering over her midsection. If everything went perfectly in a few weeks, she would give birth in the fall.

She still couldn't believe William had gone for it. But he had.

"Carmen's eggs, huh?" he had said when she'd brought up the idea. "Honey, look, I want a baby as much as you do. But I'd rather adopt. The Carmen thing seems like it could go really sideways."

"Why's that?" Elizabeth had asked defensively.

"Because she has been wanting a second for so long. Really, Elizabeth, can't you see the problem with this?"

"I think I know her better than you do," she had insisted.

"Fine, but if you're wrong, this is a really bad one to be wrong about," William had said gently, sensing how important this was to his wife.

"William, I know what you're saying, I do. But Carmen has changed. I can't really put it into words. The old Carmen is gone. There's this new one who is on fire again. The Carmen from college. The Carmen who's going for her MBA. That's the Carmen who wants to do this for us."

"Okay, then, if you want this, I'll go along. For the record, I'm delighted on the DNA front. Carmen's whip-smart and athletic too. Can't ask for better than that. But, hey, I want to be sure that we won't stop trying," he had teased her with that look in his eyes that made her feel a little dizzy.

William didn't seem phased at all by the fact that this child was not likely to look like his wife or her blond-haired, blue-eyed dad. This was the part of William that Elizabeth loved the most. He just really didn't give a shit what people might say on skin-deep issues like that.

Elizabeth had wondered if they should ask Carmen for a more detailed family history. "Like whether her dad played football?" William had laughed. So they hadn't bothered to worry about that either. The trick, of course, was whether Elizabeth's body would respond. None of them could control that part. It was up to God.

Elizabeth looked past the presents stacked on her bed at the rows of pictures lining the top of her dresser. There was one of her and William as newlyweds, looking much younger than she remembered feeling at the time. And, of course, a whole series of shots of George as a baby. And last but not least, a picture of her and her four friends on their graduation day. They were standing in front of Baker Library, their arms linked, all smiles. That had been a perfect, sunny day. She still remembered how bad the commencement speaker had been. He was the prime minister of some northern European country and had spent a good portion of his halting commencement address recounting his excellent experience at the local Ben and Jerry's ice cream shop.

Maybe she should break ranks and e-mail Heather. Her book was awful, but if this year had taught her anything, it was that she was blessed, and whatever happened with the IVF, her life was enough just as it was. Maybe it was time to bury the hatchet and forgive her old friend. She guessed it was possible that being surrounded by the rich and famous had made it impossible for Heather to realize what she had done to her real friends. She would just have to keep her peace offer a secret from Carmen and Martha.

She picked up her phone and dialed Heather's number.

Of course, it was the same old "Don't bother to leave a message, I don't check this phone" routine.

Elizabeth sighed. Heather sure didn't make it easy.

# CARMEN

It was a blessing that Dartmouth operated on a four-quarter schedule because it meant that Avery was already done with exams and was home for a long stretch over the holidays. Carmen had been worried that her Christmas without Mark would be painful, and she was relieved that she would have her daughter no matter what. Now that December was here, Carmen realized that she shouldn't have been so concerned. For the first time in a very long time, she was feeling the joy of the season. She suspected it was because she was knee-deep in planning her new life. This time, her needs and wants were at the top of the list.

Carmen was planning to take a full class load in the spring, and, if she was successful, she would graduate with her MBA from Booth in just a few short years. She was also dating a new man, her forensic investigator, Paul. He was kind and, even better, fun. She didn't have to walk around on eggshells or make elaborate plans to please him like she had done for so many years with Mark. Paul was the one who would surprise her with tickets to a great concert or convince her to do some weird, spontaneous activity like getting up early just to watch the sun rise.

Their relationship wasn't serious, and she had decided right away that she didn't want it to be. She was going to have a good time and find herself again.

Mark was coming by later in the week to finalize the divorce settlement. Paul had quickly discovered that Mark likely had substantial assets offshore. Carmen intended to confront him about them. She wasn't angry and didn't want a fight—she just wanted her fair share. And Mr. "Do the Right Thing" owed it to her.

"Mom! Did you decide how many trees you want inside the house?" yelled Avery from the front of the house.

Avery was in the foyer dangling from a stepladder while she wrapped lights around an enormous spruce. Carmen was more than satisfied with having just that one tree, but she sensed that Avery wanted to really do it up this year. She hoped Avery wasn't trying to fill a hole that was unfillable, but that wasn't something Carmen could fix. She could, however, let Avery buy as many decorations as she wanted. There were certainly worse ways for her to act out.

She had sat down with Avery after the book came out and told her the truth about her father. What an awkward conversation it had been. How do you tell your baby that no, her dad hadn't cheated, but yes, he had really wanted to? And that you hadn't had the self-respect to do anything about it? Ugh.

She had decided to tell her first thing in the morning over her favorite pancakes.

"Honey, we need to talk," she had said as soon as Avery had come into the kitchen.

"About what?" Avery had replied with her typical nonchalance.

"Well, an old friend of mine has written a book about her life. Actually, my life too. And your father's. Long story short, she sort of aired our families' dirty laundry. It wasn't just ours actually, but, well, it's a mess."

"Mom, you're not making any sense. Start from the beginning," said Avery.

"Okay. Well, the beginning is that when I was not much older than you, I had to make a tough choice about my life."

As Carmen told her daughter a slightly different version of her own history, she felt lighter and closer to her daughter than ever before. Finally, she could speak the truth about her life and her choices, even if it might cause Avery distress. Heather had forced the issue.

In the end, Avery hadn't seemed too phased by it. "Mom, I always knew our family was different," she had said. "And I stopped with the Daddy worship a long time ago. I love him because he's my dad, but he wasn't around enough to be involved in my life. I actually can't think of even one time when we did something together, just us. It is what it is, and it doesn't really have anything to do with my life now."

Carmen had felt sad that Avery had always felt that way. She really had tried to get Mark involved with her daughter more over the years. But she was also relieved. It wasn't her job anymore to try to manage her daughter's relationship with him. If Mark wanted his daughter to be a part of his life, he was going to have to do the hard work for a change.

"Come in here, and let's discuss holiday planning at a normal volume!" Carmen laughed.

"Great, because I was thinking that we should have a party," called Avery as she climbed down the stepladder. "Unless you aren't in the partying kind of mood?" she asked tentatively as she walked into the kitchen.

"No, we definitely need to have a party. Look how much we have to celebrate," replied Carmen with a sweep of her arm.

# MARTHA

Her realtor had told her (emphatically and multiple times) that the good houses didn't become available until spring. Martha had begrudgingly accepted her advice and decided to have some patience until the spring rolled around. But then a property on Cumberland Boulevard became immediately available. The realtor told her that the owner had been relocated by his company, and Martha and Robert had to move quickly.

It was a really unusual property for the Bay because it had five bedrooms and a finished attic, and it was in a highly sought-after neighborhood, particularly because of its close proximity to the village's top-notch public schools. All that said, it was in a state of some disrepair and might need a major overhaul. The kitchen was ancient, the basement was "troubled," and apparently one of the sinks in the bathroom hadn't worked in years. Robert pointed out that the property must be a real mess if the realtor herself used the word "troubled" to describe it. He thought that they should wait until the spring when there would be more choices.

Martha preferred to judge for herself and drove down to see the property in person on the first Monday in December.

As she pulled up to the curb, Martha was immediately charmed by the home's exterior. It was a classic Tudor revival built in the late twenties—dark brown half-timbering highlighting herringbone brickwork and capped with a beautiful steeply pitched roof. Sometimes the floor plans in these old homes were really strange, though, so she did her best to resist falling in love until she saw the interior.

She noted that the landscaping needed an overhaul as she

walked past the beautiful original ironwork on the porch and through the front door. When she entered the foyer, she caught her breath. To her left was a magnificent grand staircase in dark oak. On the right, a cozy living room with a fireplace. There were elements of old-world craftsmanship in every nook and cranny. Leaded stained-glass accents. Beautiful moldings. She skipped the kitchen, knowing that was going to be a tear-out, and wandered up the stairs. Upstairs, she found a spectacular den lined with the original built-in bookcases.

*Not a den*, she thought. *A library.* She closed her eyes and imagined all of her books that currently languished in storage lining the shelves. The room screamed for overstuffed leather chairs and oversized ottomans. And tea. They would drink tea like properly civilized people do every afternoon.

She called Robert as she headed to her car. She wanted to close this deal and get started right away on the renovations. Unsurprisingly, his cell went straight to voicemail. Undeterred, she left a detailed message about how much she loved the house.

As she drove down Cumberland Boulevard, she tried to peer into the other houses, looking for a sign that in one of them might be a new friend for her or for the boys. And then she saw them. A pack of kids. They were all walking home from school together. There had only been a few light dustings of snow, but the kids were already dressed for the winter weather in colorful hats and scarves. The little ones were even wearing snow pants and boots. As she got closer, she could see that they were talking and laughing and, every so often, taking a swipe at each other. Two of the little girls were holding hands.

This was it. This was home. She could feel it.

She was going to get this house ready by June, no matter how much extra she would have to pay the contractor.

# SARA

As she walked onto the work floor, three hundred screens went black and three hundred heads turned to greet her.

It was distinctly unnerving.

This was her third visit of the day. All three Indian companies she was visiting were well known in the outsourcing industry. Their businesses were much more sophisticated and complex than she had imagined. These weren't just call centers. These companies were able to reengineer company processes in almost every area—IT, finance, operations, even legal—and then execute that process cheaply and, in many cases, with greater consistency.

Also, these weren't the sweatshops she had imagined. All of the offices were fairly airy and modern. They featured the same type of cubical furniture and modern art that populated her own office space in Milwaukee. But there were differences. For one, personal space was almost nonexistent. The workers were typically lined up in rows of tables, each of which seated twenty or thirty people, side by side, with only about twelve inches separating them.

"Sorry if we startled you, Ms. Beck," said her tour guide as they stood looking out over the work floor with its three hundred members. "This team is doing document review for a very significant litigation matter. In the US, of course. When we give tours, we go black so as not to expose confidential information."

"Of course, I understand," responded Sara. She wanted the workers to turn back to their screens and stop staring at her.

"Back to screen!" her guide said sharply as they left the floor, and Sara saw three hundred heads turn back to the screens in unison. Again, unnerving.

"If you have time, I can show you our canteen and client care center. When we sit down to create and review the transferred processes, you may spend some significant time here, so we want to be sure you are comfortable."

"Sounds good," replied Sara, hoping that he was wrong about the time commitment on her part.

They walked through the canteen, which was small but, again, not that different from other cafeterias in small companies. They finally came to the client care center. Unlike the rest of the office, it was a beautifully ornate room, featuring noiseproof walls, a few original oil paintings, a large screen for presentations, a lovely mahogany conference table, and an impressive spread of colorful fruits and vegetables across a coordinating credenza.

"Thank you, this is such a nice room. I have a bit of work to do, so if you don't mind, I would like to stay here for a while."

"Yes, of course, it's our pleasure to host you," her guide replied.

Sara was finally alone and unobserved. She exhaled as she slumped into one of the plush desk chairs surrounding the conference table.

This trip was sucking the life out of her. She knew she had to select one of the three Indian outsourcing firms to partner with her company, but they were becoming a blur of sameness. Nonetheless, it was her job to differentiate them, so she had to get to it. She needed to pick a partner—the COO expected quick progress.

She booted up her laptop and made notes on all three companies she had visited. After about an hour, she packed up and headed back to the hotel. If she was lucky, she could call the kids tonight. She liked to talk to them before they headed off for school, although she could sense that Scott was annoyed by the timing. The other option was to call them in the early morning in India, but this was usually too late for them, especially on a school night. The time difference made connecting with her babies almost impossible, but she wasn't just going to give up trying.

She couldn't wait to get home in a few days. Carmen had sent out an e-mail inviting her to a Christmas party, and she was ready to get into the spirit. They had been out of touch after that night at the bar in September, but in Sara's opinion they didn't have a beef with each other, so fighting was pretty pointless. Well, except Martha. She was probably still mad at Sara.

Being in India made her almost forget that Christmas was right around the corner. Last week, she had entered a bunch of holiday-related things in her and Scott's "home to-do" spreadsheet. She was curious to see if he had completed all the tasks.

They had started the spreadsheet right after that dinner downtown three months ago. She could tell Scott wasn't excited about it, but so far the spreadsheet seemed to be working pretty well. Of course, most of the task entries were entered by her, and she had assigned the bulk of them to Scott. But he was doing them. Even the ones that he probably hadn't even realized existed before they started writing everything down. There had certainly been a few raised eyebrows, but they were on month three, and the whole thing was actually going much better than she had expected.

The others might be through with Heather, but Sara wanted to be fair. Her advice was actually helping. Ever since she had taken this job, her bills were paid in full and on time. And Scott was doing more at home. Win-win.

# Heather

**From**: Heather Hall <HHall@flash.com>

**Sent**: Sunday, 12/13 11:15 p.m.

**To**: Elizabeth Smith <ESmith@gmail.com>

Carmen Jones <MrsMarkJones@yahoo.com>

Martha Adams West <MAW@gmail.com>

Sara Beck <Sara.Beck@msn.com>

**Subject**: Hello … anybody home?

Really, no one wants to go to Carmel? NO ONE WANTS TO SAY ANYTHING NICE ABOUT MY BOOK?

REALLY?

# ELIZABETH

"Listen, I am going to need you straight through to the thirty-first. No two ways about it," Joe spat into the phone.

Elizabeth had been anticipating this call for days. The Greysteel merger was set to finally close at year-end, and she knew Joe and Kenny were planning to deliver her the short end of the stick.

"Really, are you sure you need me? How about Kenny? This is his deal now. Actually, why are you calling me anyway? Isn't Kenny flying the plane these days?"

She calmly waited for Joe's response, feeling that victory was within her grasp. This was the year she was going to really enjoy the holidays.

"Kenny is actually hosting the client at my Telluride property. He tried to call and couldn't find you, so he asked me to call you. Look, he needs your help."

"Meaning what exactly?" questioned Elizabeth, trying unsuccessfully to mask her irritation. She knew exactly what that meant, but she wanted to hear him say it.

"You know, Kenny is the big-picture guy. The strategy person. You are our executor. We need you, don't get me wrong. But Kenny is doing great with this client and will safely land this baby."

*So in other words*, thought Elizabeth, *if I were flying the plane, they would be crashing into the ocean right about now. Thank God Kenny is on board!* She thought about raising hell with Joe but realized it was a lost cause. Also, the only thing she dreaded more than work over the holidays was travel over the holidays. So she swallowed her pride and said, "Sure, Joe, I got this."

"Good girl. I knew we could count on you. Hey, Kenny asked me to have you put together a short summary of the overall deal. Be sure to include an executive summary to the summary."

"Okay, but he should already have that."

"No, this isn't just deal points—it is more of a strategy angle. You know, big picture."

Elizabeth wondered if Joe actually listened to himself when he talked. It would give Elizabeth great pleasure to point out the stunning hypocrisy of painting Kenny as the big-picture guy and then asking Elizabeth to do his "big-picture" homework for him. Of course, she knew better than to speak up. Better to spend her energy getting the next big win than being mad about the one she lost.

"You bet, Joe," she said instead.

As she settled in for the long haul, her mind drifted back to her earlier conversation with Carmen about striking out on her own. There had to be a better way. Law firms, after all, are just groups of people. She had friends at other firms who were genuinely happy with their organizations. If she wanted change here, she had to make it happen. If Joe and the Old Man weren't willing to stand up for her, maybe she would have to stand up for herself.

# CARMEN

Carmen and Avery had decided to go for it and have the party this weekend. Elizabeth and Sara were all going to be in town, and Avery had invited a bunch of her old high school friends from Chicago. A bunch of her new neighbors were coming too. Carmen had also sent an invitation to Martha, but she predicted it was going to go ignored. After the blowup in September, Martha had all but disappeared. Would she come back when she was ready, Carmen wondered, or was she done with them for good? Three months was a really long time to ignore your best friends.

Before she could relax into party planning, Carmen had to get through today's final negotiation with Mark and his attorney. There had been months of back and forth on the offshore accounts and other "discoveries" Paul had made. She was sick of it. Her goal was simple—she wanted Mark to fess up about the offshore accounts, give her half, and sign the papers. No drama, just done.

Right on cue, the doorbell rang. All three of them were standing there: her attorney, a very calm, polished woman whose serene demeanor belied the fact that she ate nails for breakfast; his attorney, a short, angry-looking man from Chicago who was sweating profusely despite the fact that it was below freezing outside; and Mark, who actually looked a little tired, which was unusual for him.

"All right then, it looks like we are all here. Let's get divorced!" Carmen said with forced enthusiasm. Her attorney gave Carmen a withering glance.

They sat at the dining room table. Once they agreed that the discussion would be open and amicable, the attorneys settled into their usual routines of bickering. After about fifteen minutes of getting nowhere, Carmen interjected, "Look, Mark, we have been at this for months. Let's end this. Just give me half of this other money you have, and let's sign the papers. Why are we making this hard?"

"Carmen, this is actually technical, complicated stuff, and I think our attorneys need to keep discussing it."

"What are you talking about? It's not complicated. It's easy. You promised me half."

"Correct, yes, half of the marital assets. These other assets your investigator identified are not marital assets. This was a side investment I made personally with a few friends totally outside of my job and our marriage."

"Mark, there wasn't a single thing you did in the last twenty years that I didn't support. Whatever investments you made were on my back. In fact, if I had not been picking up your shirts from the cleaners and cooking your food and cleaning your toilet, I doubt you would have had the time to make any investments at all, much less do so well at your regular job." Carmen's voice was beginning to rise, and she reminded herself that she wasn't going to allow herself to get upset.

"Carmen, I could have paid someone—anyone really—to do those things. They don't exactly take special skill."

"And raising your daughter? Could you have paid just anyone to do that?"

"As a matter of fact, yes, I could have," Mark said coldly.

"Wow. All I can say to that is that I hope you never decide to tell her that." Carmen always did better when she was standing up for someone she loved rather than herself.

"Look, Carmen, I'm trying to make a point. The work I did at the firm is fair game. And the retirement plan and all. But my outside investments are something that I earned fair and square on my own. Frankly, if I hadn't had to take care of you and the baby, I might have been able to do even more. I could be leading a hedge fund by now."

"And what about me? Did it ever occur to you what I might have achieved had I not raised our daughter? And supported you every day of your career?"

"I'm not going to budge on this."

"That's enough," interrupted Carmen's attorney. "I agree with Carmen. This is quite simple. Give my client half, or I expect the IRS might take an interest in your expanded portfolio."

Mark narrowed his eyes and spat at Carmen, "You've really turned into an ungrateful bitch."

*There he is*, thought Carmen. *Finally. The real Mark.*

"Mark, after this meeting I hope that we never see each other again. Good luck on your own. You look pretty tired already. Does your new woman not like to sit home and take care of you?" Mark's eyes flashed, and Carmen knew she had hit a sore point. "And while we are on the subject, please don't give yourself credit for being such a stand-up guy. If you just would have told me the truth all those years ago, my life might have been different. It doesn't matter now. I wouldn't trade what I have with Avery for anything. And who knows, I might be the one who ends up with a hedge fund in the end. But don't for a second think you're the good guy here."

Mark looked like he was going to respond, but he stopped when he saw his attorney shake his head.

His attorney said, "There is no more to discuss here. We agree to half. We will circulate revised papers later in the week and will get this wrapped up before the year is over."

Mark's attorney threw his papers in his briefcase and snapped it up as he stood. The men exited as quickly as they had entered.

Carmen's attorney turned to her and said, "Congratulations. You did well. What's next for you?"

"A Christmas party. And a really good kiss on New Year's Eve."

"When you are ready to do the prenup, call me. You're a wealthy woman now. Don't fuck it up."

*No chance of that*, thought Carmen. She had no interest in getting married again. She was going to finish her education and get a job.

# MARTHA

Martha was at her kitchen table organizing all the documents they would be required to disclose for their mortgage loan.

The banker had noted that she didn't really need to be on the loan since she had no income and wasn't relevant to the loan calculation. *Way to make a mom feel valued*, she thought. *Perhaps someday, when the time is right, I'll be able to fill in that blank next to "wife's income."* It was funny, now that she felt like Robert was on her side, she didn't feel the urgency to rush back to work. Maybe that had been all she had really wanted. His validation. The choice.

She heard Robert come in the back door and walked over to meet him with a hug.

She stopped when she saw him. "Robert, you look like someone just killed your dog! Are you feeling all right?"

"Not really. It was a frustrating day," Robert said as he shuffled to the kitchen to find a snack.

"I'm sorry. Do you want to talk about it?" Martha asked as she trailed him cautiously, considering what might be wrong.

"Not really. There was a family who was planning on adopting a girl from China. She needed a life-saving surgery. *Needs*, I mean. Anyway, I did a lot of consulting with the doctors in China, and we had a plan in place to treat her once she came over in the summer. I found out today that the adoptive parents decided to back out. They said they were worried about the cost of her care. It's just really frustrating because I know I can save this girl if I can just get my hands on her."

"I'm sorry. That's awful. I'm sure someone else will step in and adopt her."

"I doubt it. Not in time. It's a pretty fast process to adopt special needs children, but there isn't much of an appetite for their adoption. You would be amazed at the number of children waiting to come here for medical care."

"I'm sorry, that is really sad. I had no idea." Martha decided she should leave him in peace to enjoy his snack and started to leave the kitchen.

"Do you want to see her picture?" Robert asked as Martha turned to leave. Martha paused, and he took a picture out of his breast pocket. "I took it out of the file, which I really shouldn't have. I'm not sure why I did it. I think I'm turning into an old sap."

Robert handed Martha a small picture of a baby girl. Martha took it in. The little girl had wide, intelligent eyes, and her mouth was curling into a laugh as if she knew a wonderful secret and wasn't telling.

"How old?" she asked.

"About nine months."

Nine months. The same age Lucy would have been. Martha felt her heart skip a beat.

"Robert, let's take her," she gushed, the words spilling out of her before she could stop them.

Robert threw up his hands and said, "Honey, please slow down. I know this is sad, but you have no idea how difficult the process is. And don't forget that she might not make it. You aren't ready to go through that again."

Martha stood quietly, holding the picture.

"This is our baby, Robert. We are meant to be together, can't you feel it? Why would you bring this picture home? You've never done that before. It means something. It has to. Please, please, just let me look into it," Martha said urgently.

"What about going back to work? I thought that was the plan," Robert replied.

"Robert, there was so much I loved about practicing medicine. And maybe I'll go back to it someday. But I went back after Bobby more because I thought it was what I was supposed to do. You know, to please my parents and because I had done all the work for the degree. But my heart wasn't completely into it, if I'm being honest. It's true that I do want to do more in the world, but I don't have it all figured out yet. And I'm finally starting to be okay with that. It's enough for me right now that you are willing to make changes so that I can grow. But it doesn't have to be medicine. It doesn't have to be paid. Am I making any sense?"

"Yes, you are, and I'm happy that you are figuring out what you need, truly," said Robert, "but please be careful not to get too carried away on this adoption idea. Be logical. There is a reason for all the process steps. It's a serious commitment and one with no guarantees."

But his words were falling on deaf ears. Martha was already picturing how the crib would look in that house on Cumberland. She would give her baby girl the best room on the corner of the east side of the house where the sun rose.

# SARA

Sara had made her way through security and was in possession of several useless but entertaining magazines. She was sitting at the gate in the most private corner she could find while waiting for her flight back to Chicago. She figured she had time to check in at home. She hoped Scott had finished all the tasks in the tracker. There was nothing worse than coming home to a messy house after a daylong flight.

She opened Google Drive and navigated quickly to her task tracker spreadsheet and went straight to the good part—the holiday planning section.

Task - <u>Make cookies and distribute to all teachers</u>. Try to do at least six varieties. And find the nice ribbon to wrap them with.

Scott's Notes: Done. I bought them at Sendik's. They had a whole section. And they were prewrapped (nicely—don't worry).

"Nothing like that personal touch, honey," Sara typed right under his note. She rolled her eyes and went to the next item.

Task - <u>Wrap all the presents</u>. They are all in the alcove under the stairs.

Scott's Notes: If by "wrap," you mean shove in gift bags, we're done! Why does anyone bother to use wrapping paper? What a colossal waste of time.

"Really, Scott," she typed, "now the kids probably already know exactly what they're going to get. They just had to peek in the gift bag."

Task - <u>Christmas cards</u>. I put the five pictures of the kids I like best in a folder on the desktop of the family computer. Just plop them into something you like on Shutterfly and get them ordered. I know you prefer the ones that mention Christmas, but I really think it's more inclusive to just go with "Happy Holidays," especially because I want to hand them out at work. If you can print labels, too, that would be really helpful. And buy stamps.

Scott's Notes: The card plus postage is over a thousand dollars! We could buy a new bigger screen TV for the living room for that! I made a quick e-card—that will do.

"Fine," she typed. "I think everyone just looks at them for ten seconds and throws them away. But will we regret it? Hmmm."

Task - <u>Buy stocking stuffers</u>. I try to do "something to read, something to wear, something to eat" every year. If you need book ideas, e-mail me. And not too much candy. They already eat too much.

Scott's Notes: Sara, I'm just doing candy, it's so much easier and the kids will like it better anyway. It's Christmas—lighten up.

At this one, Sara teared up somewhat unexpectedly as her hands hovered over the keyboard. It was bad enough to have to hand some of these special traditions to Scott. But now he was undoing them. She had picked a special book for their stockings every year since Tommy was born twelve years ago. She remembered the very first book she had chosen, the classic *Moo, Baa, La La La!* by Sandra Boynton. She could still recite it by heart. She loved the last bit—"It's quiet now, what do you say?" It made Tommy giggle every time. She would have to fix this one when she got home. What was wrong with Scott? She didn't type a comment to that one and instead read on.

180

Task – <u>Wash wedding china and crystal and polish silver</u>. I want to get out all the good stuff for Christmas Eve dinner with your parents. I know it's a pain, but it makes things so special. Also, either wash and iron linen tablecloth or take to cleaners.

Scott's Notes: NFW. Let's watch football and have a normal meal like the rest of America. Also, I hope you know that there are like fifty other things I have always done around the house that you don't have on your tracker. Man stuff, I guess. I thought about adding them, but I have better things to do with my time.

Sara typed, "Scott, I love getting the wedding china and silver out every year for Christmas dinner. Don't you remember how much fun we had picking it all out when we were engaged? At least, I thought we were having fun! Honestly, what else are you doing at home all day while the kids are in school? Get 'er done!"

The airport announcer called out the time, ten p.m. in Delhi, which would make it late Friday morning back home. Sara decided she would give Scott a call.

Someone picked up on the first ring, but it wasn't Scott.

It was their neighbor Amy.

"Hey, Sara, namaste," Amy said.

"Amy, the India jokes aren't funny yet. You have no idea. Hey, what are you doing at our house? I hope Scott has invited you over to show him how to polish silver."

"Um, no. Although thanks for reminding me. We were thinking about doing an open house over the break, and I really should set aside some time to get the silver ready."

"Where is Scott, Amy?" she asked suspiciously.

Amy paused and then said carefully, "Sara, it's no big deal, don't worry. He had to take one of the boys over to the hospital."

"What?" demanded Sara with surprise, feeling her chest tighten with worry.

"Nathan is fine. He fell on the playground and broke his

arm. It wasn't a really bad break. He's fine, I promise. I'm here with Mikey. I'm going to pick up your other kids and take care of things tonight." Amy paused and then continued in a more serious voice. "Look, Sara, Scott was going to call you, but he decided it would be better not to make you worry while you have to sit on the flight. And what can you do from Delhi anyway?"

*Indeed, there's nothing I can do,* thought Sara miserably.

"Thanks for saving us, Amy. I really appreciate it." Sara tried to control herself and keep the worry out of her voice—as well as the touch of anger at Amy's dismissal of Nathan's injury as "fine." That would not be the word she would have used if it were her kid.

"Anytime. You can always give me a call when you need help. Scott too. Frankly, he should have asked me for help on the cookie thing. He bought the teachers those store-bought ones from Sendik's! The other mommies are never going to let you guys live that one down," she pointed out with a laugh.

"Guess we wiffed on that one." Sara laughed, cringing a little inside but also feeling like she should be defending Scott. What was wrong with store-bought cookies? "Bye, Amy. Thanks again."

Sara pressed "end" and put her face in her hands. She didn't want the other passengers to see her cry. She had been there for every hospital trip. She knew what to do and what to say to make her kids feel better. Did Scott even know which one of Nathan's loveys to bring with them to the hospital? She doubted it. Scott would handle everything just fine, but there are some times when only a mom will do, full stop.

These were the kind of days that made Sara really want her old job back. As it was, the COO expected at least four trips to India just this year alone. She thought it might break her. On the plus side, they had some serious cash coming in the door. She would take the family to Disney, she decided. That would make things right. Or at least easier to swallow, for all of them.

# HEATHER

**Text from Heather Hall to Elizabeth Smith**

OK, I get it. You guys are ignoring me. Are the girls jealous or something? And you, Elizabeth, are you siding with them? Maybe someone else is jealous too. I'm actually kind of too busy to care. Let me know when you guys get over yourselves. H

# ELIZABETH

It was finally Saturday night. Elizabeth had made it to the weekend in one piece, but barely.

Earlier in the day, after reading Heather's latest pathetic attempt to reach out to them, she had turned to the merger documents one last time and fired them back to the other side in New York. She knew that they would be coming right back to her tomorrow morning, sitting in her e-mail bright and early. Those New York guys loved to work all night and then hit you first thing the next day, just because they could. *That's one way to bill three thousand hours a year*, she mused to herself. And she knew their client was paying through the nose for it. *Did they care?* she wondered.

In any case, Saturday evening was going to belong to her. Her and William, that is. They had left George with William's mom and dad and driven down to Carmen's place for the evening. Carmen had invited Elizabeth, Martha, and Sara to have a little after-party and spend the night as well.

Martha had already begged off. She had apparently had her offer on the Cumberland house accepted and was in a frenzy of planning for renovations. Well, that was her excuse anyway. Elizabeth was pretty sure that she still just didn't want to be around them after their fight in September. Or maybe she was still sad about Lucy. Elizabeth thought she'd come around, but if she wanted space, she would get it. So it was down to Carmen, Elizabeth, and Sara. William and Scott were taking one of the cars back together and leaving the other vehicle for the girls.

Elizabeth was looking forward to her chance to blow off a little steam.

As she and William pulled up to Carmen's gorgeous lake

house, Elizabeth was embarrassed to realize that this was her first time visiting. It was true that Carmen hadn't been living there long, but Elizabeth should have gotten down there earlier. Her excuses were equally plentiful and pitiful. Just another casualty of law firm life, she thought.

Carmen had gone all out on the decorations. Elizabeth could see from outside the house that they had decorated at least three trees inside. And someone must have spent hours outside stringing lights. The party was already going strong. Laughter and music floated through the air as the lights and ornaments twinkled inside and out. Avery's friends must have been in charge of the music because it sounded like a downtown Chicago club in there. She wondered if Carmen was going to get a call from her neighbors.

As they walked up the blue stone steps to the front door, Carmen came bursting out to give Elizabeth a hug. Elizabeth was struck by how beautiful Carmen looked. It wasn't what she was wearing, although the tight red cocktail dress made her look closer to thirty than forty. Carmen had a new, relaxed glow that Elizabeth hadn't seen since, well, college. Her friend was happy for the first time in a very long time, she realized. As Paul came out to join Carmen, she could guess why.

"Carmen, you must have paid a fortune to have this place decorated," Elizabeth said as she hugged Carmen back.

"Actually, no, Avery and I did most of the interior, and Paul did the outside work."

"Wow. I'm impressed. William's a great holiday decorator, but I don't think I could get him to put up this many lights."

"It was my pleasure," said Paul. "Hey, William, good to meet you, let's get you a drink."

As Paul led William away to the bar, Elizabeth took in Paul's vanishing figure and whispered to Carmen, "Holy cow, girl. He's a serious hottie."

"I know." Carmen giggled like a twenty-year-old. "But Elizabeth, that's not even close to the best part. He wants to spend time with me. Like a lot of time. He spent two days straight stringing lights. You know how much time Mark put into this house? None. Zero. I finally found a man who wants to make my home nicer. *My home*. I keep squeezing myself to make sure it's all real."

"And how is he in bed?"

"Even better than he is at stringing lights," replied Carmen with a knowing smile.

"Honey, no one deserves it more than you. Now let's go get a drink. After the week I've had, I'm in desperate need of a strong one."

"What are you drinking? Do you want a cocktail, or do you prefer champagne or wine?"

"Yes," replied Elizabeth, and they both smiled. "This might be my last chance to get really hammered."

"It will happen for you this time. I know it will work," whispered Carmen as she squeezed Elizabeth's hand as they headed toward the bar. "This is going to be our year."

"I hope so. But let's not jinx it. Is Sara here yet?"

"Yes, Sara and Scott got here about ten minutes ago. Sara kind of looks like shit, but I think we are going to have to lie to her about that. I think that trip to India was really hard on her, and she might be a donkey on the edge."

"Did you hear about the arm?" asked Elizabeth.

"Yes, when she arrived, she told me a little bit about what happened. That must have been awful for her. I can't imagine not being there for something like that. I mean, that's why women need to be home or at least close to home. No offense."

"Hey, none taken. But William might be offended, you know," she teased.

"I have been so jealous of her four kids for so many years. It's funny, now that I'm doing my own thing, I'm not anymore. I still say she should have stopped at three. But that is not coming from a place of spite, it's coming from a place of common sense. Maybe Scott will get a new job soon so Sara can figure something else out. It can't possibly work for her to be running off to India every few months."

"Probably not," Elizabeth agreed. "You know, some days I might as well be in India for all the time I'm spending at the office. Don't get me wrong, I'm totally good with William being the at-home person. But George doesn't even call for me at night, did you know that? He calls for William. Sometimes I want to be the one he wants, Carmen."

"Don't be silly. You will be. When he grows up, you will be able to relate to him in a totally different way. He'll want to ask for your advice about work and jobs and the world. Just give it time."

"Thanks for saying that. But I'm not sure I buy it. That's what I'm afraid of. Time. Time going by. There has to be more for me."

As Elizabeth started to feel really sorry for herself yet again, Sara came up beside them. "Hey, ladies! I'm exhausted, but I'm here! I really shouldn't be spending the night since I've already been gone so long from the kids, but how many opportunities do we get to do this? Besides, I owe you guys an apology. I'm sorry that I wasn't more sympathetic about the Heather business. She was really awful to you guys. And she did abandon Martha at the worst possible time. I get it, I really do."

Elizabeth replied with a smile, "It's in the past. Let's please move on. I hope Martha will want to move on too. How was India by the way? Tell us everything."

As Sara began to recount her travel experience, Elizabeth's mind turned to Heather's book. She still couldn't shake the feeling that Heather was at least partially right about "E's" choices. Elizabeth was always letting time run away from her. She might never have that second baby. And she could live with that, whatever happened with the IVF. But she couldn't live with missing most of George's childhood. She needed to take control and start living the life she wanted—today.

# CARMEN

Carmen was confident that all three of them had each consumed at least a bottle of wine apiece.

All the other guests were gone, including Avery, who had gone to a friend's house for the rest of the weekend. Carmen was pretty sure they were going out clubbing tonight, but she didn't want to think about it. She had just handed Avery the keys, reminded her that she was still underage, and asked her to be safe. The house belonged to Carmen and her friends for the night.

The girls had changed into their pajamas, robes, and slippers the minute the last guest left and had reassembled in the den for what they expected to be the best part of the party.

"All I'm saying is that I need to make a change," Elizabeth was saying to Carmen and Sara.

"Okay, but William has no desire to work, right?" asked Sara. "You can't just up and quit without a new job lined up. What about in-house?"

"I'm not sure that's any better. I mean, look at what's happened to you."

"Point taken," replied Sara wryly.

"The truth is I like the actual work I do. I like being a partner. Technically, I'm an owner in the business. I even like a lot of the other lawyers there. I just really feel angry about what went down with Kenny."

"Why don't you start your own firm?" asked Carmen.

"Oh, sure," Elizabeth responded, laughing. "I'll just hang out my shingle and see what happens. I'm sure they will beat a path to my door."

"I'm not kidding," said Carmen. "I've read about a lot of

successful small firms going it alone. And I know you are technically an owner, but being a partner in a law firm these days is like being a stockholder in Disney. You technically get a vote, but you don't have any real control whatsoever."

"That's true, and it would be great to be a true owner," said Elizabeth. "But I have no start-up capital. And even if I did, I don't have the kind of knowledge or experience to run a business."

"But I do," Carmen pointed out, a serious tone in her voice. "I have both, actually. Mark left me a wealthy woman, as my attorney likes to say. Who better to invest in than you?" she asked, grabbing Elizabeth's hand. "You're the hardest working lady I know, and you will do everything in your power to make your firm fly."

"I do have some ideas," said Elizabeth tentatively. "For one, I would love to stop billing in six-minute increments. I'm so fucking sick of it."

"That's a no-brainer," said Sara. "Companies hate paying bills that way too. We try to get everything done by project flat fee or some other alternate billing arrangement."

"And I want to create a compensation structure that rewards teamwork and mentoring," Elizabeth explained. "Something that will cut the Kennys and Blakes of the world off at the knees."

"I have a boatload of other great ideas for you," said Sara. "My work in India showed me all kinds of ways to get work done more efficiently and cheaply. And the ideas don't always involve outsourcing. There are a lot of things you can do here to produce a very competitive product if you're willing to rethink real estate, technology, and process."

"That would be great, Sara," replied Elizabeth sincerely. "I do think firms are struggling because they're holding on to all the fancy trappings of being a lawyer. I actually don't need any of that."

"It sounds like you know exactly what you want to do," said Carmen with finality. "C'mon, let's really do this."

Elizabeth hesitated, but then, at least in Carmen's view, Elizabeth looked like she found some old courage.

"Okay, I'm in. But only if you agree to be CFO, Carmen. And we'll be sure you get a really nice return on your investment, eventually, that is." She laughed.

Carmen's eyes teared up suddenly. "Oh, Elizabeth," she said, "you can definitely have my money and my advice, but you should take some time to think about the CFO thing. If you are serious about something like this, you'll want someone with real experience. I mean, you're the breadwinner. You can't just do whatever you want and put your family at risk."

"Actually, yes I can," said Elizabeth. "I want the smartest woman I know who managed her daughter all the way to Dartmouth."

"Okay then," Carmen agreed, feeling validated in a way that she thought might never happen. "I accept your offer. What kind of maternity leave are you going to want, though?"

"Are you still trying, Elizabeth?" asked Sara.

"Well, actually, I'm planning to get pregnant with Carmen's baby," said Elizabeth.

"You are really drunk, aren't you?" Sara laughed.

"No, really," said Elizabeth as she grabbed Carmen's hand, "Carmen has given one of her eggs to William and me, and if things go the way we are planning, well, I'm going to be a mom again."

Sara's jaw dropped, and she quickly clapped her hand over her mouth in shock and glee. The room went very quiet as a full five beats passed among the women. It was one of those moments when the best thing to say was nothing at all. A rare moment among their group. They all knew the procedure was no guarantee, but for a moment they could imagine a future in which their little group would knit itself back together again, albeit as a foursome, but four was better than none.

Sara was the first one to speak. "Well, if you ladies are writing your own maternity policy, I recommend a fully funded twelve-month leave."

"Are you kidding?" said Elizabeth. "I want one of those nurseries next to my office like Heather has."

"I wonder if she makes her husband come fuck her in her office as well. You know, for the sake of efficiency," said Sara with her most serious face on.

The women burst into laughter and started shoving each other until they were rolling around on the floor like it was a third-grade slumber party.

"We are having so much fun, I had almost forgotten about Heather," said Carmen. "Did any of you fold and respond to her asinine e-mails?"

"Not me," said Elizabeth. "She still doesn't even know I lost the baby."

"Not me three," Sara agreed. "Elizabeth, you were always the closest to her. I can't believe she hasn't tried to call when she realized you weren't going to e-mail her."

"I actually tried her phone, but she has it set up so you can't even leave a message if you wanted to," Elizabeth replied.

"Of course she does," deadpanned Carmen.

"I'm just not interested in talking to her unless it's to accept her apology," continued Elizabeth. "But I might e-mail her back and let her know that she should really consider why we might be upset with her. I'm not sure I want to cut her off forever without even an explanation. That feels really wrong."

"I do!" said Carmen. "And it feels really right to me!"

"Heather's not a monster," countered Sara. "She may be just really low empathy. And her advice has actually been kind of helpful for me in the last few months."

Carmen just rolled her eyes. "Please don't start again, Sara. My ears might literally bleed."

"I'm just sad that we've ended up here," said Elizabeth. "Can you really imagine our girls' weekends without Heather? Or

Martha? She may not come back to us, you know. She's been weird and quiet since the fight."

"Maybe it's time we all grow up," said Carmen quietly. "Nothing lasts forever. Anyway, let's talk about what we are going to name our baby."

And with that, all the talk of Heather was done.

# MARTHA

Martha and Robert were on their way back from a dinner date. They had been making a conscious effort to spend more time together since the summer, and particularly time for just the two of them.

Robert hadn't had even one drink during dinner. He rarely drank, probably an old habit from his days as a young doctor when he might be urgently needed with no advance notice.

Martha had stuck to just one glass because she wanted to get up early tomorrow and start taking pictures in the new house. She was delighted that they were letting her in before the closing. The family had moved out already and didn't seem to care either way. She needed to get the contractors lined up quickly if they were going to get into the house before summer.

She felt a pang of guilt for avoiding Carmen's party, but everything had changed after that night out in September, and she wasn't sure if she could go back to how things had been before.

In any case, she needed to focus on her family now. She hoped it would be five of them moving in over the summer. In addition to working on the house stuff, she had been feverishly researching the fastest way to adopt that little girl from China. She had been pleased to learn that there was a real chance that they could be in a position to go get her by the end of the summer. That would be perfect. The boys would be settled and ready to go back to school. She would have the whole school day, every school day, to bond with her new daughter.

She just needed Robert to say yes. Martha decided it was now or never.

"Robert, I want to adopt that little girl. I've done all my research. I know the risks, and the costs. I know we will live with uncertainty about her health. I know all those things, but I can't ignore my heart. My heart tells me that we are hers and she is ours."

Martha braced herself for a long debate. Robert wasn't a big talker, but he managed to find his words when it was something that was important to him.

"I already knew all that, Martha. You don't have the poker face you think you do," he teased. Looking more serious, he sighed and then continued, "I've thought a lot about it too. If you are sure that it's what you want, then I want it too. But you will have to take the brunt of the responsibility. There's only so much I can do and keep up at work. I know you want to do more outside the home, but I don't know how much I can promise in terms of help."

"I'm not going back to medicine, Robert. I might do some volunteering at the boys' school, but I know I'll need all my energy to take care of her and the boys."

"What if you change your mind?"

"Maybe I'll change my mind later, but for now I want this baby."

"Okay," he said. "Then I will support it—and you—totally. What should we name her?"

"I think we should pick a name from your side of the family. But can her middle name be Adams, just like Lucy? I know she won't look like me or anything, but, you know, she will become part of me."

"That sounds perfect," said Robert with a smile. "What about Mildred for the first name? That was my grandmother's name."

"Okay, we're going to need to negotiate that one."

And for the first time in a very long time, they had a laugh together.

# SARA

"I will never, ever drink champagne again," groaned Sara into her pillow as she lay in her bed after coming home the next morning after the party.

The kids had been delighted to see her when she got home, and she did her very best to look enthused, but she hadn't lasted more than fifteen minutes before hitting the bed.

Scott softened the blow by leaning down to give her a kiss. "How was the girls' night?" he teased as he ran his hand along the hem of her shirt.

"Well, you can clearly see that it was super fun. Because I have never felt more hungover in my life. I need an IV. And stop hitting on me. If we have sex, that might do me in permanently."

"Your thirteen-hour flight the day before might also have something to do with your predicament, you know," he said, ignoring her instructions and slipping his hand under her shirt.

"I know. I hate my new job. I don't know what to do. I'm trapped," she moaned into the pillow.

"You're not trapped. But it would help me if you did stay in a stable job for just a little longer. I have an idea, but it might be kind of stupid."

"Hit me. This is your big chance. I don't have the strength to defend myself."

"I want to do IT consulting." His hand circled higher and higher.

"Meaning what exactly?" asked Sara.

"Meaning I work for myself on a project basis." His hand was fumbling to unhook her bra.

"So basically, totally no safety net. No insurance. No medical. No retirement plan."

"I guess, if you see it that way. The way I see it, if I'm successful, you can cut back at work or downshift into a different job. I will keep doing more at home. I think it might be a win all around."

"Okay, but you still have to take seventy-five percent on the task tracker." Sara felt Scott's caresses stop immediately, and then his hand was gone. *Shit, I shouldn't have said that.*

"Sara, just so you know, no one wants to fuck mean mommy."

"Scott! Seriously? What if the kids heard you!" Sara rolled up and sat up, fixing Scott with an irritated look.

"Look, I'll do seventy-five percent. For now. Until I get up and running. Then you need to cut back because I can't do both."

"*I* used to do both."

"Not well, you didn't. And you were always complaining to me that you were exhausted and fat and didn't have any time for yourself."

*Asshole*, thought Sara.

"I complained because I actually didn't have time for myself. And I wasn't fat. I was thick."

"Okay, Kim Kardashian. For the record, you've always looked great to me. I want us to find a third way. Let me give it a try. Maybe we can both work and split things more fifty-fifty."

"Fine, maybe, but if I have to do laundry and dishes all by myself on Sunday night again I'm going to be pissed."

"Noted," said Scott. "Why don't you take that nap? You really are unpleasant when you're tired."

*Consulting work*, she thought as she closed her eyes. *Huh. Maybe Scott can be the IT guy for Elizabeth and Carmen's new firm.* And that's as far as she got because within seconds she was in a deep sleep.

# MARCH

# HEATHER

**From**: Elizabeth Smith <ESmith@gmail.com>
**Sent**: Sun. 3/27 4:15 p.m.
**To**: Heather Hall <HHall@flash.com>
**Subject**: Re: I need you

Heather, I have to be honest, I'm surprised to hear from you. I would have thought that you have some closer friends to help you out. But I'm not going to say no to you. There's too much history between us, and you can count on me, even if I can't count on you.

I'll be on the first flight tomorrow morning. Find the resort doctor and have him prescribe you a sedative. Then go to bed. See you soon. And Heather, please don't worry. Everything's going to be fine. We'll get you through this.

**From**: Heather Hall <HHall@flash.com>
**Sent**: Sun. 3/27 4:00 p.m.
**To**: Elizabeth Smith <ESmith@gmail.com>
**Subject**: I need you

Elizabeth, something terrible has happened. I don't even know where to start. Phil is dead. We were skiing, and I saw him lose control. It all happened so fast.

I know you've been busy—probably with your new baby, right? I'm sorry I haven't visited or even sent a present or anything. I've been so busy too. And now this.

I don't know what to do, Elizabeth. You know me. I always know what to do. I'm a little lost. Can you come to Colorado? Please. I don't know who else to ask.

Heather

# ELIZABETH

Elizabeth landed in Montrose late Monday. After a fifty-minute drive, she steered her rented Jeep toward Heather's Telluride home, which was a bit outside of town. Just like her getaway "cottage" in Carmel, the Telluride house featured the best of everything in its ten-thousand-square-feet sprawl. Unlike the pale, beachy vibe of the cottage, this home was distinctly earthy. The exterior was lined with beautiful stonework that blended seamlessly into the surrounding forest.

Elizabeth walked up to the front door and rang the bell a few times. Silence. She decided to see if it was unlocked. It was, and she opened it a crack and called, "Heather? I'm here."

Still nothing.

*I'm going in*, thought Elizabeth, and she walked through the door to look for her friend. The interior of the house was as charming as its exterior. It featured dark wood beams, lovely handcrafted furniture in leather and natural wood, wool blankets, and even a standard-issue bear-skinned rug positioned in front of the large fireplace at the center of the living room. That's where she found Heather, in the living room, lying on the couch in front of the fireplace. She wasn't asleep. She was just staring at the fire.

If Heather had the wherewithal to make a fire, perhaps things were not as bad as she feared, thought Elizabeth.

"Hi," Heather said flatly, without making eye contact.

"Honey, I'm so sorry," Elizabeth said, and she moved quickly to envelop Heather in a hug.

As she pulled Heather into her arms, Heather lost her composure and began heaving with tears. Elizabeth held her for a few minutes until Heather seemed to calm down.

"Finally! I can cry," said Heather with a relieved sigh. "I just couldn't cry yesterday at all. I thought I was broken. Or just heartless."

"You're not broken. You lost your husband. You're in shock. Let's go in the kitchen and have some coffee and talk."

"I'll go to the kitchen, but only if we can have a drink," replied Heather, and she gave Elizabeth a little smile. *Okay*, thought Elizabeth, *she's going to get through this*.

"Deal. I want to hear all about your kids. We haven't seen each other in so long. We are way overdue for a catch-up."

"I know, that's my bad. The book was so successful, and the time just slipped away from me. The kids are doing pretty well, everything considered. They're so busy, and I think it helped them to just keep going with all their activities. Everybody is always busy." Heather seemed to trail off, but then she refocused on Elizabeth. "But you must be so busy, too, with the new baby and all."

Elizabeth stiffened in spite of the fact that she knew Heather would bring this up. She couldn't fault her really; Heather was just picking up where they had left off, more than nine months ago now.

"Heather, I lost the baby last June. Right after I told you. After what happened with Lucy, I forgot to circle back with you. It was a bad time."

"Oh God, Elizabeth, why didn't you call me? I'm so sorry," said Heather, taken aback.

"Well, I would have probably called eventually, but the summer flew by and then September came and, well, I read your book. I'm sure you can imagine how sad I was to lose the baby. Your book didn't help."

After an awkward pause, Elizabeth continued, "But, look, the book is a conversation for another day. Let's talk about you."

"No, no, I want to understand why the book upset you. You said that you couldn't count on me. What does that mean exactly?

I've always been in your corner," Heather said slowly, looking confused. "Look, every bit of the book was true. I was very careful about that when I wrote it."

Elizabeth didn't think this was the time to get into this with Heather. Her old friend's lack of empathy (not to mention lack of imagination) was astounding, but this wasn't the moment to point it out. She had just lost her husband.

"Look, Heather, let's talk about the book another time."

"No, I want to talk about it now," Heather said with some of her old confidence. "I'm the one with the dead husband, so I get to decide."

"Heather, I'm not sure I can be polite about it yet, regardless of the fact that you lost your husband. I really think we should save the conversation for another day. The harm is already done anyway. There's nothing either of us can do to change it now."

"I'm not taking no for an answer, Elizabeth," Heather replied, looking for a second like the world-beating Heather.

*Okay*, thought Elizabeth. *Here we go.*

"Fine. The book really hurt all of our feelings, Heather. You just don't go telling other people's secrets like that."

"Come on!" Heather started defensively, leaning away from Elizabeth and crossing her arms, her bright blue eyes flashing with annoyance. "I didn't write anything that wasn't true, and there wasn't anything in there that everyone in the world doesn't already know. I get that no one likes to have their mistakes pointed out to them, but I wrote the book for the young girls coming up in the workplace now. And for our children. And no one even knows I'm talking about any of you, anyway. I anonymized it."

Elizabeth took a deep breath. Heather was all the way up her own ass. This might take some time.

"Heather, first, just because something is true and obvious doesn't mean you have to say it, particularly if it's hurtful. Knock yourself out writing about your own mistakes, but you should think twice before you sit in judgment of others. Second, you did disclose information that was private. I hadn't told anyone at work that I was pregnant again. Or that I lost the baby, for that matter."

"You can't hold the pregnancy thing against me. That was your fault for not telling me."

Elizabeth ignored her and kept going.

"The stuff about Mark was also out of bounds."

"Please," said Heather, rolling her eyes. "If I can't call out a guy like Mark, then the sisterhood is really dead. And everyone knew what he was up to. It wasn't a secret."

Elizabeth pressed on, "Third, even if we could get comfortable with your idea that we need to share our mistakes with the next generation, I am in violent disagreement with your entire thesis that women should follow a prescribed path to be successful. Life is full of things we can't control and shouldn't try to. Look at what just happened to you."

"Well, I am also—how did you put it—'in violent disagreement' with you," Heather said as she made air quotes with her fingers. "I will be able to handle this situation better because of all my planning."

"We'll see," Elizabeth responded tightly. "By the way, Heather, I hope that you recognize that the outcomes of our lives aren't fixed at forty. When you wrote the book, we may have been struggling at that particular point in our lives. Just so you know, some pretty great things have happened for us all since then. Carmen will be graduating with her MBA soon. I'm planning to open my own law firm with Carmen as my partner. Sara has gotten a big promotion at work. And Martha and Robert are adopting a baby from China."

"That's wonderful to hear," said Heather. "But you haven't changed my mind. Wouldn't you agree that all of that success happened in spite of your choices, not because of them? Think where you might have been if you had been successful from the start. Think about your lives in that context. I mean, when you compare your lives to my life, it's pretty clear, right? Be honest, Elizabeth."

"No, Heather, I wouldn't agree at all. Some of us just dealt with our share of adversity earlier than you did. That's the only difference. But we are succeeding, too, just in our own time and in our own way. And we're helping each other do it. Your adversity just arrived. Are you so sure you'll come out the other end beautifully? Especially going it alone?"

"Please," said Heather, "don't insult me."

*This is getting out of control*, thought Elizabeth. *Time to back off.*

"Heather, you just lost your husband. I'm not here to insult you or judge you. I'm here to help."

"Well, I'm just fine. I'm going to go home and sort everything out. I have to admit, Phil chose a spectacularly bad time to die. FLASH has been getting some heat on our labor practices. I think it's just disgruntled workers bitching, but this is the kind of stuff that really throws a wrench into operations when it goes sideways. In any case, everything will be fine. I actually don't need help from any of you. You guys clearly have your hands full as it is. And besides, if I need help, I can hire it."

Elizabeth wondered if Heather believed any of the bullshit she was spewing. Especially about the timing of Phil's death. That was cold. She made one more try to bring Heather back to earth.

"Heather, we have all been friends too long for us not to forgive you. All you need to do is say you're sorry. Hired help is not the same as family."

"You don't get it, Elizabeth. I'm not sorry. My book is my gift to the world. I wish you guys could be proud of it, too, instead of jealous. I'm so happy that your lives are on track now, truly. But you all really did make mistakes. We owe it to our daughters to be honest about them."

Elizabeth sensed she wasn't going to get anywhere today,

maybe ever. Maybe it would just be better to leave and try again tomorrow. She had booked a hotel in town in case the conversation with Heather went south. *Good instincts*, she thought.

"Heather, I'm going to go back to the hotel. I'll be there tonight and most of the morning before my flight. Please call me if you change your mind," Elizabeth told her, walking toward the front door.

"Ditto," called Heather somewhat coldly, but then she seemed to deflate a bit and followed after Elizabeth.

"Elizabeth, please wait. I am so sorry about your baby. Truly."

Elizabeth grinned and said, "Don't worry about me, Heather. I'm actually pregnant with Carmen's baby now. Life is good."

And with that, Elizabeth pushed on her aviators, turned quickly away from a confused and slack-jawed Heather, and returned to her rental car.

As she drove back to town to find her hotel, she thought about Heather's arguments. *No, Heather is just wrong this time*, she decided. Maybe they wouldn't be friends anymore after all. It wasn't her choice, but it was her reality. *People do change*, she supposed. *Or maybe we start to see them for who they really are as we age, as opposed to who we want them to be. The truth is often painful—just another one of the realities of turning forty*, she decided.

Elizabeth waited by the phone all night and all the next morning for the call from Heather that never came.

# CARMEN

Paul had sweet-talked Carmen into spending a week with him in San Diego. Carmen had never been to that part of California, and Paul had successfully convinced her that it was a must-see. Not that it was a particularly hard task when the ocean (and Paul, of course) was involved.

As they drove their rented convertible over the Coronado Bridge, Carmen had to agree with Paul's assessment. The view from the two-mile bridge that connected San Diego Bay with Coronado Island was uniquely spectacular; they could see the San Diego skyline, sailboats in the harbor, and the vastness of the Pacific Ocean in the distance. Paul said that at night you could see the lights of Tijuana, and Carmen made him promise that they would make time to drive back over at night. Breathing in the sea air, Carmen slipped into an even deeper state of relaxation.

She loved this new life. Mark was gone, forever. Good riddance. Avery, on the other hand, was closer to her than ever. She was blossoming into a really wonderful adult. And Carmen may have lost her marriage, but she wasn't wanting for romantic love. Not even close. Paul was becoming an integral part of her life. She didn't want to marry him, though. She just wanted to be with him.

Carmen wasn't sure she would ever be interested in marriage again. She was just starting to get to know herself again, and she didn't want anything to get in the way of that. Besides, she thought, marriage wouldn't be right for Paul either. Paul had lost his first wife to breast cancer, just as they were planning to start a family. Carmen would never want to replace her in his memory.

No, she and Paul were going to enjoy each other and keep things simple.

After a bit longer in the car, Carmen and Paul pulled up to a beautiful beachfront resort on Coronado Island. The large resort was decorated in the traditional wooden Victorian style of beachfront resorts of the past. It was love at first sight for Carmen.

Paul insisted that Carmen have a drink at the bar while he checked them in. She thought about arguing and then decided that was the old Carmen talking. Instead, she ordered a glass of champagne at the comfortable lobby bar and settled in to enjoy the ambiance of the hotel.

About fifteen minutes later, a butler approached her and said he was there to escort her to her room.

*Weird*, thought Carmen.

The pair made their way to the ocean suite Paul had booked. When they arrived at the suite, the butler opened the door and quickly slipped away.

"Paul? Did you get a load of my escort?" Carmen laughed as she walked into the suite. She caught her breath as she saw their stunning view of the Pacific Ocean for the first time. And then she saw Paul, kneeling with a small box in his hand.

*No, no, no, no, no*, thought Carmen.

"Carmen, I know you said you didn't want to get married again. And I get that, after what happened with Mark. But I wanted to bring you here this weekend to convince you that you are wrong. I'm not Mark. I don't believe that marriage is about money or babies or obligation. That may be what Mark thought it was about, but he was wrong. And it's not about sex or travel or fun either. Marriage is about picking a person to be a witness to your life, whatever that life looks like. I didn't think I would ever find a person I wanted to share the rest of my life with again after losing Jill. But then you walked into my office, and here we are. Carmen, will you marry me?"

Carmen sucked in her breath, slowly exhaled, and pulled

Paul to his feet. His surprised and disappointed expression made her heart hurt.

"Paul, let's not ruin what we have. I do love you, completely. And I love being with you. I want to share our lives. But you don't need to marry me. I don't want to replace your wife." Now she was going to say the difficult stuff. "You should think long and hard about the future you want. You're only thirty-nine. You could decide that you want a family someday. If you marry me, that's probably not in the cards. Let's just enjoy the time we have," she said with a sad smile.

"No, Carmen, I don't accept that. I will have a family with you. I want to have a real relationship with Avery. I want to be the grandfather to her babies. Hell, we can adopt if you want. That part isn't what this is about. Let me at least show you the ring." And with that, he started opening the box.

"No, Paul, stop. This isn't about a ring. Or Mark. Or even you. This is about me. I'm still recovering and getting to know myself. I'm not ready for marriage. I might never be. Please don't show me the ring. I might not have the strength to say no."

Paul flashed her a smile, but she could see the sadness behind it.

"Look, if that's how you want things, okay. It's not what I want, but I'll take what I can get, I guess."

Paul tucked the box back into his pocket and turned to start unpacking their luggage. Carmen grabbed his arm and pulled him to her. She hoped he would not see the tears in her eyes. She thought she was doing the right thing, but it sure felt wrong.

Carmen wondered if she was making a mistake, but she knew that whether it was one or not, her chance for a fairy-tale ending was probably over now.

# MARTHA

Martha was also on a trip, not that any of her friends would know about it. They were trying to pull off a perfect family week in Paris.

They were staying at a small boutique hotel in the sixth arrondissement. She loved that section of Paris—the architecture, the history, the food. It was a perfect little corner of the world. Even better, the hotel offered a babysitter, and Martha and Robert had taken advantage of the service so that they could go for a walk. They were all still a little jet-lagged, and Martha was looking forward to her favorite Parisian walking route along the Seine from the Louvre to the Eiffel Tower, unless they were too tired to make it all the way there.

They walked in silence for the beginning of the route, enjoying the calm and cool of March before the tourists descended in earnest. As they approached the Champs Elysees, Martha was ready to talk.

"Thanks for doing this, Robert. It's really perfect."

"It's been more fun than I thought," he agreed. "It's funny. I've been here so many times for work, but this is the first time I've really seen Paris, you know?"

"I love that. And I think the boys will remember this."

"God, I hope so, after you made me climb to the top of the Eiffel Tower," he teased.

"You know, this might be our last trip together as a foursome," Martha pointed out.

"I hoped they would be able to fast-track our application and home study."

"Well, you were right about that. And if you are right about the overall timing, it will only be a few more months until we get her."

"Hope," he said.

"Hope *Adams* West," she reminded him.

"Well, at least Hope was Mildred's middle name," he joked. "Hey, we should turn back soon if we are going to make dinner."

"I guess," said Martha, "but can we just walk until we can see the tower a little closer?"

"Okay," Robert agreed. "Remind me, where did you make reservations?"

"That place at the top of the Pompidou. I thought the boys would find the whole 'inside out' thing fun. I also wouldn't mind seeing their modern art collection."

"That sounds good. I'm a little nervous to tell them about Hope."

"Me, too, but I think they will be excited."

"I bet your friends are excited for you."

"I haven't really had time to talk much to them," replied Martha. She hadn't told Robert the whole sordid tale of Heather. She just didn't want to get into all the drama with him.

"I'm sure when she's here, you won't be able to beat them off," said Robert pleasantly.

"I'm sure you're right," said Martha, but of course she wasn't sure at all.

She and Carmen still talked, of course; their bond would not be ruined by Heather, but after what happened, their conversations had been much less frequent and strained. And Carmen was busy. She had her new man, Paul, for one. And she was going to school. Also, Carmen and Elizabeth seemed to be spending more time together now, and Martha studiously avoided any interaction where there was any chance of Sara or Elizabeth being around, including Carmen's big holiday party. And just like that she felt a familiar pain in her chest. She missed her friends. She had been wrong. They were family.

# SARA

They had arrived at Disney World on Saturday, and it was their third day in the parks. The younger kids had wanted to return to the Magic Kingdom over the strong objection of Tommy, who wanted to get over to Hollywood Studios for the new Star Wars attractions. Sara had decided to let the little ones win, so they were now standing in line at the Dumbo ride. Emma was practically buzzing with excitement.

Sara had a love-hate relationship with Disney World. This was their fourth time since starting their family over ten years ago. It was hard not to admire the incredible amount of effort and creativity Disney put into making the spot the happiest place on Earth. On the other hand, keeping six people happy and on track in a place like Disney was next to impossible. She was pretty sure that if she took just one child at a time for an individualized Disney experience, it would indeed be pure magic.

For now, though, she had a teen staring down at his phone in annoyance, a little one almost asleep in his stroller, and a husband who looked like he would rather be anywhere but in line next to the flying elephants. Sara decided that they should return to the Poly after the ride for pool time and a nap for Mikey. That would make everyone happy, even if it was a bit on the chilly side to be swimming.

"This is the last time," said Scott softly in her ear, in a slightly menacing tone.

"Yes, it probably is," Sara quietly scolded him, "so let's enjoy it and have a magical day."

Scott rolled his eyes in reply.

She hated to think Scott might be right. Even though these

trips were exhausting, she intended to make the most of it because she didn't know if she would be able to interest him in
coming back. Not that she wasn't giving it her all. In the past,
they had stayed off-property to do the trip more cheaply. This
time, Sara was making the big bucks and feeling guilty that she
had been spending so much time away from the family. The net
result of all of this was that they were staying in one of the luxury lagoon villas for a full week of high-end togetherness.

As the line wound back and forth endlessly (they had blown
their FastPasses earlier in the day), Sara decided to join her oldest and pulled out her own device.

She scrolled through her messages and saw that she had received an e-mail from her old boss earlier that morning.

She opened the e-mail.

Sara,
I've heard from our COO how successful you are in the
new position. I'm not surprised, of course. I knew you
had it in you.

*Right*, thought Sara, *that's why you put me on the fast track,
buddy.*

It seems to me that you have gotten everything set for
them over there. I haven't told John yet, but I want you
back. Like yesterday. It's a mess without you, and I can't
keep up. You're an attorney, and you should be in legal.
I'm sure your boss can find another ops guy to replace
you. Also, I've had to fire the attorney we brought in to
take over for you. That man asked me about thirty
questions a day. I couldn't get a damn thing done.

*This e-mail's getting good*, she thought.

On to brass tacks. I can't pay you what they are paying
you. Legal doesn't have the budget of ops. But I think I
can do 1.3 times your old salary. Let me know if you are
interested.

*Wow*. This was incredibly validating, but she wasn't sure she
wanted to go back. She was kind of a rock star now, and it actually
felt really good (just like Heather said it would). She didn't want
to divert back to the mommy track just yet. But then she looked
down at Nathan's slim little arm that had been put in a cast when
she was in India, and she felt a pang of regret. The cast was
gone, but the memory would linger.

She would talk about it with Scott tonight. Tommy had
agreed to oversee a movie pizza party in their villa while Scott
and Sara had a date night. Maybe having a teen wasn't so bad
after all.

# HEATHER

**From Heather Hall's Twitter**

**Heather Hall** @therealheatherhall · March 29

The truest wisdom is a resolute determination #favoritequotes #Frenchwisdom #napoleonbonaparte

← Reply   ↔ Retweet   ♥ Favorite   ⋯ More

# ELIZABETH

Elizabeth was back at her desk bright and early on Wednesday.

Unlike Martha and Sara, she had wanted to keep things simple for spring break. And, truth be told, she didn't want the headache associated with a longer vacation. She and William were planning to head up to one of the big indoor water park resorts in the Wisconsin Dells tomorrow for a long weekend before school started again next week. It wasn't Florida, but the snowy wilderness was equally enjoyable in Elizabeth's opinion. And who didn't get excited about the world's longest indoor water slide?

Her phone rang and she answered, seeing it was her husband.

"Hey, honey," she said.

"Did you book the regular cabin or the one with the theater room?" asked William.

"Theater room," replied Elizabeth.

"Awesome, because George and I agreed that we need to watch all the Star Wars episodes in order. But do we start with four or one? We can't decide."

"Uh-huh." Elizabeth laughed. "I'm sure George is an expert on that. Look, I have to run. I'm trying to wrap things up here, and I promise I'll help you pack when I get home. But I've got to tell you, George told me last night that he was really interested in watching *Steel Magnolias*."

"Maybe we put George to bed and watch something else," teased William.

"I'm at work, babe," Elizabeth said, but she couldn't help smiling.

Elizabeth sighed as she turned back to her desk. She really wasn't in the mood to get started on her actual work, so she decided to try to warm up her brain by reading the business journal.

She grabbed the paper and started on the top of A1. The lead story read, "Department of Labor and EEOC Open Joint Investigation into FLASH's Labor Practices." *Not great*, thought Elizabeth, remembering the comment Heather had made about labor issues when they had talked in Colorado.

Everyone on the planet knew that FLASH had gradually been working toward faster and faster delivery. They were famous for it. According to the news article, the speedy delivery FLASH promised wasn't just costing its customers. It employees paid the price, too, in exhaustion and stress. The article painted a pretty dismal picture of their workplace. The paper reported that the DOL and EEOC were launching companion probes into the company's hiring practices and their compliance with a multitude of labor laws, particularly wage and hour laws.

Elizabeth actually laughed out loud at one of the quotes the paper had gotten from an anonymous FLASH employee who alleged that he had "epic burnout" and that when he asked for some flexibility he was told to work "the one hundred hours of his choice" during the week. *That's a familiar sentiment*, she thought.

Not great for Heather, though. *Whatever, I'm sure she will have a plan for that too.*

Out of curiosity, she checked the stock price and noted that FLASH had taken a 15 percent hit already. Ouch. Elizabeth remembered Heather telling her and the other girls a few years ago that she would never sell her shares in FLASH because it was "a rocket ship" and she wasn't going to bail "before they got to the moon." Elizabeth hoped she had gotten smart and diversified.

Elizabeth would never have wished this on Heather, but at the same time, she felt a quiet satisfaction knowing that Heather was getting at least a little bit of her karmic due.

After finishing the last piece of her work, Elizabeth sighed with satisfaction and got ready to check off the last item on her to-do list. It was a good one, and she had been saving it as her reward for finishing the long day of work.

# CARMEN

Carmen was sitting on one of the hotel's beautiful decks enjoying the ocean when the phone rang.

"Hey, Elizabeth," she answered.

"Hi, Carmen," Elizabeth replied. "How's the trip?"

"It's gorgeous out here."

"And Paul?"

"Also gorgeous." Carmen giggled.

"I'm calling with some good news," said Elizabeth.

"Good, because I could use some."

"What does that mean?"

"Nothing, really. It's just that Paul asked me to marry him, and I said no, and now it's like it didn't even happen."

"What? Start over. Why did you say no?"

"I need to be by myself for a while, Elizabeth. I don't even know who I am yet."

"I understand," said Elizabeth quietly. "I'm sorry."

"Don't be sorry. It's not sad. It's not like he dumped me or anything. I just need some time to sort things out. You know, I have so many ideas for our business. I've been reading all about law-firm management. Timekeeping, billing, compensation methods . . ."

"Stop!" Elizabeth laughed. "We have plenty of time to figure this out, and I'm thinking that we shouldn't really get going until January anyway."

"Oh, why is that?" asked Carmen. "You don't think I'll be ready?"

"No, it's not you," Elizabeth assured her. "That's my happy news. Carmen, we're having a baby."

Carmen starting whooping into the phone, and a couple a few tables over looked at her in concern.

"Sorry, but my friend is having my baby," she explained. "I mean, her baby. Never mind."

She said back in the phone, "Are you sure you'll be ready by January to launch?"

"Oh yeah, I've got you in my corner, so I know it will get done," replied Elizabeth. "Hey, I've got to go. I promised William I would get home and help him pack."

"Don't go down any waterslides," admonished Carmen.

"Okay, Mom," replied Elizabeth.

Carmen smiled as she pressed "end" and relaxed back into her chair. She was going to stop worrying. She had a great guy, and, married or not, she was going to stand on her own two feet.

# MARTHA

The boys had taken the news remarkably well. It never failed to amaze her how resilient and open children were—they had so much more to teach their parents than their parents had to teach them.

They had gotten a rare, sunny day for March, and they decided to spend it at Versailles. Martha had hired a private guide, and so far, he had been worth every penny.

The guide had held the boys' attention through room after room of the country palace, regaling them with stories of its famous royal inhabitants. Just when their attention had started to wane, the guide announced that they were ready for their tour of the gardens. Minutes before they began that part of the tour, the fountains turned on. The vast expanse of symmetrical rows of hedges and trees were now punctuated by dancing water. It was one of those magical moments that no one had anticipated. The boys cheered with glee as the guide announced, "The fountains will be on for only one hour. Let's see how many we can find!"

As they jogged through the seemingly endless maze that encompassed the two-thousand-acre spread, their guide shouted out the name of every hidden garden, fountain, and statue. At the end of the hour, they had slowed their pace and were at the last of the fountains they would see for the day.

It was the Fountain of Flora, an allegory of spring. The fountain features the goddess Flora sitting among her cherubs, all sculpted in gold.

While the guide detailed the history of the fountain, Martha saw that Jack was standing quietly to the side looking closely at one of the cherubs. Martha walked over to stand beside him.

"Mommy, do you think that is what Lucy looks like now?"

Martha's breath caught in her throat.

"Yes, I think so, honey. But probably more beautiful, though, don't you think?"

"If she's really an angel now, she will watch over Hope until she can come for her surgery, right, Mommy?"

"Of course she will, honey."

"What if Hope dies too?"

He had verbalized the thought that had taken up permanent residence in the darkest corner of her heart.

"That might happen, Jack. Hope's heart needs repair, and sometimes the repair doesn't work. Your daddy is going to make sure she has the best surgeons in the country working on her, I can promise you that. But only God can decide the outcome." *Carmen would be so proud of me*, she thought wryly.

"So God wanted Lucy to come be with him?" Jack asked.

"Yes, he did. And when it's our turn, we'll meet her again," said Martha.

"Cool! I'm going to tell her all about these gardens. They're wicked awesome!" And with that, Jack ran over and started a game of tag with his brother.

Martha chuckled as she watched Jack sprint away. "Wicked awesome"?—he must have picked that up from a phone call with his cousins in Boston.

*Yes*, thought Martha again, *the kids are okay*.

# SARA

Sara and Scott had chosen to go to one of the few adults-only restaurants in the resort.

Sara was zipping up her little black dress in the villa. She hadn't dressed for dinner in ages. She was pleased to notice that her go-to dress was substantially looser than it had been the last time she wore it. She might have actually lost some of the baby weight that had been dogging her for the last several years. She had been so busy that she hadn't even noticed.

"Ready to go, hon?" Scott asked as he poked his head into the bathroom. "Hey, hot mama! You're looking great."

"Thanks," said Sara, genuinely pleased and making a note to get her skinny jeans out of storage when they got home.

After a less-than-romantic monorail excursion with sweaty families slumped over strollers, Sara and Scott were seated at a corner table in the quiet and softly lit restaurant.

"God, the silence is blissful, isn't it?" said Scott with a happy sigh.

"C'mon, it hasn't been that bad!" Sara laughed.

"Speak for yourself," replied Scott, but this time with a smile.

*I was right*, Sara thought. *This vacation was just what the doctor ordered.*

"I got an amusing e-mail today," she said to Scott as their first course arrived.

"Oh, yeah, what was that?"

"My old boss wants me back. He apparently can't live without me."

"Huh. What did you say?"

"Well, I haven't said anything yet. But I'm not going to take the bait. He said he could only pay me at 1.3 times my old salary. I mean, please. I'm not giving up the money I'm making now."

"Sara," said Scott quietly, "I think we should seriously discuss his offer."

"Why?" Sara asked. "We need the bigger salary. Case closed."

"No, it's not case closed. In case you haven't noticed, the last six months have been really hard for me. I've been trying to get my consulting business going while keeping up with your crazy demands in that stupid task tracker."

"What are you talking about? You don't have to get up and go to work every day. And the baby goes to day care. Seriously, what's the problem?"

"Sara, even with the kids at school and day care, I can't keep up. I have three projects I'm working on, but I barely have a five-hour stretch to devote to them because I have to pick the older kids up at three and then go back and forth to the day care. Then I have to make dinner, do dishes, and put everyone to bed. And that's on an easy day where there are no sports practices, no laundry, no volunteering at the school, no puking, and no random drama. So when I refuse to polish the silver, that's why. I have dreams, too, you know. I want to have a successful business. Something that belongs to me and that I control. I'm happy to help at home, but not at the rate I'm going now."

After an uncomfortable silence, Scott continued, "Sara, when you were in your old job, we split the burden. Life was busy, but I didn't feel like I was drowning."

"You know why that was, Scott? It was because I was the one doing the drowning, and you were the one shining at work. And now you know what it feels like," she argued back. "Maybe this is my turn to be the star at work."

Several beats passed between them.

"Sara, look, I know I should have been doing more in the

past. I get it now. I hate that stupid tracker, but it did make me understand how much you quietly got done before. But I also think you were doing a bunch of stuff that is unnecessary. And I do plenty that's not on your list. There is a middle ground here where we both share the work—the important work, not the stupid stuff like polishing silver—so that we can both be professionally successful and have time for the kids too. People do it all the time."

"Scott, I do want to be there at home more. Of course I do. I know what I'm missing. But I'm scared that if I go back, I'll never be looked at as a high performer again. It will be back to the old Sara that they can underpay and underpromote. I don't know if I can bring myself to be that person again."

"Don't be that person then. You know what a guy would do? He would ask for exactly what he wants. Demand what you deserve. Hey, you managed to do it on the task tracker. You clearly have it in you," he teased.

"You know what, you're exactly right," said Sara quietly. "But what about the money? It is nice to have extra."

"Sure it is. But if you get your way, you can make more in your old position. And I have faith in my little business. I think I can make a real go at it if you're home more. There's more to life than money, you know."

"Okay, I'll e-mail him back and see what happens," Sara agreed. "But don't get your hopes up—these things never work for me."

# HEATHER

**From Heather Hall's Twitter**

**Heather Hall** @therealheatherhall · March 30

Jealousy contains more of self-love than of love #favoritequotes #Frenchwisdom #Francoisdelarochefoucauld

← Reply  ↔ Retweet  ♥ Favorite  ••• More

# ELIZABETH

They had returned from their weekend in the Dells refreshed and ready to go. Well, everyone except for Elizabeth. Every day that went by brought her to a new level of morning sickness. *It shouldn't be called morning sickness*, she thought, *it should be called all-day-and-night-without-reprieve sickness.* She had started to carry extra air-sickness bags in her purse for when the lingering nausea overwhelmed her.

She wasn't too bothered by the nausea today, though, because today was the day she was going to meet her baby.

She was doing a scan for genetic abnormalities, which was standard practice given her age. She had found a doctor who would actually do the scan himself and, according to her friends who had used him, detail all his findings even as he was performing the scan. She hated to wait for results, so this doctor sounded perfect.

She had finished the check-in process and the dreaded weigh-in in short order and was soon on the examination table waiting for her scan to begin. Dr. Musser came in and introduced himself. He was originally from Germany, and he had not lost his thick accent. Somehow, it was oddly reassuring.

"Would you like to watch?" he asked. It sounded like "Vould you like to vatch?" which made Elizabeth smile.

"Oh, yes," replied Elizabeth.

As he began the procedure, her mood quickly shifted, and Elizabeth suddenly felt very nervous about the possibility that she was carrying a child with an abnormality. Or, much worse, a child that wasn't going to make it at all.

The doctor turned the screen to her, and she looked wildly

for any sign of trouble. After a few minutes, he froze the screen and said, "And what do you see here?"

Elizabeth focused on the screen and saw two roundish circles nested side by side.

"Is that what I think it is?" Elizabeth asked, starting to feel a little faint. "Is that twins?"

"Very good!" enthused Dr. Musser. "And now we will see if they are fraternal or identical."

Elizabeth felt a buzzing in her ears. *Twins!* Her mind was rushing with a million questions.

"Yes, there we are. Two placentas, so fraternal then."

"Fraternal," Elizabeth repeated slowly.

"Yes, yes, fraternal. Two placentas, always fraternal."

"So it could be one of each?"

"Of course. Or two girls or two boys. We can determine boys or girls in another month or so."

*So I might have three boys*, thought Elizabeth as Dr. Musser began to take more measurements. *That would be an interesting life. Or maybe one of them will be a girl. It would be lovely to have a chance to parent a girl too.* It was all too much.

After another ten minutes or so, Dr. Musser said, "This is all looking very good. No signs of abnormalities. You won't need to see me again, but I would suggest finding a hospital that specializes in multiple deliveries."

"Of course, thank you, Doctor," said Elizabeth, realizing she had forgotten all about her fears of the babies being unhealthy. They were perfect, and keeping them healthy was her job now. Her very next stop would be to gather every book available on twins. Forget the women's advice books—there was a whole new genre she needed to devour.

"Okay, you are done then. These are the appointments I enjoy. Such good news for you! Please take care of yourself. You rest and give those babies lots of time to grow," he said kindly as he left the exam room.

Elizabeth had a flash of worry as she thought about how she was going to actually rest and keep things going at work, but then she suppressed the thought. Today was a happy day, and she wasn't going to let her work worries spoil it.

# CARMEN

Carmen was back home after the whirlwind trip to San Diego.

Carmen might not be a bride, but she was going to be an MBA. She planned to be in the best shape of her life for this next phase, and she was forcing herself to go to one of those trendy exercise classes. The class went by quickly, and Carmen was grateful when it ended. The class never failed to transform, but the transformation never failed to be painful.

As she walked back to her car, Carmen's cell rang. Elizabeth. She hoped that Elizabeth didn't want to talk business. She wasn't fully prepared with her thoughts yet after their last business conversation, and she wanted to avoid a misstep at this stage.

"Hi, Elizabeth. Hey, can I call you later? I just got out of class," said Carmen.

"You are going to want to talk to me now," replied Elizabeth. "Because we are having twins!" she screamed into Carmen's ear.

Carmen laughed with joy. "No way!" she replied. "Maybe we should press pause on the whole law firm thing. This changes everything, doesn't it?"

"No, we must certainly not press pause," said Elizabeth. "But I agree it does change everything. Carmen, I'm ready to go all in. I owe it to these babies to get out of the firm sooner rather than later and into a place that will allow me to be a part of their lives. I've spent too much time thinking and waiting in the past. I'm not going to repeat that mistake."

"You got it, boss, burn those ships," said Carmen. "And by the way, if you made mistakes, they were all the right ones. Look how great everything has turned out for you. For all of us, really."

"Agreed. Wouldn't it be nice if Heather agreed too?"

"Fat chance," replied Carmen.

"I don't know. Have you been keeping up with the news about her and her company?"

"Yeah, that's a no," replied Carmen.

"Well, you won't believe what's happening to her," said Elizabeth, and she started to tell her old friend all about Heather's woes.

# MARTHA

Her time in Paris had made Martha realize that she wanted to make an effort to move past all the anger and pain of the last year before she brought her new daughter home. She had thought that she could simply move past the friendship, move on with her new life. But in her quiet moments she felt a loss and a sadness she couldn't shake off. This was not something she wanted to live with, to leave behind. She decided it was time to face her old friends and try to reconcile with them.

Martha thought her best move was to host a girls' night in her new home on Cumberland. Definitely no husbands or kids. Things were tricky enough as it was.

Martha debated how to reach out to them for several days. Carmen she could just call, but Sara and Elizabeth, that would be trickier. E-mailing or texting them was out. Even calling them felt wrong. She needed to set a more serious tone without going totally over the top.

Martha settled on sending a very fancy invitation to them for a decidedly unfancy event—a housewarming slumber party. *Really, how could they resist?* she thought, even as she had some apprehension about whether she was doing this right at all.

She imagined them finding the creamy invitation in their mailboxes and smiling when they realized it was from their old friend. Or would they smile? In truth, she wasn't sure of how they would react at all. So much time had gone by. She and Robert had changed a lot in that time. Her friends had probably changed too. And it wasn't like they could just pick up where they left off. Things had been left very badly.

Martha knew she couldn't fix any of that, so she put her energy into making the evening a success.

Martha and Robert hadn't moved in to the Cumberland house yet, and there was ongoing construction, but Martha decided that might make it interesting. A fresh space for a new start. She set up the library with candles and giant floor pillows. And booze. If this was going to work, there would have to be a lot of booze.

As the appointed time drew near, Martha felt a growing knot of apprehension in the pit of her stomach. She poured herself a glass of wine and considered that maybe this was all too little, too late.

Carmen was the first to arrive, and she gave Martha a big hug and said, "It's going to be great tonight. You'll see."

"I don't know, Carmen. I feel like I ruined everything."

But then she saw Sara turn up the walk. And as she opened the door to greet Sara, Elizabeth pulled up in her BMW.

As Elizabeth exited the car, Martha noticed a very discernable bump and gasped. Sara smiled as she watched Martha discover that Elizabeth was pregnant.

"Elizabeth! I'm so happy for you!" Martha exclaimed.

"Martha, we are going to catch you up!" responded Elizabeth with a smile.

"You look like you are pretty far along. It's so wonderful!"

"It's twins!" trilled Elizabeth. "And there's a back story you are going to love," she added with a laugh as the four women walked into the house.

As the girls gathered for dinner, Elizabeth told Martha all about her pregnancy, and Martha told the girls all about Hope. As the dinner wore on, the conversation was polite and safe. No mention of Heather. No mention of Lucy. And no mention of the fight last September. But unless they planned to be familiar strangers, they had to discuss those things. Martha kept pouring more and more wine in the hopes that the small talk would turn back to real talk.

As they pushed aside their food and stretched out on the

floor pillows, Carmen tried to help her friend by breaking the ice.

"Martha, this house is perfect for you," she said. "I would modernize it personally, but it fits with your whole New England, stick-up-the-ass vibe."

"Don't be such a bitch," Martha replied with some relief. "I'm all Wisconsin now, baby. And I've become much less intense over the years. All of us have, I think."

At this, all four women fell into an awkward silence.

Martha dove in.

"I'm sorry. I probably overreacted that day at the bar. I love you guys. Heather was the one at fault. Us being apart doesn't help the pain she caused. It just makes it worse."

"Martha, you know I'm sorry about what I said about my job," started Elizabeth. "That job might be history for me anyway. Carmen and I may be breaking off on our own now."

"Wow," said Martha. "I'll need an update on that."

Sara added, "I'm sorry too. Sometimes I can't see past my own nose."

Carmen finished, "Martha, you know I'm on your side one hundred percent no matter what. And I'm so happy for you and the new baby."

Martha felt the knot at the pit of her stomach start to loosen.

"Do you think we'll ever hear from Heather again?" asked Martha. "I do feel bad about her husband."

"I have to confess, I sent her a huge bouquet of flowers," said Sara.

"Me, too, believe it or not," said Martha with a sad smile. "I am still my mother's daughter in some ways. Even at my most bitter."

"Well, you are both better people than I am. I just think all the years of her crap finally got to me. Anyway, it's over. The days of free Heather swag and girls' weekends are gone now,"

Carmen declared. "But the four of us should start new traditions. Put the past behind us."

"And the best are yet to come," finished Elizabeth, rubbing her tummy.

Elizabeth was sipping a La Croix and enjoying watching her friends get drunk. Finally, she had the very best reason not to drink. She remarked, "You know, in a few months, we will have three new children and maybe a new business. It's kind of crazy. Everything is happening all at once."

"I wish Heather could have been part of this night," said Sara sadly. "She's not a bad person, you know. She just lost her way."

"I told her all she has to do is apologize," Elizabeth responded sharply. "She never will. She truly believes her book is a great act of generosity."

"What a load of horseshit," said Carmen with a laugh. "If our mistakes are what brought us to this moment, then I would make every one of them all over again."

"Me too," said Martha. "I'll never regret staying home with my boys."

"Me three," chimed in Sara. "My life is a mess sometimes, but it's mine and I love it."

"Me four," agreed Elizabeth. "I'm right where I always wanted to be. Well, I'm on my way. What did you say yesterday, Carmen? Oh yeah, we made all the right mistakes."

"To all the right mistakes!" cheered Carmen as she raised her glass.

"To friendship!" replied Elizabeth as she raised her La Croix.

"Okay, enough screwing around," said Sara, "it's time for the movie. And we are not watching *Heathers* again, Martha and Carmen."

"What's your damage, Heather?" they yelled back at her.

It wasn't the same, Martha thought, but it was getting a little better. Sara was right, though. It would always be a little sad that they had lost Heather. Or, rather, that she had lost them.

# SARA

**From**: Phil Smith
**Sent**: Sun. 4/3 2:15 p.m.
**To**: Sara Beck
**Subject**: Re: Counteroffer

Fine. Consider it done.

Please note you may have to stay in your cube for a few months until I can arrange for a suitable office. And I don't know much about that touchy-feely successor business, so you'll have to bear with me on that score. Let's agree no HR, OK?

See you Monday.

P


**From**: Sara Beck
**Sent**: Sun. 4/3 2:00 p.m.
**To**: Phil Smith
**Subject**: Counteroffer

Phil, I received your e-mail last week. I'm sorry my replacement did not work out and that you are in a tight spot.

I have really been enjoying my time with operations. That said, I am willing to consider returning to your team. Here are my terms:

1.5 times my old salary (I know exactly how much is in your budget now, and I know you can afford it);

VP title and all associated benefits, including participation in the company's stock option program;

36 vacation days to be taken at my discretion;

Work from home option as needed, not to exceed two days a week; and

Quarterly meetings to discuss and implement a development plan for me as your successor.

Let me know.

Best regards,

Sara Beck

# JUNE

# HEATHER

**From Heather Hall's Twitter**

**Heather Hall** @therealheatherhall ·June 2

Tune in for my interview with 20/20 for the truth about FLASH's labor practices #factsnotspin #workinghardiswhatIdoforfun

← Reply   ↔ Retweet   ♥ Favorite   ··· More

# ELIZABETH

Elizabeth was terrified to think how big she was going to be by September. As it was, just about every person who crossed her path said some version of "You must be due any day now!" She wanted to hang a sign around her neck that said, "Not until September and, yes, it is twins, thanks for asking."

With every pound that she added to the scale, she felt more urgency to be ready to launch her firm.

She and Carmen had put the finishing touches on their business plan for the new firm last week. She felt like they were turning in their group project for economics class and leaving for summer vacation, but this time the work wasn't hypothetical. It was going to be a real business. They were going to be owners. She loved that word. *Owners*.

They agreed that they would officially launch in late January to allow Elizabeth some time with her babies. She was confident in William's ability to manage the baby factory, but she was still the mom, and she wanted to enjoy those first few months with no distractions.

Quitting was most definitely a leap of faith. She was going to be in a tough place if the new firm wasn't successful pretty quickly, but she was feeling brave. Elizabeth's goal for June was to tie up all the loose ends at work in the next week or so and then announce her intentions to Joe. She wanted to spend the last few months of her pregnancy resting to give her babies their best chance at being full-term.

Although she was already fantasizing about announcing her departure, she wanted to take the high road. And she was realistic. No matter what she said on the way out, she knew the firm would hardly skip a beat. She had seen too many people quit to think otherwise. She knew that Kenny in particular would be measuring for new drapes within minutes of her announcement and instructing Linda to transfer all her files to his office. He could have it, she thought. She was going to be on to bigger and better things.

Today was Wednesday, which meant that she would be expected at the weekly all-attorney lunch and learn. She would have preferred to sit at her desk, but she decided to be a good sport and attend. It would do all those guys good to have to hang out with a pregnant woman now and then anyway.

They always had the lunch in the same room, and they were always organized pretty much exactly like the high school cafeteria had been. The popular kids always sat together, even if one of them had to squeeze in an extra chair rather than sit at a lesser table. It was Elizabeth's strong suspicion that none of these lawyers had ever been anywhere close to the cool-kid table in high school. This was their big chance to right that wrong, and they weren't going to let that chance pass them by this time around.

Elizabeth walked past them toward a group of older associates, mostly women, positioned in the far corner. She checked under the table to make sure none of them were wearing red patent leather heels.

"Hi, guys. Is this seat taken?"

"No, but you know this isn't the table for management," one of the young men joked. The women gave him a sharp look and said, "Of course you're welcome, Elizabeth, please join us."

The guy shrugged and went back to looking unimpressed by Elizabeth.

"Well, thank you, and I'm just here as a person, not as a partner," replied Elizabeth awkwardly. She probably sounded like a total idiot to these attorneys who were a good ten years younger than she was.

"When's the baby due?" asked one of the women with interest. "I know you're not ever supposed to ask that, but, well, it's pretty obvious now, isn't it?"

Elizabeth had never noticed this woman before. She was dressed plainly but attractively, and her intelligence radiated from behind her tortoiseshell glasses. So pretty much the opposite of Blake.

"September. I know, I'm big as a house already. In my defense, it's twins."

"I think you look great," the woman replied sincerely.

*Huh, this woman is either really kind or a really good liar,* thought Elizabeth.

The woman continued, "You should really be nicer to yourself. Women get enough negative messages from the media that we don't need to add our own voices to the chorus."

Elizabeth wondered how in the world this woman was surviving the firm.

"What practice area are you in?" asked Elizabeth.

"Litigation. I've actually been here for nine years. I was passed over last year, but I'm hoping this is my year."

Nine years and Elizabeth had never noticed her. The firm was big, but not that big. Elizabeth knew with near-certainty that this woman would never be selected to make partner. She didn't have that aggressive bearing that every litigation partner seemed to have. She had nine years of disappearing into the background. She must be an excellent researcher and writer if they were keeping her around, though. It was a shame. She probably added great value to the firm, but because she wouldn't attract clients or be a star in the courtroom (or in Joe's office), she probably wouldn't be valued properly here, assuming they could convince her to transition into a salaried non-partner role.

"I got passed over my first year, too," said Elizabeth. "Hang in there."

"You'll make it next time, Jenny," said a younger-looking blond associate from corporate.

"You're Cassie, right?" asked Elizabeth. "How are things going for you in the group?" She was surprised Cassie wasn't hanging with Blake and the other girls. She certainly had the looks for it.

"Well, I've been working a lot with Kenny," said Cassie tentatively, as she pulled nervously on her long blond hair.

"He'll get you working on some top-drawer stuff," replied Elizabeth.

The young man seemed to decide he was going to mostly ignore Elizabeth and get back to their original conversation.

"Cassie, you need to just get on with it."

"Jeff!" she said sharply, and looked in Elizabeth's direction.

"Hey, she's pregnant, maybe she'll be sympathetic," said Jeff, his eyes flashing with mischief.

"Sympathetic about what?" asked Elizabeth.

"Thanks a lot, Jeff," said Cassie. "Who needs enemies when I have you as my friend?" But she didn't actually look angry. She looked like she wanted to talk. Elizabeth knew that look well.

"Well, I'm pregnant too," said Cassie defensively, turning to Elizabeth.

*Ah*, thought Elizabeth. *That would certainly explain why she's not hanging with Blake.*

"Congratulations!" said Elizabeth. "Good for you."

"No, not good for me," said Cassie and her checks started to get red. "I want to go part-time, and when I talked to Kenny about it, he said I would be dead in the water if I went down that road."

"Well, Cassie, that's a little harsh, but there is some truth there," said Elizabeth. "It's not easy to become a mom for the first time and practice here. But it is doable."

"I want the option of part-time, maybe a telecommute day. I don't know exactly what I want, but it can't be the way I work now. I just want a more human schedule in general. My husband is a teacher, and he'll do a lot, but I'm still the mom, you know? I want to be a good mom. My mom worked, and she was gone, all the time, practically all day long. I love her, but I don't want to be like her, in that way at least. Please don't take that the wrong way, Elizabeth. You seem really nice. I'm sure you're a great mom. My mom was in that first generation of women, you know. They had to be hard as nails. I'm probably going to be a big disappointment to her. God, I'm sorry. Talk about TMI." Cassie went quiet and looked at her hands.

"I get it," said Elizabeth softly, and someone quickly changed the subject.

Did she ever get it. Elizabeth made a mental note to give Cassie and Jenny a call in a few months. And maybe even Jeff, too, if he could be a little friendlier. She didn't blame him for his hostility. She remembered that Kenny had recently taken him off a deal because he was "too soft," whatever that meant. These were the people she wanted at her firm. She was going to make them the workplace they wanted. No, she corrected herself, it was the workplace they deserved.

# CARMEN

She and Paul had been discussing where they should live for the last few months. Carmen may not have wanted to marry him, but she was more than willing to shack up. Paul was a master of breakfast, and Carmen loved being the one sitting on the stool at the kitchen island for a change. Plus, there weren't many things sexier than watching a man make a frittata.

Paul had been campaigning for them to move to a new home in the Milwaukee area. Carmen was torn. She loved the Lake Geneva home, but she could understand why Paul wanted to start fresh in a new house. And Paul had pointed out that if Carmen and Elizabeth were going to make a go of the new firm in Milwaukee, she would have to move anyway. Finally, Paul liked the idea of having some land, and the Texas girl in Carmen had a hard time arguing with him.

Paul had taken the day off work so that they could go look at houses. They were looking around Fredonia in Ozaukee County because there were a lot of properties there with substantial acreage, many of them backing up to the Milwaukee River.

They pulled up in his black truck to a property with a long, winding drive. In the distance, she could see a beautiful old farmhouse. Old, but very spacious and well-kept, at least from the outside. To the left of the main house was a riding complex and a neighboring field for the horses to graze.

It had been so long since she'd been on a horse, thought Carmen. She had grown up riding in Texas and had nothing but fond memories of those weekends with her dad and her horse, Trudy. City living had pretty much made riding impossible, and once Avery was born, she had never gotten back to it.

As they drove down the winding path, Carmen thought

about what her life could be like here. Different, she thought. Very different. They keyed in the code on the realtor's lock and started to explore the main house. It was exceptional, she had to admit. There wasn't a lot she would have to change.

Paul was interested in taking a look at the woodshop that was supposed to be in the little shed neighboring the barns. Carmen decided to check out the stables.

She walked in to find a cream-colored dappled mare standing calmly in her stall. She looked like she could be Trudy's foal. Carmen grabbed an apple from a nearby bushel and walked over to feed it to the lovely animal. As she fed the mare with her left hand, she reached up with her right to stroke the animal's neck. The mare seemed to welcome Carmen's caress. Carmen flashed back to the feeling she used to get as a child when she was on Trudy's back, galloping through the Texas fields. Free and wild and full of life.

*I used to be fearless*, thought Carmen. *What happened to me? Why am I willing to move, to live with Paul, but not marry him?* It was a nonsensical boundary, really. Avery had been on her case about it ever since she had told her what happened in Coronado.

"Mom! Don't be stupid. Paul loves you. You love him. What else is there?" she had said. "Just because you're over forty doesn't mean your life is over. Look at all the couples who got married after waiting decades for the laws to change. Appreciate your right to be with the person you love. And Mom, it will be different this time. Paul is not Daddy."

Maybe her daughter was right. Carmen was finally finishing her education, and this time, she was the one with the dream job lined up. Not to mention that she didn't have a newborn, which was definitely going to make things easier. Maybe it was time to finally let down her guard and let herself be happy. Maybe someday, she thought as she left to find Paul.

"Well, what do you think?" he asked when she met him outside the shed.

"About what?" Carmen responded.

"The house, what else?" said Paul with a laugh. "Are you thinking about the firm again? You're going to need to learn to compartmentalize if you're going to be a successful CFO, you know."

"Actually, I was thinking we should get married someday. And we should definitely buy the house too."

Paul stood there blinking slowly.

"I'm sorry," he said. "Did you just propose to me?" He laughed with delight.

*Oh, crap*, thought Carmen. *Can't turn back now.*

"Yeah, I guess I did. Paul, will you marry me?" asked Carmen, softly smiling.

Paul grinned and said, "I thought you would never ask. Would you like your ring now?"

"Are you carrying it around in your pocket?" asked Carmen incredulously.

"Well, sort of. It's in the truck. I didn't want to let it go just yet."

Paul jogged over to find the box.

As she watched him retreat, Carmen started to doubt herself. What if this was a horrible mistake? Maybe it was too soon. Why was she so impulsive?

As he walked slowly back over, Carmen tried to calm her nerves. He was soon standing in front of her holding a familiar box, the same one he had been holding in San Diego.

He handed it to her. She took a deep breath and opened it. She didn't know what to expect. She had seen a lot of bad engagement rings in her days, and she hoped Paul had just gone simple and classic.

Nestled in the white satin was a ring that was most definitely not bad. It was stunning, in fact. It had a beautiful art deco design that was unique but still clean and elegant in its design. The ring looked familiar, but she couldn't quite place it. And then she knew. "This is my grandmother's ring!" she said with surprise. "How did you . . ."

"I asked your father for permission back in March," Paul explained quietly. "We had a long talk. He's such a good man, Carmen. He loves you so much and wants you to be happy. And he wants you to have his mother's ring. He said that he would have given it to Mark if he had thought to ask."

Carmen was overcome with emotion. She couldn't wait to show the girls. And Avery. Avery would love this. It was all too much. She started to cry despite her best efforts to hold it together.

"One thing," said Paul. "Your mom wants to be part of planning the wedding this time. I said that was fine by me. I hope that's acceptable."

"Sure," Carmen replied, laughing through her tears. "She's certainly waited long enough. But we are having it in Milwaukee because Elizabeth will be too pregnant to travel."

"I'll let your mom down gently," said Paul, joining in her laughter. "So we have another hour to tour the place. Let's walk through the main house one more time. There's one room I think we should pay particular attention to. We're going to be spending a lot of time in there if I have my way."

"Actually, I'm more a fan of the stables," teased Carmen.

"Well, then," said Paul, "let's check out both." He pulled Carmen into his arms for a kiss, and she felt the defenses she had so carefully crafted over the long years with Mark begin to melt away. She was ready to trust again.

# MARTHA

The contractors had outdone themselves and finished all their renovations by June, which turned out to be just in the nick of time because Martha had returned from China with Hope just last week. The trip to China had been quick and uneventful, and their little family had gone from four to five in the blink of an eye. In some ways, it felt like she had always been there.

Even though the renovations were complete, Martha was still unpacking boxes. She didn't mind. This move was permanent, and she wanted it done right. She would take all the time she needed and make sure everything was in its proper place.

Hope was down for her afternoon nap. Martha was being very strict about Hope's nutrition and nap schedule because her heart surgery was scheduled for Friday, and she wanted Hope to be as strong as possible for it.

Martha was unpacking and organizing today in her favorite room in the new house—the library. She had tried to make minimal changes to the space. Just a fresh coat of paint to highlight the gorgeous built-ins. It took her a while to decide upon a scheme for which books would go where, but she had it figured out now and was ready to load the shelves. It would be going much faster, though, if she could stop lingering over every book that she unpacked.

Her books were the thumbnail history of her life. There were her favorite novels, of course. But there were also hundreds of biographies, obscure histories, travel books, her old favorites from her childhood, and even her old textbooks. As she took them out of the boxes one by one, she would run her hand over their spines and sometimes sit and leaf through her favorites for a while. At the rate she was going, it would take her a month to get all the books shelved.

She was nervous about Hope's surgery. While the travel and pickup had gone remarkably smoothly, the medical process had been a little rocky.

To begin with, it had taken a great deal of planning to get the right doctors together at the right time for Hope. Robert had been instrumental in getting an A team for their baby. She wondered how regular families navigated that process. Then there was the wrangling with her insurance company. And finally, there was the startling lack of information on the specifics of Hope's condition—both the procedures required to treat it and the prognosis. Part of this was because things might change when the doctors saw what they were dealing with when they opened her up. Martha understood that full well, but she still wanted every piece of information she could get her hands on to help Hope. And she disliked uncertainty, particularly if she wasn't able to directly manage it herself.

Martha understood now why people were reluctant to adopt children with special needs. The system was indeed not easy to navigate, as Robert had said at the outset, even for someone like her with a medical degree. She was trying to be patient, but the waiting and the wondering were emotionally exhausting.

As she fished through the next box of books, she looked outside her window and scanned around for the boys. School was finally out, and she knew they were somewhere outside playing. She hadn't seen them in a while, though, so she decided to go check on them. She started to turn toward the door to make her way outside, but then she saw them out of the corner of her eye.

They were with those same kids she had seen all those months ago walking home from school. There were maybe seven of them today, and they all appeared to be on scooters. Maybe racing? Bobby and Jack didn't have scooters, so the kids must have lent them a couple. Her boys were both smiling broadly as they whizzed down the sidewalk. She couldn't remember the last time she had seen them looking so happy and unburdened.

She made a mental note to buy popsicles the next time she was at the grocery store. A box big enough to share.

# SARA

Sara was back in her old cube while her boss negotiated for her new office.

It was amazing how easily she fell back into her old routine. She had forgotten how much she enjoyed legal work. It was only Wednesday, but she had planned a long lunch anyway. She had decided to take Katherine out to lunch, and her old friend had Sara in stitches with the stories of the various screw-ups her colleagues had endured at the hands of Sara's temporary replacement.

"I promise, I won't leave again!" Sara had said through her laughter.

"You better not!" Katherine had replied. "And by the way, he also clipped his toenails in the cube. His toenails, Sara. And don't even get me started on the weird food he brought from home. And then there was this time at the Thai place when the waiter asked if I wanted to take my leftovers home, and after I said no, he asked to have them wrapped up for him. I mean, seriously, how gross is that!"

This was the part of work she had missed. Operations was so go, go, go that they hardly had time to interact with one another, much less go to lunch together.

Sara was planning to leave soon to pick Mikey up from day care. She had taken that duty back over, much to Scott's relief. She was happy to do it. She had missed that sweet baby face staring at her in the rearview mirror.

As she was tidying up her desk in preparation to leave, her phone rang.

"Hey, Scott," she answered, trying to sound like she needed

to be walking out the door. "What's up? Did the babysitter leave early?"

They had agreed that they would hire a college student to help keep the kids entertained over the summer so that Scott could have a solid eight hours for his consulting work during the workweek. So far, it seemed to be going really well. But that's always when something would go wrong in the past—just when you started to think you had things figured out and could relax.

"No, she's with the kids at the zoo. She's great. I hardly have to lift a finger. That's not why I'm calling."

"Did you want me to pick something up on the way home?"

"No, Sara, it's nothing like that. It's work stuff. I just got a call from one of my clients. They want me on staff full-time. It's actually at a bigger company than the one I left last year."

*Oh boy*, thought Sara.

"Scott, I thought we agreed that neither of us would go back to a big job."

"Hey, they came to me. I wasn't out looking. I know what we said, but how can I say no to this, Sara? I mean, come on. They want me to run the whole IT operation, worldwide. That's huge."

"Uh, you do it the same way I did. You just say no."

"But it's different for you."

"Why is that exactly, because I'm a woman? We had a deal, Scott."

"I guess," said Scott quietly. "I need to think about it. It just seems like something I shouldn't just reject out of hand. We can get more help, you know."

"Okay," said Sara, "but please don't forget your advice to me at Disney. Think about what you really want. If you do go back to a demanding job, you won't have to do as much at home, but you will also start to miss seeing your kids grow up. You can't have it both ways, Scott. Nobody can."

As they hung up, Sara wondered if she was naive to think she understood what Scott wanted. Maybe he found working at home emasculating. He would be great in the job they were of-fering him. And he deserved to go for his dreams too. She really should hear him out. He wasn't her, and maybe they wanted dif-ferent things.

She was right, anyway, that things always went haywire just as you figure out your family rhythm. *Why does everything always have to be so hard?* she wondered as she headed for the door.

# HEATHER

**From Heather Hall's Twitter**

**Heather Hall** @therealheatherhall ·June 4

If you're going through hell, keep going #favoritequotes #thefrenchingoodtimesthebritsinbad #winstonchurchill

← Reply   ↔ Retweet   ♥ Favorite   ••• More

# ELIZABETH

Today was the day. *Bombs away*, thought Elizabeth.

She had gotten on Joe's calendar for ten o'clock that Thursday morning. She knew most people liked to quit on a Friday, but she planned to come in tomorrow with her head held high and no drama. Not that she wasn't planning to celebrate tonight, of course. She was meeting Carmen and Martha at the bridal salon after the fireworks and intended to drink exactly one sip of champagne followed by multiple flutes of sparkling water.

It was five minutes until ten, and it was time for her to get her game face on. She opened the closet in her office and took out a shoebox. It had been uncharacteristic of her, but she had bought new shoes for the occasion. It was her homage to Blake, she thought with amusement. She planned to wear the gorgeous new heels for exactly the amount of time it took her to tell Joe the news (she was figuring less than five minutes if history was any guide). The shoes were wildly expensive, and she didn't want to stretch them out too much. She would want to wear them again next year when she launched her business.

She slipped the heels on and considered whether she should do any of the power poses she had read about in one of those women's career books. *Nah*, she thought. *I'm pregnant with twins. I'm going to be a presence no matter how I'm standing.*

She checked her makeup one last time, put on one more swipe of lipstick, and rose to walk over to Joe's office.

The heels bit into her swollen feet as she walked down the hall, but she ignored the pain.

As she rounded the corner, she ran into none other than Blake, who said as she breezed past Elizabeth, "Great shoes, mama! Hey, you haven't called me about lunch!"

*And I never will*, thought Elizabeth as she arrived at Joe's door.

Before Elizabeth could even knock, she heard Joe bark, "Come!"

"Hi, Joe," began Elizabeth as she opened the door and walked in with as much authority as she could muster. "Thanks for making time for me."

"Listen, I really don't have more than five minutes. Things are really on fire today," Joe said with his back turned to her, organizing a stack a documents.

Sure they were, thought Elizabeth. When were things not on fire in Joe's world?

"No problem, Joe. I'll be brief. Effective tomorrow, I am leaving the firm. I will have my office cleaned out and my files transferred by Monday."

Joe whipped around to face her, and after about three beats he snapped, "Well, that would be really stupid. You are one of our most valuable partners."

"Joe, respectfully, then you should have fixed the situation with Grey."

"Elizabeth, I had no choice, you know that."

"Joe, we always have a choice."

Joe's eyes flashed, but he seemed to compose himself. "Well, what are your plans?" he asked. "Going to take some time with the babies, I suppose?"

"Quite the opposite actually. I'm opening up a new firm in January."

"That's not going to last," said Joe, sounding a little harsher than he probably had intended.

He sighed and continued, "I don't mean to be a jerk, but you need to rethink before you leap. What client would want some no-name firm doing their work? None of ours, that's for sure. Really, Elizabeth, don't make decisions while you're pregnant. Go have your babies and come back to us when you're ready."

"I appreciate your support, Joe, but I've made up my mind—

and I have a great business plan," said Elizabeth. "I have a good friend who practices in-house, and she has informed me that clients are more open to taking a risk on an unknown firm if they are offering something different than the standard by-the-hour model. Our bill rates have become quite impressive, I'm sure you'd agree."

"You get what you pay for," said Joe, now with some irritation. "Clients know it, and that's why they pay up in the end. Hey, best of luck to you, I just hope you realize what you're setting yourself up for."

"It will be a success, Joe. And, by the way, it won't just be me. It will be a team. I'm going to make the place a fun, relaxed, flexible place to work. I think there will be a lot of interest. And that will make us a name eventually. Every business has to start somewhere."

Elizabeth moved to leave but then paused. She had so much she wanted to say and decided not to, but maybe she could make a little headway for the next generation. "By the way, I hope you realize that you're ignoring a lot of good people because your evaluation and promotion structure can overlook some real strengths."

"Like who are we ignoring exactly?" asked Joe.

"How about Jenny? She's up for partner this year. She's not in my group, but she seems great."

"Yeah, I remember her from last year. She's definitely not partner material. But don't get me wrong—we love having her around. She's a workhorse, and smart. Otherwise we would have gotten rid of her a long time ago. We have her on a fixed salary. I think it works for both of us."

*Well, that's short-sighted*, Elizabeth thought.

"What about Cassie?" she countered.

"Yeah. Kenny told me she's pregnant. That takes her off track for at least a year, but we'll see what happens when she comes back."

"Okay, Joe, what about Jeff? He's not pregnant," Elizabeth said sarcastically, starting to lose her cool.

Joe gave her a disapproving frown.

"He's smart and does good work, I guess. But he doesn't have the killer instinct. Kenny tells me he's soft. Look, Elizabeth, whatever you think about me personally, and I'm starting to suspect you think I am a first-class asshole, the reality is that clients want assholes like me in their corner. The day I go soft is the day I go to the bottom of their list."

"I think reality is changing, Joe, and I'm part of a better way that's coming," replied Elizabeth.

"We'll see. Hey, keep in touch. If you do make a go, let's talk down the road."

*Isn't that funny*, thought Elizabeth. *In the end, success always gets their attention.* Who knows, maybe there was a deal to be made in the future.

Elizabeth walked back to her office, feeling more and more free with every step she took. A few minutes later, she was seated at her desk with the tortuous heels kicked off. She decided to calm herself by reading the paper for a while.

She found it right where her assistant placed it every morning. She noticed immediately that FLASH was back above the fold. The headline read, "FLASH Stock in Free Fall after Earnings Restatements." *Whoa*, thought Elizabeth. Heather's company was in really big trouble, way beyond their labor issues. She read on.

The article described how FLASH had voluntarily made filings with the SEC restating their earnings for the last two years, resulting in disclosure of losses in the hundreds of millions of dollars. Apparently, FLASH's investments in service delivery and speed had been both expensive and, in many cases, not sufficiently successful for them to recoup their investment. At the same time, the company had been quietly losing market share to a rival who used a proprietary algorithm to drive lower prices through bundling and delivery efficiencies, albeit with delivery times being much slower.

According to the article, it turned out that most everyday Americans would rather pay less and receive their stuff a few days later than get it lightning fast from the comparatively over-priced FLASH. They also probably liked the social responsibility message from FLASH's rival that the human impact of business was important. The paper got a quote from the rival stating that they would be pleased to waive the initial subscription fee for any customer who had been disappointed by FLASH's labor practices and wanted to have a new experience based on provid-ing a quality service without impacting the human rights of its workers and suppliers.

The article wasn't clear on how the massive losses had gone unreported for so long. The SEC was launching an investigation into FLASH's accounting practices and was also planning to in-vestigate the involvement of its auditors.

In sum, it was a mess.

When things went badly in business these days, they sure went badly fast, thought Elizabeth.

# Carmen

Carmen was standing in front of the full-length mirror admiring the pink tulle dress and the body that was filling it. *Not bad for forty*, she thought.

"It's a little unseemly to stare at yourself so long," Martha pointed out wryly.

"Shush," said Carmen. "This is my princess moment, and what the princess wants, the princess gets."

"If you go bridezilla on us, I'm out," replied Martha.

"Martha, why can't you just be a friend? Why do you have to be such a megabitch?" Carmen asked.

"Because I can be," Martha responded, continuing the scene.

"You guys need to knock it off. You're embarrassing yourselves," said Elizabeth. "It wasn't even funny in college."

"Lick it up, baby. Lick it up," Carmen replied as she twirled in front of the mirror.

"You look lovely in that one, dear," said the elderly saleswoman as she walked by, perfectly turned out in her Chanel suit, pearls, gray bun, and sensible heels. "You know we have a very generous layaway plan, in case you are worried that this one is too costly."

As soon as the saleswoman was out of range, Carmen said sweetly, "Martha, can you please let her know I'm filthy rich. I swear, some things never change."

"You got it," said Martha, and headed off to strike another blow against profiling.

"Hey, while we're alone, Carmen, I have something I'd like to ask you," started Elizabeth.

"No, you are not getting out of being a bridesmaid just because you are enormous. I already ordered extra material. We'll just wrap it around you mummy-style if we have to."

"No, it's not about the wedding. It's about the babies," said Elizabeth.

"Oh, God, is something wrong with the babies?" asked Carmen with fear in her voice.

"No, no, everything's great. They're great. I was hoping you would agree to be their godmother. They are practically half yours anyway."

"Oh, Elizabeth, I would be honored. I really hoped I could be part of their lives, but I didn't want to be pushy." Tears started tracking down Carmen's face, and she came down off her pedestal to hug Elizabeth.

"I see that I upset you greatly, please accept my heartfelt apology," came a tight voice from the door. "We old women can be rather stupid sometimes, you know."

Martha was standing behind the saleswoman with her hands on her hips, having taken care of business.

"Oh, no," said Carmen, "these tears aren't about that at all. I'm going to be a godmother—twice!"

"Congratulations, dear," the saleswoman said with relief. "Let me get another bottle of champagne for you ladies. Then we can move on to the dresses for the bridesmaids. We'll need some extra time for this situation," she continued as she sized up Elizabeth's belly.

# Martha

Martha was not accustomed to being the one sitting in the waiting area. She was usually the one behind closed doors calling the shots, holding the patient's life in her hands.

This must be how the families of her patients felt every time, she thought. It was terrible.

She decided to shake off her anxiety and go for a walk around the hospital. She knew from experience that it would be easy to do a few miles without passing the same place twice.

After about thirty minutes, she turned the corner and saw that she would be walking by the hospital's chapel. She decided to go in and sit for a bit.

She noticed an older woman sitting nearby wearing the ubiquitous Packers sweatshirt that was part of the official uniform of the citizens of Wisconsin. She didn't want to disturb her, so she sat a fair distance away.

After a few minutes, the woman got up to leave. On her way out, she said, "I hope your prayers are answered."

Martha replied kindly, "Yours too."

"Pardon me for asking, but do you know where I could go to get some information about the surgery they are performing on my daughter?"

"Actually, yes," said Martha. "Believe it or not, I am a doctor myself. I'm happy to try to answer your questions, at a general level anyway."

"Oh, I'm sorry. I didn't mean to disturb you. I'll ask someone else."

"Why? I'm sitting right here."

"You must be busy, since you're a doctor and all."

"I'm actually just a mom these days. Shoot."

"All right then," the woman said tentatively as she sat down. "Thank you, Doctor."

"Call me Martha."

The woman started talking to Martha about her daughter. As Martha listened to her, it occurred to her how she could use her skill set to be part of the world again. She might not save another patient, but perhaps she could find a way to help give comfort to their families and maybe even provide some medical counseling. It was so hard to be the one sitting in the waiting room. Especially for the families who were adopting special needs children like Hope. If she'd had a buddy during the process that specialized in medical issues, it would have been very helpful.

As she talked with the woman, her idea began to take on more definite shape. Martha had never been very religious, and when she had lost Lucy, she had turned her back completely to God, but sitting in the chapel that day, she felt a presence. As she looked up to the stained-glass window in the front of the room, she found herself thanking God for the shape her new life was taking. Her God was definitely not a guy, though, she decided.

# SARA

Sara and Scott hadn't talked about his offer since their conversation earlier in the week. It was Friday, and she was ready to get the issue settled. She didn't want it hanging over their heads all weekend.

She decided that she had to bring it up straight away when she got home, so she was rehearsing her arguments with Mikey on the ride home. He wasn't a very good proxy for Scott because all she got in response to her serious conversation was a happy smile.

She walked in the door with Mikey on her hip and saw a printout of a letter Scott had written to his client. She couldn't resist reading it.

> . . . regret to decline your offer . . . pleased to provide services to you as an independent consultant . . . I look forward to continuing our relationship . . .

*Holy cow. He's going to say no after all. Crap.* She hoped he wasn't doing it for her. That wouldn't work long-term. She felt bad. She shouldn't have guilted him into this.

As she was thinking about what to say to him, he suddenly appeared in the kitchen.

"Caught you," he teased.

"I'm sorry," she said. "It was right there, and I just started reading."

"I left it there for you to read. I thought you would be pleased."

"Scott, of course I'm delighted. You know I love our setup

now. But if you need to get back to a big job to be happy, you should take it. We'll figure it out. We will have more money than we know what to do with, and we can hire help. Hell, we can even move into a new house. You should rip up that letter and just take the job."

"Well, at first, I wanted to take it," Scott conceded. "But then I took your advice and thought about why. It was pride, mostly, I think. I wanted to show everyone at my old job that the higher-ups had been wrong about me. And maybe I could have brought in some of my old friends. That would have been very satisfying. At least for a few days. But then I would be working nonstop. And my old friends don't want new jobs anyway. They've moved on." Scott sighed and continued.

"Sara, I need to work. I need to be out of the house. But I also want to be a good dad. When you were in India, I was pretty agitated and thinking I just wanted to go back to a regular desk job. But now that things are settled, I can see all the great stuff that's coming from me being closer to the kids. Did you know that Tommy talks to me for almost a half hour every day when he gets home? He's a teen. They're not supposed to talk to you at all. And Emma draws me pictures every day saying, 'I love you.' Every day, Sara. And I actually love consulting. I can set my own schedule and take the work I like, not the work that is thrust on me."

Sara exhaled and said, "I feel like you should still wait a few days to be sure it's what you want."

"Look, I know it's what I want. But I do have a request for you."

"All right," said Sara tentatively.

"No more task tracker. Ever."

"But . . ." Sara started, and then she changed her mind. A decent sex life had to be more important than a perfectly organized home. "You got it. But since we're negotiating, I have a request too. I want to go to Disney one more time. No, two more times. For Mikey."

Scott sighed and said, "Okay, honey, I guess it's worth it if I never have to see that tracker again." And with that, he came in for a hug, and Mikey squealed his delight as he was sandwiched between them and enveloped in the love of his parents.

# HEATHER

**From Heather Hall's Twitter**

**Heather Hall** @therealheatherhall ·June 5

Sometimes you win, sometimes you learn

← Reply   ↔ Retweet   ♥ Favorite   ⋯ More

# ELIZABETH

Elizabeth was unemployed for the first time in her life. It was very strange. She had always had some sort of a job from the time she had started babysitting at age twelve. Growing two babies should count as work, she thought. Actually, it should be overtime. At least the way it was going these days.

She didn't know if she was going to make it to September. She had developed sciatica and, unlike when she had been pregnant with George, was finding it difficult to get in her three-mile daily walk. It was a good thing she didn't have to get dressed anymore for work because her options for both professional-looking outfits and footwear that fit were dwindling.

For their part, William and George were delighted that she was home. She was trying to stay off her feet as much as possible for the rest of the pregnancy, but George had figured out that this in no way impeded her from playing board games. She was beginning to question the wisdom of her decision to quit the firm after her fifteenth game of Candyland. If this was what William did all day, she had zero interest in ever doing his job.

"Honey, Mommy needs to check her e-mail quickly," she said to George after he drew double purple for the win. She was ashamed of herself, but she had stacked the deck to give him a quick win. It was pretty low, she had to admit.

"Okay, Mommy. I'm going to find Daddy. I'm ready to paint."

If she were the stay-at-home parent, they would never paint, she thought. *What a mess! No way.* George was lucky he had William instead of her.

She grabbed her phone and started glancing at her e-mails. She was still getting lots of e-mails from a variety of partners bitching about all the things they hated about the firm. Elizabeth thought they were all very unprofessional, but she guessed that they figured that now that she had quit, they could let it rip. She noticed that Heather had sent her a message too.

She wasn't sure she wanted to read it, but it couldn't be any worse than the crazy partner e-mails.

Elizabeth,

What can I say? I was wrong. Wrong about all of it.

It does take a village. And my village is gone. Being a single mom to three kids turns out to be harder than anything I have ever done in my life.

Also, I'm sure you've read the papers. I might be doing it without a job.

I shouldn't be talking about this, but I know you can keep a secret, and it will be all over the news Monday anyway (Just don't trade, OK?). It looks like the board is going to sell to our rival and at a bargain-basement price. It's too late for me to sell my shares, of course. My net worth is set to take a beating, and there's nothing I can do now. It's killing me that I didn't take your advice all those years ago and diversify. I didn't want to miss out on FLASH's growth, you know?

What's worse, I don't think the new company will want me either. Because of my stupid book, they think I'm a know-it-all prima donna.

So that's the measure of it.

I will still have some wealth, of course, but I probably won't be left with much other than our family home and maybe the Carmel home if I can figure out how to rent it out from time to time. I already let all my help go.

You probably think I deserve this. Go ahead and say I
told you so. I'll be OK, I always am.

Can we start over, the five of us? I hope so. Come to
Carmel for a weekend and let's see.

Love and kisses,

Heather

*Finally*, thought Elizabeth. Maybe there was a chance to get
the band back together after all. She typed a response.

Heather,

Nobody deserves something like this. As I said when we
spoke in March, these things happen no matter how
much planning you do. That's why you have your friends
and family. Don't be proud—you are going to find raising
a family takes a village, job or no job. And of course we
can start over. I'm a big believer in second chances.
Please realize, though, that you have work to do with the
others.

E

Elizabeth picked up the phone to call Carmen.

# CARMEN

"No way," said Carmen. "We're busy, and she's a big snobby bitch who doesn't deserve us. I am living a new life now, and it doesn't include Heather, period."

"Come on," pleaded Elizabeth. "Everyone deserves a second chance. Let's hear her out at least. I don't want to go alone when I'm this pregnant. Please?"

"Fine, but if you give birth to my godbabies three months early on the plane, there's going to be hell to pay," Carmen retorted.

Carmen pressed "end" on her phone and smiled despite herself. It would be fun to witness a little Heather groveling for a change. And anyway, she needed to shop for her honeymoon wardrobe, and those lovely shops in Carmel would be perfect for that. Whatever happened with Heather, it wasn't going to be a total loss.

The landline rang. Probably another telemarketer, she thought with annoyance. No one else ever used that number. Except one person, she corrected herself as she saw the number pop up on the television screen.

"Hi, Mom," she answered, vowing to be patient.

"Carmen! I'm so glad I caught you! Oh, honey, I'm so excited about the wedding, I just can't stand it. I was thinking it might be the right time to show you some of my ideas. I'm on Pinterest now, you know."

"That's great, Mom," Carmen replied, wanting to be irritated but not being able to resist enjoying her mother's happiness. "I'll take a look tonight, promise. Hey, Mom, can I call you later? I have my realtor coming over soon. Paul and I found the greatest little farmhouse. You're going to love it. Anyway, I have to get this Lake Geneva property on the market ASAP."

"Of course, honey. I'll try you later. But Carmen, may I please say something now?"

"Sure, Mom." It had become nearly impossible to hang up on her mom since she had announced her engagement to Paul.

"Honey, I'm sorry for how your dad and I behaved all those years ago at your graduation. I was so worried for you when you told us about your pregnancy and Mark and all. I should have been more supportive."

"Ancient history, Mom," said Carmen.

Her mom plowed ahead, ignoring her. "And Carmen, you have been the very best mom for Avery. She was such a lucky little girl to get you. I know you wanted more babies, but you are going to have the time of your life with Paul. And you'll finally get your chance to run a company. I knew that would happen for you someday. My smart girl. We love Paul, by the way. He is such a well-mannered young man. You won't miss the mom thing even for a second."

"Actually, Mom, I'm going to be a godmother to Elizabeth's twins! So I'm not totally giving up the mom thing," said Carmen.

"It's not really the same, though, honey," her mom said carefully.

"Actually, it sort of is. She used my eggs. I will explain later, I see my realtor pulling up."

"What do you mean 'used your eggs'?" replied her mom in confusion.

"Gotta go, Mom, talk later."

"Carmen, you can definitely expect a call later," her mom said with a note of concern in her voice as they both hung up.

As the realtor approached with the "For Sale" sign in her hands, Carmen smiled. Her mom hadn't needed to apologize. Carmen knew that her mom had only ever wanted the very best for her. But she had to admit it had really felt good. *Do any of us really get over not having our parents' unconditional love and approval?* Carmen wondered. She hoped that Avery knew Carmen was proud of her and approved of her choices. When the rest of the world was so judgmental of women, it was nice to be able to count on your mom no matter what. And the family you make too—Martha, Elizabeth, Sara, and, possibly, even Heather.

# MARTHA

Martha's initial instinct was to decline the invitation to go to Carmel. When she got the invitation, it had gone right into the trash. Robert had actually spied it, fished it out, and had been urging her to go for days. She had reflexively replied that she didn't want to leave Hope so soon after her surgery.

She couldn't help but remember what had happened the last time she had gone to Carmel. She had left a thriving, beautiful baby, and when she'd returned, that baby was gone. She would be beyond devastated if the same thing happened again.

But her rational side knew that one had nothing to do with the other. And she needed to telegraph to Robert that she trusted him, completely, to care for Hope. Also, the truth was Hope was recovering nicely.

In the end, she had given in to Robert's pleas. And if she was being honest with herself, she had more than a little curiosity about how Heather was going to handle the whole situation.

As she walked out the front door to the car waiting to drive her down to O'Hare, Robert came out to say goodbye.

"Thanks, Martha," he said.

They both understood exactly what he was talking about.

"It's all in God's hands, isn't it?" replied Martha.

"Sometimes it is," said Robert. "But occasionally he needs us doctors to give him a helping hand."

Martha smiled, gave Robert another kiss goodbye, and jumped into her ride to the airport.

She and her three friends had booked themselves on the same flight, and before they knew it, they were driving down Highway 1 with the ocean outside the passenger window. Martha enjoyed every second of breathing the healing ocean air.

They pulled into the cottage around two o'clock. Heather was due to arrive any minute now.

Martha perused the wine selection with Carmen while Sara started digging through the fridge for a Diet Coke. Elizabeth headed directly to the couch and plopped down in exhaustion.

"I'm not moving from this spot, so if you people want to talk, you will have to come to me," she joked.

They all joined Elizabeth in the living room and had just started to relax when they heard the front door close.

"That's her," hissed Martha.

"No shit, Sherlock," replied Carmen.

"Who's going to start talking?" Sara asked. "Elizabeth, you were her closest friend."

"Fine," said Elizabeth with annoyance. "But I can't be responsible for anything I say when I'm in this state."

And then Heather walked into the living room, and the four of them immediately fell silent.

# SARA

Sara thought Heather looked great, all things considered. She wasn't dressed like the woman on the front of her book. And she certainly didn't look like the kind of person who hobnobbed with celebrities. She looked pretty and soft in dark jeans, a white peasant top, and plain white sandals.

"I'm sorry," said Heather simply and directly to her old friends.

Nobody spoke for several moments. And then the dam broke. Elizabeth managed to haul herself off the couch to hug Heather. Sara went next.

Carmen came forward and said, "Look, you're on double secret probation. But I'm willing to hear you out."

It appeared that they were all terrible at holding a grudge.

Except one of them.

Martha stood quietly to the side. She clearly wasn't there yet.

"Ladies, I need your tips on how to manage three kids without a husband and without a budget," Heather said with as much confidence as she could muster. "My life is one big hot mess."

"I can certainly help on the multiple kids on a budget part," offered Sara kindly. "But I don't know how I would do it without Scott. I'm so sorry about Phil, Heather. I don't know what else to say."

"Well, I know how to get by without any help from a man," said Carmen wryly. "I did that for the better part of twenty years. You might have been up your ass in general when you wrote your book, but you were sure right about Mark. That guy was a big fucking mistake."

Heather reddened and said, "I'm really sorry about what I

said in the book. All of it. I don't know what I was thinking. None of your lives are mistakes. And you didn't deserve having them characterized that way. I was, as you put it so delicately, Carmen, totally up my own ass. I want to rewrite your stories someday. No, I don't want to. I'm going to. I owe you that much at least. But probably no one will want to read it after everything that's happened. And I wouldn't blame them."

"Heather, maybe you should just focus on rebuilding your life," Elizabeth suggested gently. "You don't need to correct the record. It's in the past. Let's just try to move on."

"Let's not beat around the bush," said Carmen. "Listen, Heather, you really can't just write about someone else's experience like you did. It's just not right."

"I know that now. I'm so sorry," repeated Heather.

"But if you do want to write something," said Carmen playfully, "we did come up with a title."

Sara smiled and said, "All the Right Mistakes."

"I love it!" enthused Heather. "Please, let's catch up. I missed you guys so much. And I need to know exactly how it is that Elizabeth is having Carmen's baby. That's been bugging me since your visit in March, Elizabeth. It's got to be a good story. And by the way, I think I'm moving with the kids back to Oconomowoc before school starts again in the fall. There's nothing for us anymore in California. I'll get a normal job and live in a normal house and live a normal life for a change."

"You'd better not be selling this cottage," said Elizabeth in mock pain. "We're just getting used to it."

"Well, we'll see. I'm not totally wiped out, and I do love this place. I was thinking about trying to rent it out," said Heather. "Except in June. That month is reserved for you guys and your families. If you would like to come, that is. Consider it your royalties from the book."

"Make it all summer, and we might find it in our hearts to forgive you," Carmen replied with smile.

Carmen grabbed two bottles of champagne out of the fridge, and the girls instinctively formed a little conversation circle. Except one. Martha sat a little outside the group and was far quieter than the others. But she was there, and that was something.

# SEPTEMBER

# Heather

**From Heather Hall's Twitter**

**Heather Hall** @therealheatherhall · September 5

Tune in for my interview with 20/20 tonight—might be the last you see of me for a long time #lessonslearned #meaculpa #secondchances #goinghometoWisconsin

← Reply   ↔ Retweet   ♥ Favorite   ⋯ More

# ELIZABETH

*If this were for anyone else other than Carmen, it so wouldn't be happening*, Elizabeth thought as she sat with the girls in the styling salon. They planned to spend the balance of the afternoon in the small, lovely shop getting ready for Carmen's big day. They had arranged to have the run of the place, including a manicurist brought in for the occasion and, of course, champagne.

As Elizabeth sat in the styling chair, she had a good look at her substantial baby belly. She was exactly thirty-seven weeks today and was pretty confident that she was over fifty inches around by now. Carmen had been true to her word and had insisted Elizabeth be a bridesmaid no matter how big she had gotten. Elizabeth had decided to be a good sport and had spent most of the day yesterday being fitted by the seamstress for the fourth time. The poor woman had basically resorted to draping yard after yard of the sheer maroon fabric from an impressively wide empire waist.

Elizabeth was more than ready for her babies to be born. She finally knew what she was having. A boy *and* a girl. Every time she got frustrated about being so pregnant, she would pull out one of the many twin books she had collected to read the chapter on the importance of carrying the babies as long as possible. Her goal had been to hit the thirty-seven-week mark. When she looked at the probable size of the head and the feet before that milestone, it worried her enough to slow her down. She planned to give these babies every advantage she could, even if it meant staying off her feet twenty-three hours out of the day.

Now that she had hit her goal, though, she planned to enjoy herself at the wedding. Hell, she might even try to dance.

All five of them would be at the wedding, but Heather had been excused from bridesmaid duty. She had started the process of moving to Oconomowoc and was still overwhelmed by all the recent events of her life. Plus, she was still a minor celebrity, even in Wisconsin. The last thing she wanted was to take even a smidgeon of the spotlight from Carmen. She planned to quietly sneak into the back row right before the ceremony started and slip out before the reception got underway. Her family would keep the kids back home in Oconomowoc.

It was Elizabeth's turn to have her hair done, and after thirty minutes she was feeling at least marginally more fabulous. Carmen snuck up on her and said, "Looking great!"

"Not bad for being so pregnant—but you still owe me big-time for this," replied Elizabeth.

"Besides giving you my unborn? Can't top that gift! Hey, that reminds me. I have your bridesmaids' gifts."

Carmen left to retrieve the gifts and was back a few minutes later with a stack of three telltale-blue boxes.

"Okay, girls, open them together please."

"Well, there's nothing that comes in a box this color that isn't fantastic," Sara declared excitedly.

The three of them pulled off the white bows and lifted the blue lids simultaneously.

Inside their boxes was a small silver object, an artfully curving oval, strung on a thin chain.

"Oh, it's lovely," said Martha. "What do they call it?"

"I have no idea," replied Carmen. "I'm calling it the bean. I bought one for myself and Heather too. It reminds me that we will keep growing and changing as long as we keep planting seeds for our future."

"I love that," said Elizabeth, tearing up. She cried at the drop of a hat these days. But she was genuinely touched by the gift.

"If you make me cry and ruin my makeup, I'll never forgive

you," said Carmen as she glared at Elizabeth. "Get it together, woman. Now let's get back to the important stuff—what color do we want on our nails?"

"Anything that distracts from the belly," replied Elizabeth with a laugh.

*One day I'll be here with my little girl getting our nails done together*, Elizabeth thought happily as she watched her friends evaluate the various nail colors.

# CARMEN

Carmen felt nervous. And she felt stupid for feeling nervous. But there was something about the thought of a hundred pairs of eyes looking at you as you walked down the aisle that did make a girl anxious.

The setting was everything she had hoped for. They had considered a number of venues in the city. She had really liked a beautiful spot called Villa Terrace, but Paul was all about the food, so they ended up at Lake Park Bistro. The ceremony would be conducted outside with cocktail hour following on the beautiful stairs behind the restaurant, which ran down the gently sloping hill toward Lake Michigan. Finally, dinner would be served in the French bistro before dancing and cake.

Carmen had always fantasized about the perfect June wedding, but she now thought fall was an even better time, especially for a more sophisticated wedding like this one. She had put her mother in charge of the flowers and told her to use all her creativity to make a unique and beautiful look. To say her mom had delivered would have been a gross understatement.

Carmen's bouquet was a masterwork. Her mother had rejected the typical white bride's bouquet for a stunning arrangement of stems in deep fall shades. Carmen's pale pink dress was made even more beautiful by the fiery flowers. The girls carried miniature versions of Carmen's arrangement, and the venue was accented by larger versions in varied, unexpected arrangements. Definitely Pinterest-worthy.

Carmen heard her cue, but she felt like she couldn't move. She stood frozen clutching her bouquet and looking for her father, who was going to walk her down the aisle. And then she saw him. He was walking toward her wearing his new Stetson. Her mom informed her not to worry about her dad's attire because she had vetted it all in advance. Twenty years ago, she would have been annoyed by the hat. Now, she found it endearing. *Same old Dad*, she thought. *The one guy I can count on not to show up a different person*. She hoped he wouldn't say something to make her cry. She had been on the edge all day.

"Ready, cowgirl?" he asked with a smile as he took her arm.

"Giddy up," replied a grinning Carmen. And she started down the aisle and toward her new future.

# MARTHA

Robert had been assigned the first reading of the wedding. It was a classic and one of Martha's enduring favorites.

*Love is patient, love is kind. It does not envy, it does not boast, it is not proud. It does not dishonor others, it is not self-seeking, it is not easily angered, it keeps no record of wrongs. Love does not delight in evil but rejoices with the truth. It always protects, always trusts, always hopes, always perseveres.*
*Love never fails . . .*

*No, it doesn't,* agreed Martha.

Martha felt closer to God now than she ever had before in her life, and certainly closer than she ever had when she was a doctor. *Perhaps we get so caught up in our paid work and our kids' schedules and our narcissistic pursuits that we make it impossible to let love in,* thought Martha. She had certainly been pretty closed off. Hope had put her on a different path.

She was at the beginning of an exciting new phase in her life. She had begun to provide medical counseling and support for prospective adoptive parents of children with special needs. She had a lot to learn about the process and the organizations she would be working with, but she finally felt that the missing piece had fallen into place. She had found a way to use her hard-earned knowledge on her own terms.

She glanced at Hope sitting peacefully on her chair next to Bobby and Jack as she listened to the end of the reading.

*When I was a child, I talked like a child, I thought like a child, I reasoned like a child. When I became a man, I put the ways of childhood behind me. For now we see only a reflection as in a mirror; then we shall see face to face. Now I know in part; then I shall know fully, even as I am fully known.*

*And now these three remain: faith, hope, and love. But the greatest of these is love.*

*Sometimes the old words are the best words*, she remarked to herself.

# SARA

Sara was listening to the reading as well.

*Keeps no record of wrongs.*

*That's a tough one for us married folk,* she thought. Especially ones who are trying to split the work fifty-fifty.

She had really hated giving up the tracker. It had been comforting to have been able to assure herself that everything was fair. But it had been a wedge between her and Scott. Lists are almost never a prescription for happiness. Especially lists of past wrongs. Life is fluid, messy, and sometimes impossible to quantify. Sara knew the way forward for them was love and kindness, not measurement.

Happiness was a choice they were making every day, and she knew from past experience how easy it would be to have things go the other way. It was the little stuff. Carrying your dirty dish to the sink. Emptying the garbage just because you have a spare ten minutes. Folding the socks that end up in a jumbled pile in the laundry basket. Some days were certainly easier than others, but every day that they made the choice to love each other by *doing*, she felt their roots growing stronger as they continued to entwine, more unbreakable every day.

*We've been at this an awful long time,* she realized as she glanced at her children sitting in a neat line next to Scott in the audience, tallest to shortest. Her oldest was about ready to pass her in height. He would be off to college in five years. They would all be gone in about ten. And then it would be just the two of them, Sara and Scott, alone in the house, just as they had been in the beginning. If they kept going the way they were going now, she had faith the best was yet to come—graduations, marriages, grandchildren.

As Robert finished his reading, she caught Scott's eye. He smiled at her, and she smiled back, thinking how truly blessed she was.

# HEATHER

**From Heather Hall's Twitter**

**Heather Hall** @therealheatherhall · September 9

Sometimes people have to fall apart to realize how much they have to fall back together #favoritequotes #secondchances

← Reply    ↔ Retweet    ♥ Favorite    ••• More

# ELIZABETH

The wedding had been pretty perfect, Elizabeth decided as she propped her feet up on the chair next to hers. In addition to the indignity of the bridesmaid dress, Carmen had seated her at the "wedding party table." To be fair, this was probably all Carmen's mom's doing. Elizabeth was relieved that at least she had chosen floor-length tablecloths. Her feet had been stuffed in heels (albeit, very low ones) for the ceremony, but they were now spread into flip-flops, and the throbbing was starting to ease.

Carmen was cutting the cake. Another perfect creation arranged by Mom. It featured five tiers, probably two more than she needed, and was thoughtfully accented with the same flowers that were in Carmen's bouquet. She fed a small piece to Paul, and then it was his turn. Elizabeth always found this part of the ceremony very telling. Any groom that thought it was funny to smash the cake into the bride's mouth gave Elizabeth great pause for the future of their union.

As expected, Paul was the perfect gentlemen, and as he finished gingerly feeding Carmen, the waiters swept the cake away to be cut and the DJ announced that it was time to dance. Up until this point, the music had been tastefully performed by a string quartet followed by a great local jazz band over dinner. But Carmen had insisted on a DJ for the dancing, over her mother's strong objection.

As she heard the notes of the DJ's first selection, Elizabeth threw back her head and laughed. "Bizarre Love Triangle." What else could it be? She let the girls drag her onto the dance floor, and it felt like college all over again. She imagined that she was quite the sight for the audience.

The party was still going strong several hours later. Paul, William, Robert, and Scott were nowhere to be seen. They were probably enjoying a scotch and cigar outside, Elizabeth decided. The various children had been taken home or to their hotel hours ago by babysitters and by now should be safely tucked in their beds.

Elizabeth was ready to pack it in. The night was an unmitigated success, but it was time for her and her babies to go get some rest. And then, suddenly, she knew that she wouldn't be going home tonight.

She looked around for William as calmly as she could. She spied Sara and pulled her aside, saying, "I need a ride. Like right now. And it would be great if that ride included my husband."

Sara started to object but then suddenly nodded in understanding and took off to find the guys. Elizabeth sat down and tried to relax. William would be back in a few minutes, and then they could make their way to the hospital.

Carmen noticed Elizabeth and walked over to check on her. "Honey, you look tired. You should go home."

"Actually, I need to make one stop first."

Carmen sensed immediately what was happening and yelled loudly, "It's time!"

Paul, Robert, William, and Scott appeared suddenly along with Martha, who had noticed the commotion. They all surrounded Elizabeth in a bit of a panic.

William said, "Elizabeth, I've had too many drinks. I really shouldn't drive." He looked over at the other three men.

"Same boat, man," said Scott.

"Me too," agreed Robert. "I never drink, but I was having so much fun . . ."

Paul shrugged. "Hey, it's my wedding—what was I supposed to do?"

"Okay, so which of us three ladies is in shape to drive?" Carmen demanded.

Martha and Sara shook their heads, and Carmen sighed in exasperation.

Martha said, "I've only had two glasses of champagne, but I hardly ate at all today, and you guys know I'm a lightweight."

Sara said a little drunkenly, "Not even close, sorry Elizabeth!"

"Okay, then," said Carmen with a deep sigh. "Apparently I'm the only sober one at my own wedding. Good thing for all of you I was too nervous to drink today."

The atmosphere shifted as Carmen took charge.

"This is what we are going to do. Paul, give me the keys to the truck. It seats three, so that's me, Elizabeth, and William. Sara, stay here and get Paul a cup of coffee and a ride to the hospital. You'll also need to get Scott to Elizabeth's to relieve their babysitter. Paul, you need to call the travel agent and tell her we need to reschedule the flight to Bali for tomorrow. We're having a baby tonight. Right, I think that covers it. Let's get going."

And with that, she grabbed Elizabeth's hand and dragged her toward the parking lot.

"I'm coming with!" shouted Martha. "William, I'm voting you off the island. Your wife needs a doctor more than a husband. You come with Paul on the next bus. Sara, can you handle everything here?"

"Of course—go!" Sara replied.

"She's going to be a kick-ass CFO," Paul declared with a smile as his bride hustled Elizabeth out the door.

# CARMEN

Carmen was behind the wheel of Paul's black truck and was trying to figure out which hospital to go to.

"Columbia Saint Mary's is right down the street," Martha pointed out.

"No, no, that's not where my doctor is! And not in-network. I'm not paying full freight for a twin birth," wailed Elizabeth. "We need to get up to Mequon."

"Christ on a cross," said Carmen, and she headed for Interstate 43.

They made it no more than five miles when Elizabeth said, "Carmen, pull over, they're coming now. I can't make it stop."

"Yes, let's pull over," agreed Martha quickly as she looked Elizabeth over. Carmen took the next exit and pulled into a strip mall right off the highway.

"Oh my God," said Elizabeth. "My babies are going to be born at the mall. In a truck."

# MARTHA

Martha felt the old calm settle over her just as it did before every medical procedure. Although the last baby she had delivered was during her OB rotation many, many years ago. The champagne buzz was long gone. She was going to bring these babies into the world, safe and sound. And she was going to make sure Elizabeth was taken care of too.

Three lives, all in her hands. Just like old times.

"Carmen, call an ambulance," Martha quietly instructed. "I'll do what I can until they get here. Elizabeth, let's put you in the bed of the truck and help you relax."

Elizabeth looked at Martha like she was crazy, but she started to edge out of the truck. Carmen found some blankets in the front of the truck and tried to make things more comfortable for her friend.

Once Elizabeth was settled in the truck bed, Martha said, "I'm going to take a peek."

After a few moments she said, "Okay, Elizabeth, you were right. Baby number one is crowning. Give a good push."

"No, no. I'm scared, Martha. What if the babies don't make it?"

Martha locked eyes with her old friend and said, "Elizabeth, I've got this, and so do you. Trust me, and trust yourself. Now push."

Elizabeth bore down with all her strength, and a few seconds later she heard a strong cry.

"It's a girl, Elizabeth!" cried Carmen.

Martha could hear the ambulance in the distance coming to rescue Elizabeth—and her, as well, if she was honest. Delivering twins was not exactly a run-of-the-mill event. Things were going well, but she knew all the risks with a twin delivery.

In mere minutes, the paramedics were rushing toward the three women. They tried to push Martha out of the way, but Martha quickly explained that she was a doctor and gave them quick orders for what she needed from the ambulance.

"Okay, baby number two is here. One more time, Elizabeth."

And then another cry joined the first. This one was a little weaker, but thankfully still there.

"This one's your boy!" cheered Carmen as she held her cell to her ear. She was on the phone now with the hospital, making sure they had a room ready for Elizabeth. Martha thought she heard her say, "Money is no object." *Good old Carmen*, she thought.

After some awkward wrangling, the paramedics and Martha got Elizabeth and her babies into the ambulance. The vehicle quickly took off for the hospital and Carmen followed in the truck.

William, Paul, and Robert were there looking for them when they all rolled in.

"Where were you guys?" they demanded in unison, taking in the motley crew of Carmen and Martha.

"We had to make a pit stop," said Carmen wryly. Everyone in the emergency department was taking in the disheveled layers of pink tulle. This was one they had never seen before.

"Robert, who is with Hope and the boys?" demanded Martha.

"It's good—the babysitter is spending the night. She's delighted actually. I promised her an obscene amount of money."

"Where's Elizabeth?" asked William anxiously.

"She and the babies are being taken to her room. Everybody's healthy and happy," replied Martha with a smile.

Robert looked over at Martha, and said "You?"

"Still got it!" replied Martha, her smile growing bigger. "I'm going to stay with Elizabeth and William for a while and make sure they have the right medical care lined up for them. Why don't you guys go home, get some sleep, and maybe come back tomorrow."

"Well, I'm staying here with my godbabies as well," insisted Carmen passionately. "Wild dogs couldn't drag me away."

"I'll go home and get you a change of clothes," said Paul with an amused smile. "Unless you just want to stay in the dress. You still look spectacular, you know."

Carmen wrapped her arms around her groom and laid a long, romantic kiss on him. Half of the emergency department personnel and nearly the whole waiting room started cheering and applauding.

"Well, I'll always have a great story to tell the twins about their birthday," William said with a smile as he turned to go find his wife and his new daughter and son.

# SARA

Sara left her hotel and was at the hospital bright and early to relieve Martha and Carmen. Martha had not had a problem staying up. Just like her days as a resident. Carmen, on the other hand, was slumped in the rocking chair in the corner looking like an exhausted teenager who had just come home from prom.

Sara managed to get the old roommates out the door and into a cab without disturbing Elizabeth. When she returned to the room, Elizabeth was awake, and two clear plastic bassinets had been placed on either side of her bed. The babies were both wrapped in the standard-issue blue-and-pink-striped blanket. Their tiny heads were encased in little knit caps, one blue and one pink.

"Can you believe this, Sara?" breathed Elizabeth. "I knew that they were going to be beautiful, but nothing really prepares you for this, does it?"

"Happens every time," responded Sara with a quiet smile. "Elizabeth, let's take some pictures."

"Oh, God, no," said Elizabeth. "I probably look a fright."

"Actually, you look quite beautiful. And you'll want these pictures when you're old and gray. You'll think back fondly on how young and beautiful you were when your twins were born. Be in the picture, mama."

"You're right," agreed Elizabeth.

Sara handed her each of the babies in turn and began snapping pictures.

"Have you picked out names?" she asked.

"No. We talked about a few, but I wanted to wait and get a good look at them."

"All right—let's do it!" Sara declared with a laugh.

They unbundled the babies and laid them side by side.

The baby girl definitely favored Carmen. She had a shock of dark hair and beautiful creamy skin. The boy was almost all William. Fair and blotchy.

"What do you think about Margaret for the girl? After Margaret Thatcher. The Iron Lady."

"A little Cold War, but I like it. And the boy?"

"I'm thinking Winston," said Elizabeth. "You know, after Winston Churchill, never give up—never, never, never. Heather has been quoting him a lot these days. I think she's on to something."

"Maggie and Win. Sounds like people who are ready to take on the world."

"That's the idea," said Elizabeth softly. "We can't do it all in our generation."

As Elizabeth and Sara continued to admire the babies, a nurse carried in a stunning flower arrangement that was so large she could hardly see around it.

"You have quite an admirer," she teased Elizabeth.

Elizabeth grabbed the card and read:

*Sorry I left the party and missed the fireworks. I couldn't be happier for you. By the way, I wanted to tell you something at the wedding. I've gone ahead with that new book, and it should be ready by June. It will be our twentieth college reunion in June—can you believe that? The reunion committee has asked me if I would like to host a lecture for students and interested alumni while I'm there. They wanted me to talk about The Four BIG Mistakes. That book keeps going and going. I told them that I would be happy to speak, but that I would have a new book to discuss. I hope to see all four of you in the audience.*

# EPILOGUE

**From Heather Hall's Twitter**

**Heather Hall** @therealheatherhall · June 9

Today's the day—download All the Right Mistakes
#NowDartmouthCollege #Nextreallife #seeyouinWisconsin

← Reply ↔ Retweet ♥ Favorite ••• More

# HEATHER

Heather stood at the podium in one of the college's lecture halls. Her twentieth reunion was finally here. She still couldn't believe that it had been twenty years since they had left.

Her "class" was packed. There were a handful of alumni there, but it was mostly full of graduating seniors and a few underclassmen who had stuck around to hear Heather. It wasn't every day that you got to be face-to-face with someone famous. And most of them had a lot of interest in her life advice. They were an ambitious group and wanted every advantage as they headed out into the real world.

Heather began, "I know many of you are here because of *The Four BIG Mistakes of Women Who Will Never Lead or Win*. I'm also here, at least in part, because of the success of that book.

"It's a comforting thought, isn't it, to think that if you just avoid a handful of pitfalls, if you make the right moves, if you architect your life in just the right way, that you will be successful. I used to think that way.

"And why not? Most of you probably know I grew up in a small town in Wisconsin. In my hometown, most people think Dartmouth is a dental school."

The crowd chuckled at the old, worn joke.

Heather continued, "I came here as a freshman with a duffel bag full of all the wrong clothes and the will to succeed. And you all know the story from there.

"What can I say? When you arrive here at Dartmouth, they tell you that you are special. You have been chosen. And you believe it.

"They tell you that again at your graduate school or consulting firm or whatever important place you land.

"Then you get promoted. Other good things continue to happen.

"One day, you find yourself surrounded by people telling you how amazing you are on a daily basis. After a while you think that you possess some secret recipe for success, and you decide to share it. To help the world, you tell yourself."

Heather paused and looked for her friends in the audience.

"'The road to hell is paved with good intentions,' as they say.

"First, I have come to realize that while the experience here at Dartmouth is truly a wonderful one, it is no more special than that of hundreds of other colleges and universities. Graduating from this institution will not protect you from life's obstacles, and it certainly won't impress fate.

"Likewise, making a particular set of choices about your life both personally and professionally doesn't guarantee success either. The events of the last two years have taught me that in spades.

"No matter how hard you plan, life is unpredictable and messy. There's no getting around it.

"You are probably thinking at this point that you shouldn't have bothered to come hear me speak. I know you are looking for specific guidance on how to be successful and how to navigate the choppy waters out there. Well, I would like to offer you an alternative to the suggestions I wrote in my first book.

"Under your chair, each of you will find a copy of my new book, *All the Right Mistakes*. You'll recognize the characters in there—my friends 'E,' 'C,' 'M,' and 'S.'

"You will remember the things I said about their lives. How I simplified each of their lives under the umbrella of one overarching mistake.

"The truth is that each of them, like all of us, is a work in progress. And if any of them made mistakes, they were the right ones because, today, each of them is living the life she was meant to lead. I had a wonderful elementary school teacher that liked to tell us that none of us were good or bad at anything. We were just practicing. Mistakes are part of the process of practicing, and you can't really plan in advance how exactly you will handle them.

"I'm sure some of you out there are asking yourself what then is left for you to employ to help you live your best life if planning isn't such a great option. I'd like to offer you this.

"My four friends have shown me the importance of four qualities that will be the touchstones for your future success, no matter which path you take. We all have the ability to possess and nurture these qualities, in ourselves and in each other.

"Let's start with my friend 'C.' Those of you who read the book know she had a difficult start, forced to begin her young life as a mother. She is now the CFO of a wildly successful new law firm. Why? Because she created an innovative business model that her firm's competitors are scrambling to keep up with. And she did it at forty. And, by the way, she was a pretty great mom too. Her daughter landed right here at the college. The thing that made the difference for my friend's life was her resilience and the faith of a good friend.

"Each of you is going to face bumps in the road. They may not be as early and as profound as 'C's' was, but trust me, they are coming. The thing that will get you through is your ability to bounce back—your resilience.

"Let's turn next to my friend 'M,' who I criticized for dropping out of her profession. She's just at the start of an amazing new project. She's using her unique skills in a new and creative way to bring children who might otherwise not survive to this country where they can receive life-changing surgeries and an American education—which is still the envy of the world, despite what you read in the papers. One by one, my friend is adding brainpower to the next generation. Those children might be the very ones who cure cancer or who take us to Mars.

"My friend 'M' also experienced the loss of her third child

recently, the pain of which I can't even fathom. But she never lost her optimism. The same optimism that made her a brilliant doctor who always worked with the belief she could heal her patient is now leading her down this new path where she is healing lives in a different way. When fate deals you a bad card, it's your optimism that will help you move forward to better days.

"You will all be happy to hear that 'S' has been promoted. You remember 'S,' right? The friend I thought didn't work hard enough and would never get ahead? She's ahead now. But that's not the whole story. You might also be surprised to hear that she turned down an even bigger promotion as part of her getting ahead process. Why did she say no to the even bigger job? Because she had the courage not to walk down a path that would have impressed the outside world but that would have taken away from her family time, which is very important to her in these next years. She had the courage to say no to something for which the time was not right, and to put her family first. I'm pretty confident that she'll get the even bigger job someday. And when she's ready, and if she wants to, she'll say yes.

"Life will give you so many choices, so many opportunities. Have the courage to carefully consider all the people in your life when you weigh them and make your decisions. And please have the courage to ask not just for what you need, but also what you want.

"Lastly, there's 'E.' She is one of the hardest workers I know. I criticized her for not balancing her private life the same way I did. Everyone does things in their own time and at their own speed. 'E' never gave up on her goals, and she has reached them, both personally and professionally, with the help of her friends and with her persistence. Sometimes life requires you to just keep going even when you can't quite see clear to your destination. That's where persistence will fill the gap.

"You can read more about my friends' stories in my new book. Please remember, though, their lives aren't perfect. No one's is. But they are using their resilience, optimism, courage, and persistence to create lives that are perfect for them.

"I'd like to leave you with one more thought.

"My book includes one last lesson from a fifth life—mine.

"That lesson is to be humble and ask for help. I'm sure all of you are well aware that humility is not a natural state for me. It never has been. But I am in the process of figuring out how to learn from my mistakes. To ask for help and to give it. And to recognize that we are all in this life journey together.

"I was lucky enough to make four amazing friends here at the college. People who knew me right at the beginning of my journey. They wanted to be there for me in the years after we left this place, but my pride got the best of me, and I let myself lose hold of those friendships.

"And worse, I had the temerity to think that it was okay to tell their stories without their permission, and in such an ugly way.

"Each of you here today knows the truth of who you are and what you want your life to look like. You don't need someone like me to tell you what to do. Trust yourselves. Go out and find your tribe. They will help you remember who you are when the world starts to pull you apart. And don't wait for the opportunities to come. Make them. Change the existing institutions. Create new ones. Lend a hand. Cheer each other on. Lower a ladder.

"I wish I had not treated my friends the way I did. But I have also learned that life finds a way to give you a second chance. I plan to spend the next twenty years enjoying mine."

The audience sat a little stunned. And then someone started to slowly clap. Others quickly joined. After a minute, everyone was on their feet giving Heather a standing ovation. She finally spotted her four friends in the back and gave them a nod. She knew her new book was going to be the beginning of her next chapter, and, this time, she wouldn't be writing it alone.

# ELIZABETH

As Elizabeth left the lecture hall, she realized that she had actually enjoyed listening to Heather's speech. Even though she no longer needed the validation from Heather, it sure felt good to hear it.

She was enjoying this baby-free weekend even more, though. William's parents had volunteered to take Maggie and Win for the weekend, and Elizabeth felt a wonderful sense of freedom.

It had been only about six months since she and Carmen had gotten the firm up and running, but those six months had exceeded expectations in every way. She had enjoyed figuring out how best to use every contributor's particular talent—and compensate them fairly. They called their approach "one size fits one," and it was a smashing success.

They had people working in their new office in the Third Ward—a funky loft space that they had converted into their permanent offices. They also had people working remotely, part-time and full-time. They typically tracked and billed work by matter or piece, but also tracked some work by the hour if it made more sense. The people who were good at client development (like Jeff, it turned out) spent more time on that, and the people who preferred a more introverted existence (like Jenny) were treated with equal importance. Everyone had the ability to receive compensation for individual achievement, but they could also be rewarded for being part of a successful client service team. Elizabeth was also developing a unique approach to talent acquisition, with a particular focus on finding older women who wanted to ramp back into private law practice from a number of workplaces, including the home.

In short, Elizabeth was breaking all the "firm" rules and adjusting as she went along. Elizabeth had made several mistakes, but the beauty of the system was that these mistakes were almost always quickly brought to her attention, and she had the power to fix them immediately.

Elizabeth was a little exhausted, but it was worth it to create the life she wanted.

William was fully in control of what should have been a chaotic home front with two infants. And he even managed to visit Elizabeth with her babies almost every day at lunch. The three of them were always on the way to somewhere for a day of fun.

And Carmen—without Carmen, the thing wouldn't have flown. The tough part about one size fits one is that someone has to be sure the numbers all add up. And Carmen did. Every time.

She saw Carmen, Martha, and Sara leaving the lecture hall and waved for them to come take a walk with her.

# CARMEN

The four of them decided to go take a look at their old dorm. As the Choates came into view, Carmen flashed back to that first day over twenty years ago when she was meeting Martha for the first time.

*The skinny, embarrassed girl sure has turned into a powerhouse,* she thought.

*And me, well, I'm still Carmen from Texas. But I'm also Carmen who went to Dartmouth. And Carmen the CFO. And Paul's wife. And Avery's mother. I'm all of them. And proud to be all of them.*

*And I'm not embarrassed to say Choates out loud anymore,* she thought with a smile.

# MARTHA

Martha was having similar thoughts as they walked up to her old dorm. *My parents were so happy when I chose Dartmouth*, she thought. *My dad's school. And his dad's school.*

Another strong branch on the family tree.

She had just recently accepted that her new life might not measure up to what her parents had in mind for her. She had decided that it was just fine because you truly can't please everyone.

But then her dad had gone and surprised her. As she was pulling together her plans for a foundation or nonprofit to support her new work, she had gotten a card in the mail with a Boston postmark.

In it she found a note. Her father said that Robert had told him all about what she was doing and that he wanted to help in any way he could. He had also written a check for $1,500,000 and said that she should consider it an advance on her inheritance. "Wish big," he had written, adding that he had never been prouder of her.

Her mom wrote at the bottom that she was planning to give Wisconsin another chance because she wanted to be a part of her granddaughter's life (starting with shopping).

That had been a very good day.

# SARA

Sara, Elizabeth, Carmen, and Martha decided to end their walk around the Green so they could hear the Baker Bell Tower play the alma mater, which happened without fail at 6:00 p.m. every day. The Green was the heart of the campus, with Baker Library on one end and the Hanover Inn at the other end. Its crisscrossing paths led the way to every corner of campus, or every corner of the world, as the song went. As they got closer to the library, they saw Heather approaching.

"I can't believe you have a daughter here, Carmen," said Heather. "It feels like just yesterday we were walking across the stage to get our diploma, doesn't it?"

"Indeed," agreed Carmen.

"Yes, but they didn't tell us the road was long and winding, did they?" said Heather.

"Amen, sister. To be fair, our alma mater does mention roaming the girdled earth. I think we checked the 'roaming' box." Carmen laughed. Then she said more seriously, "I wonder if things will be easier for Avery than they were for us."

"I don't know," said Martha. "I'm not sure we are where we need to be on women's issues at all."

"Agreed," replied Heather a little sadly. "And you and I aren't where we need to be. I know that, and I promise to work on it. Missing your daughter's funeral was a terrible thing. Please let me make it up to you."

"Thanks, Heather," said Martha, "I'd like that. And I'm sorry I wasn't there for you when Phil died."

"Well, women may not be where we want to be, but we are trying," Elizabeth pointed out with optimism in her voice. "At

315

least I am, in my own limited way. I think we women are just at the beginning of our moment. I mean, think about it—our own mothers wouldn't have been able to go to college here. And their mothers were born just as women were getting the right to vote."

As the chimes rang out over their alma mater, the women fell into a contemplative silence.

"I wonder what's next for us," said Heather.

"I really thought when I was Avery's age that you sort of fell off a cliff after forty, you know, in terms of doing anything interesting," replied Sara.

"Speak for yourself," said Carmen. "My life is beginning at forty. And trust me, it's very, very interesting," Carmen teased.

"Gross," Martha complained as one of the reunion photographers ran up to take their picture in front of Baker Library.

As he lifted his camera, the five of them linked arms and Heather said, "You know, that whole rebirth at forty gives me a great idea for my next book."

"Heather!" they all exclaimed at her in unison as the photographer snapped the picture of them glaring at their friend.

*No biggie*, thought Sara. *Our twenty-fifth is right around the corner. We'll get another chance at the picture.*

## ACKNOWLEDGMENTS

A heartfelt thank-you to the following members of my far-flung tribe, many of whose stories inspired this book, and all of whom believed in it, right from the start: Elizabeth, Kathleen, Donna, Dermot, Anita, Adie, Brandy, Jackson, Niamh, Dana, Angela, Cat, Heidi, Jessie, Mary, Deborah, Erin, Holly, Brian, Amy, Ellen, and whomever else my mom-brain forgot!

And thank you to my parents and especially my husband, who have always supported my big dreams.

# ABOUT THE AUTHOR

Photo credit: Amy Pearson Studios, LLC

Laura Jamison is an attorney from Whitefish Bay, Wisconsin, where she lives with her husband and their four children. When she is not practicing law or writing, she is driving her kids to one of their many activities in her minivan. Laura is a graduate of Dartmouth College and the University of Michigan Law School. This is her first book.

# SELECTED TITLES FROM SHE WRITES PRESS

She Writes Press is an independent publishing company
founded to serve women writers everywhere.
Visit us at www.shewritespress.com.

*Center Ring* by Nicole Waggoner. $17.95, 978-1-63152-034-1. When a startling confession rattles a group of tightly knit women to its core, the friends are left analyzing their own roads not taken and the vastly different choices they've made in life and love.

*Play for Me* by Céline Keating. $16.95, 978-1-63152-972-6. Middle-aged Lily impulsively joins a touring folk-rock band, leaving her job and marriage behind in an attempt to find a second chance at life, passion, and art.

*Again and Again* by Ellen Bravo. $16.95, 978-1-63152-939-9. When the man who raped her roommate in college becomes a Senate candidate, women's rights leader Deborah Borenstein must make a choice—one that could determine control of the Senate, the course of a friendship, and the fate of a marriage.

*Stella Rose* by Tammy Flanders Hetrick. $16.95, 978-1-63152-921-4. When her dying best friend asks her to take care of her sixteen-year-old daughter, Abby says yes—but as she grapples with raising a grieving teenager, she realizes she didn't know her best friend as well as she thought she did.

*In the Heart of Texas* by Ginger McKnight-Chavers. $16.95, 978-1-63152-159-1. After spicy, forty-something soap star Jo Randolph manages in twenty-four hours to burn all her bridges in Hollywood, along with her director/boyfriend's beach house, she spends a crazy summer back in her West Texas hometown—and it makes her question whether her life in the limelight is worth reclaiming.

*Wishful Thinking* by Kamy Wicoff. $16.95, 978-1-63152-976-4. A divorced mother of two gets an app on her phone that lets her be in more than one place at the same time, and quickly goes from zero to hero in her personal and professional life—but at what cost?